BUtterfield 8

BUtterfield 8

—

John O'Hara

Introduction by
John Sacret Young

Random House

New York

Introduction

It's easy to write about John O'Hara's faults. Read him, read all of him—402 stories and fourteen novels—and you get saturated. He had this matter-of-fact, uniform tone, this baritone, that pushes his prose toward a middle and seems to do the same with the contents and subject matter. In many respects it is an illusion. The variety of his work and the range of his characters are, among his generation, second to none.

He created, populated, and made infamous a third-class city, Gibbsville, P.A., but he also gave rich definition to any number of other regions of Pennsylvania, New Jersey, New York, and Hollywood. His characters go to Yale, or (like O'Hara) wish they had, but they are also gangsters or tend bars, own car dealerships, practice the law, run beauty parlors, shoot their husbands, waltz in the afternoon, and play jazz. They are Skull and Bones and they are hepcats. He said once in *Pal Joey* that he had created Frank Sinatra before Frank Sinatra and, in Gloria Wandrous in *BUtterfield 8,* Elizabeth Taylor before Elizabeth Taylor.

BUtterfield 8 was his second novel and he wrote it fast. "Zip zip," he said years later in an introduction to a collection that included it. Fast was his style and he was legendary for infuriating other writers at *The New Yorker* when he briefly had an office there. He would come in, take his jacket off, loosen his tie, sit down, roll paper into the typewriter, and begin. The keys did not stop. They hardly hesitated. They fired away until in a single sitting out rolled a story complete and with hardly a need of pencil or proofing. Done, ready to be published. Often extraordinary. His editor Albert Erskine wrote that that was how O'Hara stories came out of the typewriter but was not the way they went in. By the time he sat down they already existed fully formed, nearly finished in his mind, and there his work never stopped.

O'Hara had written *Appointment in Samarra* in less than four months the year before in 1934 and it had been a terrific success. It sold well, it was talked about good and bad; it created Noise. Dorothy Parker ("Mr. O'Hara's eyes and ears have been spared nothing") and Ernest Hemingway ("a man who knows exactly what he is writing about and has written it marvelously well") gave thumbs-up, Sinclair Lewis thumbs-down ("Nothing but infantilism—the erotic visions of a hobbledehoy behind the barn"). Despite Lewis, the novel has lasted. It alone made its author famous, and it remains remarkable and in print to this day.

Before and after this first flush of success O'Hara was always on the move. Addresses piled up. He never stayed at one place long. In the short time it took to complete *BUtterfield 8* there was an apartment he shared at 103 E. 55th Street in Manhattan, a spot in Miami while on an ill-fated trip to visit Hemingway, the Oceanside Inn in East Sandwich, Massachusetts, the ship *Conti di Savoia,* and the last page of the final typescript is dated "exactly 2 o'clock p.m., August 5, 1935/Paris France." He burned through jobs at a litany of magazines and newspapers at the same rate. *The Pottsville Journal, The Tamaqua Courier, The New York Herald Tribune, Time,* and *The New Yorker* are just a sampling. He was full of himself and hypersensitive, and he took offense quickly and unforgivingly ("the master of the fancied slight" was how Brendan Gill characterized him). His Irish and his insecurity would get up, and he would be out of work and would move on.

These were the years he was living late hours on too little money and drinking too much, and yet simultaneously he was whetting his observation of others and himself and gathering the experience that laid the foundation of his writing. He was still not yet thirty years old. "You never quite get over the degrading, debasing experience of going hungry. You learn to see things very plain, and not only things but people, and not only people but a city," he wrote in a second unpublished introduction to *BUtterfield 8* written twenty-five years after its initial publication. The city he meant was of course New York, including the middle upper East Side that is the locus of the title of the novel, and it was New York he sought to capture as he had captured Pottsville, the town where he was born, in *Appointment in Samarra.*

BUtterfield 8 is O'Hara's only roman à clef. On June 8, 1931, a twenty-five-year-old woman with the astonishing name of Starr Faithfull washed up on Long Beach, Long Island. Her death created a sensation that was never resolved: accident, suicide, or murder? The papers had a field day. It came out that she had hung out in speakeasies, dried out at Bellevue, been in therapy, lived a while on St. Luke's Place a couple of doors from Mayor Jimmy Walker, and been sexually abused as a girl by Andrew J. Peters, the former mayor of Boston.

O'Hara re-created her in Gloria Wandrous, who wakes in despair on page one, sentence one of the novel. Listen to her spinning into self-destruction: "It's awful when you think that you've stayed with so many men and made such a mess of your life, and then someone you really want to stay with because you love him, that person is the one person you mustn't stay with because if you do he immediately becomes like the rest, and you don't want him to become like the rest."

The book's title reflects the azimuths of her world, and the pages are alive with the specificity of that time and place. They breathe with a nasty, chilling authenticity. John Dos Passos, for example, in the three volumes of *U.S.A.* offers a far wider, greater, more passionate and political vision of America in the twenties and thirties, but nowhere in our literature is prose wielded about those years with a sharper scalpel than in O'Hara's first two novels.

The brilliant, rather brittle surface of *BUtterfield 8* deflects some shortcomings. Around the vivid portrait of a doomed young woman, the book has a tendency to centrifuge. The principals ping-pong off one another, but their interplay seems arbitrary, almost haphazard, without deeper meaning. It is true that structure and plot are not great O'Hara strengths. He didn't believe in cause and effect. He wrote once to his brother "you must let something hang . . . people die, love dies, but life does not die, and so long as people live, stories must have life at the end."

What is most often celebrated about O'Hara's work is his dialogue. How real it is. It's not, in fact; it's a stylized tool, an artist's rendering, that especially here seems chewy with the brand names and rhythms of right there and then, and has a speed and a directness that gives it a force at times almost like a slap.

Love of language might be what his art lacked, John Updike wrote: "language as a semi-opaque medium whose colors and connotations can be worked in a supernatural, super mimetic bliss." Yes, he lacks Updike's opulent virtuosity, or John Cheever's lapidary dark-and-light radiance. Equally, his language is far from carrying the stark vigor of Raymond Carver's or Cormac McCarthy's. The baritone has aged and dated a bit now, many of its references long gone to museum or heirloom. Time has subtracted its currency and its pertinence, but given it another value—the apprehension of that moment. The thirties. Speakeasies. New York. The lusts and lack of moral compass that abounded.

Jim Malloy, O'Hara's autobiographical voice, makes his first appearance in a novel in *BUtterfield 8,* and twenty-five years later in the fine novella "Imagine Kissing Pete" Malloy speaks trenchantly of that same time: "We knew everything, everything there was to know. We knew so much, and since what we knew seemed to be all there was to know, we were shockproof. . . . Prohibition, the zealots' attempt to force total abstinence on a temperate nation, made liars of a hundred million men and cheats of their children; the West Point cadets who cheated in examinations, the basketball players who connived with gamblers, the thousands of uncaught cheats in the high schools and colleges. We had grown up and away from our earlier esteem of God and country and valor, and had matured at a moment when riches were vanishing for reasons that we could not understand. We were the losing, not the lost, generation. . . . We knew everything, but we were incapable of recognizing the meaning of our complacency."

The early, young Jim Malloy who appears in *BUtterfield 8* is somehow cocky and insecure at once, and he lets loose in the novel about his Irish background: "I want to tell you something about myself that will help explain a lot of things about me. You might as well hear it now, first of all I'm a Mick. I wear Brooks clothes and I don't eat salad with a spoon and I probably could play five-goal polo in two years, but I am a Mick. . . . I'm pretty God damn American, and therefore my brothers and sisters are, and yet we're not American. We're Micks, we're non-assimible, we Micks." Far less callow, the later Jim Malloy has wrestled the chip off his shoulder, and in *Sermons and Soda Water* (which includes "Imagine Kissing Pete") O'Hara would with him then, if not create, master an easy-skipping, time-jumping narrative form that crosses times and captures lives.

In his famous introduction to *Sermons,* O'Hara sought to sum up that time, his time: "I have lived with, as well as in, the Twentieth Century from its earliest days. The United States in this Century is what I know, and it is my business to write about it to the best of my ability, with the sometimes special knowledge I have. The Twenties, the Thirties, and the Forties are already history, but I cannot be content to leave their story in the hands of the historians and the editors of picture books. I want to record the way people talked and thought and felt, and to do it with complete honesty and variety . . . within, of course, the limits of my own observations."

The depth of these collected novellas, and the too-little-known, sad and stirring *A Few Trips and Some Poetry,* isn't in their size or overt ambition, their stylistic invention or their metaphors. O'Hara's abhorrence of metaphors was for him a principle. He states it clearly in the mind of his character Weston Liggett in *BUtterfield 8:* "It is the trouble with all metaphors where human behavior is concerned. People are now ships, chess men, flowers, race horses, oil paintings, bottles of champagne, excrement, musical instruments, or anything else but people." He chose instead in his baritone to try and find a straightforward efficiency and simplicity, a kind of human story-telling as old as gatherings around the campfire and as contemporary as all the twentieth-century playing with form and literary technique.

In his later novels O'Hara could wander and become discursive, prolix, they could weigh a ton and be too quickly done—but in these stories with Jim Malloy he probes the mysterious, sometimes blessed and sometimes cursed way events and feelings tie up one with another.

The prose of this prickly man of enormous and vulnerable ego seldom shines a light on itself, and in his work, even when he couldn't in his life, he set ego and insecurity aside. His first and final interest was in other people, male and female. As much as any American writer O'Hara wrote both genders well. There are few finer chapters about a woman by a man in our literature than Chapter 5 in *Appointment in Samarra,* where Caroline English charts the history of her relationship with her husband, Julian. The taste of it comes with sympathy and skill as he sketches Paul, and especially Nancy Farley, in *BUtterfield 8* in only a page or two. His unfeigned curiosity and empathy are consummate and remarkably without preconception or judgment. He took sides—but both sides.

John O'Hara saw plainly and unscathingly into the relationship between the sexes and into intimacy with its quick impulsive excitements and its unhealing failures and desperate isolations. He saw even beyond the commandments and Catholicism that had forged him and into the despair and occasional healing where love and loneliness touch and merge.

JOHN SACRET YOUNG
Santa Monica, California
July 1994

Starting on December 16, a distinguishing numeral will be added to, and become part of, each central office name in New York City.
For example:

HAnover will become HAnover 2

*(From an advertisement of
the New York Telephone Company,
December 8, 1930.)*

1

ON THIS SUNDAY morning in May, this girl who later was to be the cause of a sensation in New York, awoke much too early for her night before. One minute she was asleep, the next she was completely awake and dumped into despair. It was the kind of despair that she had known perhaps two thousand times before, there being 365 mornings in a calendar year. In general the cause of her despair was remorse, two kinds of it: remorse because she knew that whatever she was going to do next would not be any good either. The specific causes of these minutes of terror and loneliness were not always the words or deeds which seemed to be the causes. Now, this year, she had come pretty far. She had come far enough to recognize that what she had done or said last night did not stand alone. Her behavior of a given night before, which she was liable to blame for the despair of any today, frequently was bad, but frequently was not bad enough to account for the extreme depth of her despair. She recognized, if only vaguely and then only after conquering her habit of being dishonest with herself, that she had got into the habit of despair. She had come far away from original despair, because she had hardened herself into the habit of ignoring the original, basic cause of all the despair she could have in her lifetime.

There *was* one cause.

But for years she had hardened herself against thinking of it, in the hope of pushing it away from her and drawing herself away from it. And so mornings would come, sometimes as afternoons, and she would awake in despair and begin to wonder what she had done before going to sleep that made her so full of terror today. She would recollect and for a fraction of a fraction of a second she would think, "Oh, yes, I remember," and build up an explanation on the recollection of the recognizably bad thing she had done. And then

would follow a period of inward cursing and screaming, of whisper-
ing vile self-accusation. There was nothing she knew of that she
would not call herself during these fierce rages of self-accusation.
She would whisper and whisper the things men say to other men
when they want to incite to kill. In time this would exhaust her
physically, and that left her in a state of weak defiance—but not so
weak that it would seem weak to anyone else. To anyone else she
was defiance; but she knew that it was only going on. You just go on.

For one thing, you get up and get dressed. On this Sunday morning she did something she often did, which gave her a little pleasure.
The drawstring of the pajamas she was wearing had come undone in
the night, and she opened the pajamas and laughed. She said to
herself: "I wonder where he is."

She got out of bed, holding the pajamas to her, and she was
unsteady and her body was pretty drunk, but she walked all over the
apartment and could not find him. It was a large apartment. It had
one large room with a grand piano and a lot of heavy, family furniture and in one corner of that room, where there was a bookshelf,
there were a lot of enlarged snapshots of men and women and boys
and girls on horseback or standing beside saddle horses. There was
one snapshot of a girl in a tandem cart, a hackney hitched to it, but if
you looked carefully you could see that there was a tiestrap, probably held by a groom who was not in the picture. There were a few
prize ribbons in picture frames, blues from a Connecticut county
fair. Some pictures of yachts, which, had she examined them carefully, the girl would have discovered were not many yachts but duplicate snapshots of the same Sound Inter-Club yacht. One picture of
an eight-oared shell, manned; and one picture of an oarsman holding
a sweep. This picture she inspected closely. His hair was cut short,
he was wearing short, heavy woolen socks, a cotton shirt with three
buttons at the neck, and a small letter over the heart, and his trunks
were bunched in the very center by his jock strap and what was in it.
She was surprised that he would have a picture like that hanging in
this room, where it must be seen by growing girls. "But they'd never
recognize him from that picture unless someone told them who it
was."

There was a dining-room almost as large as the first room. The room made her think of meats with thick gravy on them. There were four bedrooms besides the one where she had slept. Two of them were girls' bedrooms, the third a servant's room and the fourth was a woman's bedroom. In this she lingered.

She went through the closets and looked at the clothes. She looked at the bed, neat and cool. She took whiffs of the bottles on the dressing table, and then she opened another closet door. The first thing she saw was a mink coat, and it was the only thing she really saw.

She left the room and went back to his room and picked up her things; her shoes and stockings, her panties, her evening gown. "Well, I can't wear that. I can't go out looking like that. I can't go out in broad daylight wearing an evening gown and coat." The evening coat, more accurately a cape, was lying where it had been carefully laid in a chair. But when she took a second look at the evening gown she remembered more vividly the night before. The evening gown was torn, ripped in half down the front as far as the waist. "The son of a bitch." She threw the gown on the floor of one of his closets and she took off her pajamas—*his* pajamas. She took a shower and dried herself slowly and with many towels, which she threw on the bathroom floor, and then she took his tooth brush and put it under the hot water faucet. The water was too hot to touch, and she guessed it was hot enough to sterilize the brush. This made her laugh: "I go to bed with him and take a chance on getting anything, but I sterilize his tooth brush." She brushed her teeth and used a mouth wash, and she mixed herself a dose of fruit salts and drank it pleasurably. She felt a lot better and would feel still better soon. The despair was going away. Now that she knew what the bad thing was that she was going to do, she faced it and felt all right about it. She could hardly wait to do it.

She put on her panties and shoes and stockings and she brushed her hair and made up her face. She used little make-up. She opened a closet door and put her hand in the pockets of his evening clothes, but did not find what she wanted. She found what she wanted, cigarettes, in a case in the top drawer of a chest of drawers. She lit one and went to the kitchen. On the kitchen table was an envelope she had missed in her earlier round of the apartment. "Gloria," was written in a round, backhand style, in pencil.

She pulled open the flap which was sticky and not tightly held to the envelope, and she took out three twenty-dollar bills and a note. "Gloria—This is for the evening gown. I have to go to the country. Will phone you Tuesday or Wednesday. W." "You're telling me," she said, aloud.

Now she moved a little faster. She found two hats, almost identical black felt, in one of the girls' closets. She put one on. "She'll think she took the other to the country and lost it." She was aware of herself as a comic spectacle in shoes and stockings, panties, black hat. "But we'll soon fix that." She returned to the woman's closet and took out the mink coat and got into it. She then went to his bedroom and put the sixty dollars in her small crystal-covered evening bag. She was all set.

On the way out of the apartment she stopped and looked at herself in a full length mirror in the foyer. She was amused. "If it wasn't Spring this would be just dandy. But—not bad anyway."

She was amused going down in the elevator. The elevator operator wasn't handsome, but he was tall and young, a German, obviously. It amused her to think of what would happen to his face if she opened the mink coat. "Shall I get you a taxi, Miss?" he said, without turning all the way around.

"Yes, please," she said. He would not remember her if anyone asked him to describe her. He would remember her as pretty, as giving the impression of being pretty, but he would be a bad one to ask for a good description. All he would remember would be that she was wearing a mink coat, and anyone who wanted to get a description of her would know already that she had been wearing a mink coat. That would be the only reason anyone would ask him for a description of her. He was not the same man who had been running the elevator when she came in the apartment house the night before; that had been an oldish man who did not take his uniform cap off in the elevator. She remembered the cap. And so this young man naturally did not question her wearing a mink coat now instead of the velvet coat she had worn coming in. Why, of course! He probably didn't even know what apartment she had come from.

She waited for him to precede her to the big iron-and-glass doors of the house, and watched him holding up his finger for a taxi. She decided against tipping him for this little service—that would make him remember her—and she got in the taxi and sat back in the corner where he could not see her.

"Where to, Ma'am?" said the driver.

"Washington Square. I'll tell you where to stop." She would direct him to one of the Washington Square apartment houses and pay him off, and then go in and ask for a fictitious person, and stall long enough for the driver of this taxi to have gone away. Then she would come out and take another taxi to Horatio Street. She would pay a surprise call on Eddie. Eddie would be burned up, because he probably would have a girl there; Sunday morning. She was in good spirits and as soon as she got rid of this cab she would go to Jack's and buy a quart of Scotch to take to Eddie and Eddie's girl. At the corner of Madison the driver almost struck a man and girl, and the man yelled and the driver yelled back. "Go on, spit in their eye," called Gloria.

IN the same neighborhood another girl was sitting at one end of a rather long refectory table. She was smoking, reading the paper, and every once in a while she would lay the cigarette in an ash tray and, with her free hand, rub the damp short hair at the back of her neck. The rest of her hair was dry, but there was a line deep in the skin of her head and neck that showed where a bathing cap had been. She would rub her hair, trying to dry it, then she would wipe her fingers on the shoulder part of her dressing gown, and her fingers would slide along the front of her body and halt at her breast. She would hold her hand so that it partly covered her breast and the fingers rested under her arm, in the armpit. Then she would have to turn a page of the paper and she would pick up the cigarette again and for a while she would hold it until the heat of the lighted end warned her that it was time to get a shorter hold on the cigarette or get burned fingers. She would put it in the ash tray and start all over again with the rubbing of the hair at the back of her neck.

Presently she got up and was gone from the room. When she came back she was naked except for a brassière and panties. She did not go back to the table, but stood on one foot and knelt with the other knee on a chair and looked out the windows that ran the length of the room. She was in this position when a bell rang, and she went to the kitchen.

"Hello. . . . Ask him to come up, please."

She walked hurriedly to the bedroom and came out pulling a cashmere sweater over her shoulders and wearing a tweed skirt, light wool stockings and brogue shoes with Scotch tongues that flapped a little. Another bell rang, and she went to the door.

"Greetings. Greetings, greetings, and greetings. How is Miss Stannard? How is Miss Stannard."

"Hello, Jimmy," said the girl. She closed the door, and immediately he took her in his arms and kissed her.

"Mm. No response," he said. He tossed his hat in a chair and sat down before she did. He offered her a cigarette by gesture and she declined it with a shake of her head.

"Coffee?" she said.

"Yes, I'll have some coffee if it's any good."

"Well, I made it and I drank two cups of it. It's fit to drink, at least."

"Ah, but you made it. I doubt if you'd throw away coffee you made yourself."

"Do you want some or don't you?"

"Just a touch. Just one cup of piping hot javver for the gentleman in the blue suit."

"How *about* the blue suit? Didn't you get What's His Name's car? I thought we were going to the country." She looked down at her own clothes and then at his. He had on a blue serge suit and white starched collar and black shoes. "Did you get a job in Wall Street since I last saw you?"

"I did not. That goes for both questions. I did not get the car from Norman Goodman, not What's His Name. You met him the night we went to Michel's and you called him Norman. And as for my getting a job in Wall Street—well, I won't even answer that. Norman phoned me last night and said he had to drive his father to a circumcision or something."

"Is his father a rabbi?"

"Oh—don't be so—no, dear. His father is not a rabbi, and I made that up about the circumcision."

"What are we going to do? You didn't get someone else's car, I take it. Such a grand day to go to the country."

"I am in the chips. I thought we could go to the Plaza for breakfast, but seeing as you've had breakfast. I'm supposed to be covering a sermon, but I should cover a Protestant sermon on a nice day like this. I don't know why they ever send me anyway. They get the sermons at the office, and all I ever do is go to the damn church and then I go back to the office and copy the sermon or paste it up. All I do is write a lead, like 'The depression has awakened the faith of the American people, according to the Reverend Makepeace John Meriwether, don't spell it with an *a* or you're fired, rector of Grace Methodist Episcopal Free Patrick's Cathedral.' And so on. May I have some cream?"

"I'm afraid I've used up all the cream. Will milk do?"

"Damn, you have a nice figure, Isabel. Move around some more. Walk over to the window."

"I will not." She sat down. "What do you really contemplate doing?"

"No Plaza? Not even when I'm in the chips?"

"Why are you rich?"

"I sold something to the *New Yorker.*"

"Oh, really? What?"

"Well, about a month ago I was on a story up near Grant's Tomb and I discovered this houseboat colony across the river. People live there in these houseboats all winter long. They have gas and electricity and lights and radios, and all winter the houseboats are mounted on piles, wooden piles. Then in the Spring they get a tug to tow them out to Rockaway or some such place, and they live out there all summer. I thought it would make a good story for the Talk of the

Town department, so I found out all about it and sent it in, and yesterday I got a check for thirty-six dollars, which comes in mighty handy. They want me to do some more for them."

"You're going to do it, aren't you?"

"I guess so. Of course I can't do a great deal, because believe it or not I have a job, and the novel."

"How's the novel coming?"

"Like Santa Claus. And you know about Santa Claus."

"I think I'll leave you."

"Permanently?"

"A few more like that last one and yes, permanently. Such a lovely day to go to the country." She got up and stood at the window. "Look at those men. I never get tired of watching them."

"What men? I'm too comfortable to get up and look at men. You tell me about them."

"The men with the pigeons. They stay up on the roof all day, every Sunday, and chase the pigeons off. Our maid said the idea is that a man has a flock of pigeons, say eighteen, and the reason he chases them off is that he hopes that when they come back there'll be nineteen or twenty. A pigeon or two from another flock gets confused and joins them, and increases the man's flock. It isn't *exactly* stealing."

"But you won't have breakfast at the Plaza?"

"I've had breakfast, and I'll bet you have too."

"As much as I ever have. Orange juice, toast and marmalade, coffee. I just thought we'd have kidneys and stuff, omelette, fried potatoes. Like the English. But if you don't want to, we won't. I just thought it'd be fun, or at least different."

"Some other time. But I'll dress and we can spend your money some other way, if you insist."

"I am not unmindful of the fact that I owe you ten dollars."

"We'll spend that first. Now I'll go dress."

He picked up a few sections of the paper. "The *Times*!" he shouted. "You'll never see my stories in the *Times*. What's the idea?" But she had closed the door of the bedroom. In ten minutes she reappeared.

"Mm. Nice. Nice. Mm."

"Like it?"

"It's the best dress I've ever seen. And the hat, too. It's a cute little hat. I think girls' hats are better this year than they've ever been. They're so damn *cute*. I guess it has something to do with the way they do their hair."

"I guess it has a whole lot to do with the way they do their hair. Mine's still damp and looks like the wrath of God, and that's your fault. I wouldn't have taken a shower if I'd known we weren't going to the country. I'd have had a real bath and wouldn't have got my hair wet. Remind me to stop at a drug store—"

"Darling, I'm so glad!"

"—for a decent bathing cap. Jimmy, before we go, I want to tell you again, for the last time you've got to stop saying things like that to me. I'm not your mistress, and I'm not a girl off the streets, and I'm not accustomed to being talked to that way. It isn't funny, and no one else talks that way to me. Do you talk that way to the women on newspapers? Even if you do I'm sure they don't really like it all the time. You can't admire my dress without going into details about my figure, and—"

"Why in the name of Christ should I? Isn't the whole idea of the dress to show off your figure? Why does it look well on you? Because you have nice breasts and everything else. Now God damn it, why shouldn't I say so?"

"I think you'd better go." She took off her hat and sat down.

"All right, I'll go." He picked up his hat and walked heavily down the short hall to the door of the apartment. But he did not open the door. He put his hand on the knob, and then turned around and came back.

"I didn't say anything," she said.

"I know. And you didn't move. I know. You know I could no more walk out that door than I could walk out those windows. Will you please forgive me?"

"It will happen all over again, the same thing, the same way, same reason. And then you'll come back and ask me to forgive you, and I will. And every time I do, Jimmy, I hate myself. Not because I forgive you, but because I hate those words, I hate to be talked to that way, and I know, I *know* the only reason you do talk to me like that is because I *am* the kind of girl you talk to that way, and that's what I hate. Knowing that."

"Darling, that's not true. You're not any kind of girl. You're you, Isabel. And won't you ever believe me when I tell you what I've told you so often? That no matter what we do, whenever I see you like this, in the morning, in the daytime, when there are other people—I can't believe that you're my girl. Or that you ever were. And you're so lovely in that dress, and hat. I'm sorry I'm the way I am."

"You wouldn't talk to Lib that way. Or Caroline."

"I wouldn't talk to them *any* way. I couldn't be annoyed. Let's go before I say something else wrong."

"All right. Kiss me. Not hard." She put out her hand and he pulled her out of the chair until she stood close to him.

"I *have* to kiss you hard. Me not kiss you hard? Impossible." He laughed.

"Not quite impossible," she said. "There are times." She laughed.

"Now I don't want to go," he said.

"We're going. See if I have my key." She rummaged in her bag. "Yep. Lipstick, Jimmy. Here, I'll do it. Me your handkerchief. There."

He held the door open for her and with his free hand he made as if to take a whack at her behind, but he did not touch her. She rang for the elevator and after it groaned and whirred a while the door opened.

"Good morning, Miss Stannard," said the elevator man.

"Good morning," she said. They got in and the car began its descent, but stopped one floor below, and a man and woman got in. The man was precisely the same height as the woman, which made him seem smaller.

"Good morning, Mr. Farley, Mrs. Farley," said the elevator man.

"Good morning," said the Farleys.

None of the passengers looked at one another. They looked at the elevator man's shoulders. No one spoke until the ground floor was reached, then Isabel smiled and allowed Mrs. Farley to leave the car first, then she followed, then Farley nodded to the open door and indicated with his eyes that Jimmy should go first—and was obviously surprised when Jimmy did go first. But the Farleys beat them to the door and the doorman was standing there with the large door of their car open for them. The car, a Packard four-passenger convertible, sounded like some kind of challenge of power, and not unlike the exhaust of a speedboat gurgling into the water.

"And to think we walk while punks like those people ride in a wagon like that. Never mind, all that will be changed, all that will be changed. I guess you know who made the loudest noise in Union Square the day before yesterday."

"I guess I do," said Isabel.

"I don't think I like your tone. Somehow, I don't quite like your tone," but he began to whistle and she began to sing: "Take me back to Man-hattan, that dear-old, dirty, town."

At Madison Avenue they were almost struck by a huge Paramount taxi, and when Jimmy swore at the driver, the driver said, "Go on, I'll spit in your eye." And both Isabel and Jimmy distinctly heard the lone passenger, a girl in a fur coat, call to the driver: "Go on, spit in their eye." The cab beat the light and sped south in Madison.

"Nice girl," said Isabel. "Did you know her?"

"How would I know her? She's someone from this neighborhood obviously. Downtown we don't talk that way, not in the village."

"No, of course not, except I could point out that the taxi is on its way downtown, in a hurry."

"All right, point it out. And then for a disagreeable couple I give you the man and woman in the elevator. Mr. Princeton with the glasses and his wife. I'll bet they're battling right this minute in that beautiful big chariot. I'd rather know a girl that yells out of a taxi, 'Spit in their eye,' than two polite people that can't wait to be alone before they're at each other's throats."

"Well, that's the difference between you and me. I'd rather live in this part of town, where the people at least—"

"I didn't say anything about living with them, or having them for neighbors. All I said was I'd rather know that kind of girl—that girl —than those people. That's all I said."

"Still stick to my statement. I'd rather *know* the man and his wife. As a matter of fact I happen to know who they are. He's an architect."

"And I don't really give a damn who they are, but I do give a damn who the girl is."

"A girl who would wear a mink coat on a day like this. She's cheap."

"Well, with a mink coat she must have come high at some time."

He was silent a few seconds before continuing. "You know what I'm thinking, don't you? No, you don't. But I'd like to say it if you'd promise not to get sore? . . . I was just thinking what a powerful sexual attraction there is between us, otherwise why do we go on seeing each other when we quarrel so much?"

"We only quarrel, if you'll look back on it, we only quarrel for one reason, really, and that's the way you talk to me."

He said nothing, and they walked on in silence for several blocks.

WHEN Sunday morning came Paul Farley never liked to be alone with his wife, nor did Nancy Farley like to be alone with Paul. The Farleys were Roman Catholic, although when they were married, in the fourth summer after the war, you would not have been able to guess from their dossiers in the newspapers, without looking at their names, that the wedding was taking place in the Church of St. Vincent Ferrer. Of Paul it was said: "He attended Lawrenceville School and Princeton and served overseas as second lieutenant in a machine gun company of the 27th Division. He is a member of the Association of Ex-Members of Squadron A, the Princeton Club and the Racquet and Tennis Club." Of Nancy it said: "Miss McBride, who is a member of the Junior League, attended the Brearley School and Westover, and she was introduced to society last season at a dance at the Colony Club and later at the Bachelors' Cotillon in Baltimore, Md."

After their marriage they had children, three of them, rapid-fire;

but when the third, a girl, died, Nancy, who had wanted a girl very much, came to a decision. It was a major adjustment in her life. Up to that time Nancy had been a girl who always did what people told her to do. A succession of people: her mother, to a lesser degree her father, a nurse, a governess, her teachers, and the Church. The odor of sanctity was faint but noticeable in the McBride household, as Nancy's paternal uncle had been quite a good friend of the late Cardinal Gibbons; and the McBrides, as they themselves put it, realized their position. It was a religious household, including the servants, and at the time of Nancy's various debuts the big house in the East Seventies still had its quota of holy pictures, and there was hardly a bureau which did not contain one drawer full of broken rosary beads, crucifixes with the corpus missing, Father Lasance's *My Prayer Book, The Ordinary of the Mass,* and other prayer books for special occasions. One of Nancy's losing battles against the domination of her elders (and they were all defeats) was fought for the removal of a small, white china holywater font which hung at the door of her bedroom. She finally capitulated because a Westover friend who was visiting her was curious and delighted by the sacred article.

Nancy was the youngest of four children. The first-born, Thornton, was ten years older than Nancy. He was out of a high-priced Catholic prep school, Yale, and Fordham Law School. He was with his father in the law firm and cared about nothing except the law and golf.

Next in age was Nancy's only sister, Mollie. She was eight years older than Nancy, and when Nancy was married Mollie was in the Philippines, living the life of an army officer's wife.

Two years younger than Mollie was Jay—Joseph, but always known as Jay. He was unable to finish prep school, and had lived almost all his life, from the time he developed a case of T.B., in New Mexico. He was at work on a monumental history of the Church and the Indian in the Southwest.

There would have been a child between Jay and Nancy, but it had been a Fallopian pregnancy from which Nancy's mother almost died. This was kept from Nancy not only all through her girlhood, but

even after she was married and had her own two children. Nancy did
not know about her mother's disastrous Fallopian pregnancy for the
reason that her mother did not quite know how to explain it. It was
kept quiet until Nancy's little girl died in early infancy, and then
Mrs. McBride told her. It infuriated Nancy to be told so late in life.
It might not have made any difference in her attitude toward having
children, but it gave her the feeling of having been insulted from a
distance, this taciturnity of her mother's. People ought to tell you
things like that. Your own mother ought to tell you everything about
that—and then she would recall that what ought to be and what
actually was were two quite different things so far as her mother and
sex were concerned. Mrs. McBride accepted the working theory of
the Church that sex education of children was undesirable, unsanc-
tioned; and when Nancy was fourteen her mother told her that "this
is something that happens to girls"—and that was all she ever told
her until Paul and Nancy were to be married. Then Mrs. McBride
provided the second piece of information to her daughter: "Never let
Paul touch you when you are unwell." Whatever else Nancy learned
was from the exchange of knowledge among school acquaintances,
and from her secret reading of the informative little propaganda
pamphlets which the government got out during the World War,
telling in detail the atrocities which the Germans committed upon
Belgian maidens, nuns, priests, old women. These pamphlets did not
incite Nancy to turn her allowance into Liberty Bonds, but they
made her understand things about her anatomy and the anatomy of
the young men with whom she swam summer after summer on the
South Shore of Long Island.

Sex had been healthy and normally strong and only a trifle unpleasant for Nancy up to the time of the death of her daughter. Paul
was considerate and tender and fun. Child-bearing, the incomparable
peace of nursing the boys, the readjustment after the nursing periods
—all were accomplished with a minimum of fright and pain, and
sometimes with a pleasure that—especially at nursing time—was
heavenly joy, because at such times Nancy felt so practically religious. She wanted to have a lot of children, and she was glad that

things were that way: that the Church approved and that there was such high pleasure in motherhood. Then the little girl died and for the first time Nancy discovered that you cannot blame your body alone for the hell it sometimes gives you. Nancy broke with Rome the day her baby died. It was a secret break, but no Catholic breaks with Rome casually.

THE man carrying the black Gladstone refused the help of the Red Caps. Who wanted a little thing like that carried for him? A little thing like that. What did they think? Did they think he wasn't strong enough to carry it? Didn't he look strong enough to carry a little bag, a little Gladstone like this? Did they think he wasn't young enough to carry a bag like this? Did they think he—they didn't think he was old, did they? Huh. If they thought that they had another think coming, by Jove. Ablative of Jupiter. They were young and looked pretty strong, most of these Red Caps, but the man drew a deep breath as he walked rapidly up the ramp and out into the great station. He would wager he was as strong as most of them. He could break them in half, and they thought he was old and wanted to carry his little Gladstone! He thought of how they would look on a chain gang, with the sweat pouring down on their satiny hides. Satiny hides. That was good. Ugh. He wanted to be sick, he wanted to think away from bodies; he patted his belly and pinched his Phi Beta Kappa key and started to curl the watch-chain around his finger, but this was somehow getting back again to the things of the flesh, and he wanted to think away from things of the flesh. He wanted to think of the ablative, the passive periphrastic, the middle voice, the tangent and cotangent, the School Board meeting next Tuesday. . . . He wished he hadn't thought of the School Board meeting next Tuesday or any Tuesday. He wished he'd always thought of the School Board meeting next Tuesday.

He got into a taxi and gave the address, and the driver was so slow starting the meter that the man repeated the address. The driver nodded, showing half his face. The man looked at the face and at the driver's picture. They didn't look much alike, but they never did. He supposed this was a reputable taxicab company that operated the taxicabs at the station. Oh, well, that wasn't important.

"If only I'd always thought of the School Board meetings I wouldn't be here now, in a filthy New York taxicab, living a lie by being in this city on a cooked-up pretext. Living a worse, worse lie by having any reason to be here. God damn that girl! I am a good man. I am a bad man, a wicked man, but she is worse. She is really bad. She is bad, she is badness. She is Evil. She not only is *evil,* but she *is* Evil. Whatever I am now is her fault, because that girl is bad. Whatever I was before, the bad me, was nothing. I never was bad before I knew her. I sinned, but I was not bad. I was not corrupted. I did not want to come to New York before I knew her. She made me come to New York. She makes me trump up excuses to come to New York, makes me lie to my wife, fool my wife, that good woman, that poor good woman. That girl is bad, and hell's fire is not enough for her. Oh, *more* fresh air! It is good, this fresh air, even in a taxicab. Fresh air taxicab! God! Amos and Andy. Here I'm thinking of Amos and Andy, and all that they mean. Home. Seven o'clock. The smell of dinner in preparation, ready to be served when Amos and Andy go off the air. Am I the man who loves to listen to Amos and Andy?" The door opened and he got out and paid the driver.

2

THE YOUNG MAN got out of bed and went to the kitchenette and pushed the wall button that unlatched the front door. He was in his underwear, one-piece cotton underwear and it had not been fresh the day before. He rumpled his hair and yawned, standing at the door and waiting until whoever it was that rang would ring the apartment bell. It rang, and he opened it half a foot.

"Oh," he said, and opened the door all the way.

"Hel-lo, darling, look what I brought you." Gloria held up the parcel, a wrapped-up bottle.

"Oh," he said, and yawned again. "Thanks." He went back to the bed and lay on it face down. "I don't want any."

"Get up. It's a lovely Spring morning," said Gloria. "I didn't think you'd be alone."

"Uh, I'm alone. I haven't any soda. You'll have to drink that straight, or else with plain water. I don't want any."

"Why?"

"I got drunk."

"What for?"

"Oh, I don't know. Listen, Gloria, I'm dead. Do you mind if I go to sleep a little while?"

"Certainly I do. Where are your pajamas? Did you sleep in your underwear?"

"I haven't any pajamas. I have two pairs and they're both in the laundry. I don't even know what laundry."

"Here. Here's twenty dollars. Buy yourself some pajamas tomorrow, or else find the laundry and pay what you owe them."

"I've some money."

"How much?"

"I don't know."

"Well, take this, you'll need it. I don't believe you have any money, either."

"Why are you suddenly rich? Isn't that a new coat?"

"Yes. Brand-new. You didn't ask me to take it off. Is that hospitable?"

"Good God, you'd take it off if you wanted to. Take it off, if you want to."

"Look," she said, for he was closing his eyes again. She opened the coat.

He suddenly had the expression of a man who has been struck and cannot strike back. "All right," he said. "You stole the coat."

"He tore my dress, my new evening dress. I had to have something to wear in the daytime. All I had was my evening coat, and I couldn't go out wearing that."

"I guess I will have a drink."

"Good."

"Who is the guy?"

"You don't know him."

"How do you know I don't know him? Damn it, why don't you just tell me who it is and save time? You always do that. I ask you something and you say I wouldn't know, or you talk around it or beat about the bush for an hour, and you make me so God damn mad —and then you tell me. If you'd tell me in the first place we'd save all this."

"All right, I'll tell you."

"Well, go ahead and *tell* me!"

"His name is Weston Liggett."

"Liggett? Liggett. Weston Liggett. I do know him."

"You don't. How would you know him?"

"I don't know him, but I know who he is. He's a yacht racer and he used to be a big Yale athlete. Very social. Oh, and married. I've seen his wife's name. What about that? Where did you go?"

"His apartment."

"His apartment? Is his wife—does she like girls?" He was fully awake now. "Did she give you the coat? You're going in for that again, are you?"

"I think you're disgusting."

"You think *I'm* disgusting. That's what it is. That's started again, all over again. That's why you came here, because you thought I had someone here. You know where you ought to be? You ought to be in an insane asylum. They put people in insane asylums that don't do a tenth of what you do. Here, take your lousy money and your damn whiskey and get out of here."

She did not move. She sat there looking like someone tired of waiting for a train. She did not seem to hear him. But this mood was in such contrast to her vitality of a minute ago that there was no doubting that she had heard him, and no doubting that what he was saying had caused her mood to change.

"I'm sorry," he said. "I'm terribly sorry, Gloria. I'd rather cut my throat than say that. Do you believe me? You do believe me, don't you? You do believe I only said it because—"

"Because you believed it," she said. "No. Mrs. Liggett is not a Lesbian, if you're interested. I went to their apartment with her husband and I slept with him. She's away. I stole the coat, because he tore my clothes. He practically raped me. Huh. You think that's funny, but it's true. There are people who don't know as much about me as you do, you know. I'll go now."

He got up and stood in front of the door.

"Please," she said. "Let's not have a struggle."

"Sit down, Gloria. Please sit down."

"It's no use, Eddie, I've made up my mind. I can't have you for a friend if you're going to throw things up at me that I told you in confidence. I've told you more than I've ever told anyone else, even my psychiatrist. But at least he has professional ethics. At least he wouldn't get angry and throw it all up to me. I trusted you as a friend, and—"

"You *can* trust me. Don't go. Besides, you can't go this way. Listen, sit down, darling." He took her hand, and she allowed herself to be guided to a chair. "I'll call up a girl I know, I was out with her last night, and ask her to bring some day clothes over here. She's about your build."

"Who is she?"

"You wouldn't—her name is Norma Day. She goes to N. Y. U. She's very good-looking. I'll call her and she'll come right over. I have a sort of date with her anyway. All right?"

"Uh-huh." Gloria was pleased and bright. "I think I'll take a bath. Shall I? Okay?"

"Sure."

"Okay," she said. "You sleep."

WESTON LIGGETT walked up the platform to where the line of parked cars began, and as he reached the beginning of the line he heard a horn blown six or seven times. A Ford station wagon was just arriving. It was driven by a young girl, and two other girls about the same age were on the front seat with her. Liggett took off his hat and waved.

"Hello, pretty girls," he said. He stood beside the right front door. The girl in the driver's seat spoke to him:

"Daddy, this is Julie Rand; this is my father."

"How do you do," he said to the new girl, and then spoke to the girl in the middle: "Hello, Frances."

" 'Lomistliggett," said Frances.

"Where's Bar?" he said.

"She drove Mother over to the club. We're all going there for lunch. Get in, we're late."

"No, we're not. Mother knew I was coming out on this train."

"Well, we're late anyway," said Ruth Liggett, the driver. "We're always late. Like the late Jimmy Walker."

"Oh, ho, ho." Miss Rand laughing.

"Is that door closed, Daddy?" said Ruth.

"Think so. Yes," he said.

"It rattles so. We ought to turn this in while we can still get something on it."

"Uh-huh. We'll turn this in and sell the house. Would that suit you?" he said.

"Oh. Always talking about how broke we are. And in front of strangers."

"Who's a stranger? Oh, Miss Rand. Well, she's not exactly a stranger, is she? Aren't you Henry Rand's daughter?"

"No. I'm his niece. My father was David Rand. I'm visiting my Uncle Henry and Aunt Bess, though."

"Well, then you're not a stranger. *You* like this car, don't you?"

"Don't call it a car, Daddy," said Ruth.

"I like it very much," said Miss Rand. "It's very nice, I think."

"Ooh, what a prevaricator! She does not. She didn't want to ride in it. You should have seen her. When she came out of the house she took one look and said, 'Is this what we're going in?' Didn't you? Own up."

"Well, I never rode in a truck before."

"A truck!" said Ruth.

"Aren't there station wagons where you come from?"

"No. We just have regular cars."

"She comes from—what's the name of the place, Randy?"

"Wilkes-Barre, P A."

"And a very nice town it is," said Liggett. "I remember it very well. It's near Scranton. I have a lot of very dear friends in Scranton."

"Do you know anybody in Wilkes-Barre?" said Miss Rand.

"I don't believe so—*Ruth!*"

"Well, he ought to stay on his own side of the road."

"You can't count on that. I don't mind taking chances, but when there are other people in the car."

"Oh, he wouldn't have hit me."

"That's what you think. No wonder this car's all shot."

"Now you can't blame that on me, Daddy. I don't drive this car that much."

"Well, I'll admit you're not responsible for this car, but the Chrysler, you are responsible for that. Clutch is slipping because you ride it all the time. Fenders wrinkled."

"Who wrinkled it—not them. It. The left hind fender. That happened when someone else was driving, not me."

"Well, let's not talk about it."

"No, of course not. I'm right. That's why we won't talk about it."

"Is that fair? Do I change the subject when I'm in the wrong, Ruth? Do I?"

"No, darling. That wasn't fair." She reached her hand back to be held. He kissed it.

"Why, Daddy!" The others did not see.

"Shh," he said and then was silent until they came to the club. "Here we are. I'll go around and wash up. I'll meet you in three minutes."

In the locker room he rang for the steward and arranged to cash two checks. The club had a rule against cashing a check for more than twenty-five dollars on any single day, but he made them out as of two dates and the steward, who had done this many times before, gave him fifty dollars. The sixty dollars Liggett had left for Gloria and the other money he had spent on her had left him short, and he knew Emily would think it strange that he had spent so much in one night.

He had a highball, and as he prepared it and drank it he wondered what it was that made him feel so tender toward Emily, when he was sure that what he ought to be feeling was unwillingness to see her. Yet he wanted very much to see her. He wondered what had made him kiss Ruth's hand. He hadn't done that for a long time, and never had he done it quite so warmly and spontaneously. Always before this it had been a part of a game he played with Ruth in which Ruth played a flirtatious girl and he was a hick from the country. He joined the party in the grill.

He went straight to Emily and kissed her cheek.

"Oh-ho, somebody had a highball," she said.

"Somebody needed a highball," he said. "Somebody has a hangover and badly needed a drink. How about the rest of you? Cocktail, dear?"

"Not I, thanks," said Emily, "and I don't think the girls had better have anything if they're going to play tennis. Let's order, shall we?"

"Steak," said Ruth. "How about you, Randy? Steak?"

"Yes, please."

"We all want steak," said Ruth. "You do, don't you, Frannie?"

"I don't," said Barbara, the younger Liggett girl. "Not that it makes any difference to Miss Smarty Pants, but steak is exactly what I don't want. Julie, if you'd rather not have steak just say so. You too, Frannie. Mother, do you want steak?"

"No, dear, I think I'd rather have just a chop. Will that take too long, Harry?"

" 'Bout ten minutes, Mizz Liggett. Course you be having soup maybe, first, 'n' by the time yole get finished with your soup chop'll be ready."

"Daddy, steak?" said Ruth.

"Right. Tomato juice cocktail first for me, if that's all right, Ruth?"

"Absolutely. Have we decided? Chops for how many? Mother, chops. Miss Barbara, chops. Randy, chops. Daddy, steak. Frannie, steak, and me, steak. Have you got that, Harry?"

"Yes, Miss Liggett. What about vege'ables?"

"Just bring in a lot of vegetables," said Ruth.

All through the ordering Liggett watched Ruth and thought of

Emily. Emily—and he did not remember this at the moment—who retained the mouth, nose, chin, bone structure and, to some extent, the complexion Emily had had and that made her handsome; but she was handsome no longer. What Emily retained only made you ask what had happened that left her a plain woman with good features. The eyes, of course they made the difference. They looked nowadays like the eyes of someone who has many headaches, although this did not happen to be the case. Emily was apparently very healthy.

Now he watched her busying herself with her hands; unfolding her napkin, touching without changing the position of the silverware, folding her hands. She had a way of watching her hands when she was using them. He wondered about that, noticing it for the first time. He could not recall ever having seen her watching her hands when they were resting and still, the way she would have if she were conscious of them in the sense of being vain. What she did was to watch them as though she were checking up on their efficiency, their neatness. It was just another part of the way she lived. Her life was like that.

Often she would sit at home with a book of poems in her hand and she would be looking in the direction of the window, a dreamy look in her eyes. He would look again and again at her, wondering what pretty thoughts had been started by what line in what poem. Then she would say suddenly something like: "Do you think I ought to ask the Hobsons for Thursday night? You like her, don't you?" Liggett supposed a lot of husbands were like him; two or three, at least, of his own generation had confided to him that they didn't know their own wives. They had been married, some of them, as much as twenty years; reasonably if not strictly faithful, good providers, good fathers, hard workers, and temperate. Then after a year or so of the depression, when they saw it was not a little thing that was going to pass, these men began taking stock of what life had given them or they had taken. Usually men of this kind began counting with, "I have a wife and two children . . ." and go on from there to their "investments," cash, job, houses, cars, boats, horses, clothes, furniture, trust fund, pair of binoculars, club bonds, and so on. They were—these men—able to see right away that the tangible assets in the Spring of 1931 were worth on the whole about a quarter of what they had cost originally, and in some cases less than that. And in some cases, nothing. By the time the depression had reached that point such men accepted as fact the fact that nothing that you could buy or sell was worth what it once had been worth. At least it worked out that way. Then a few men, a few million men, asked themselves whether the things they had bought ever had been worth what had been paid for them. Ah! That was worth thinking about, worth buying heavy and expensive books to find out about. Some of the keenest practical jokers on the floor of the Stock Exchange went home nights to see what the hell John Stuart Mill said—to find out who the hell John Stuart Mill was.

But among Liggett's friends there were men who, beginning their inventories with, "I have a wife and two children—" went through the list of their worldly goods and then came back to the first item: wife. Then they discovered that they could not really be sure they had their wives. The mortality rate for marriages in Liggett's class is fairly close to 100%, but until the great depression there was no reason to find this out; most of these men believed that they were working for the happiness of their wives and children as well as for their own advancement, but an idle woman is an idle woman, whether her husband is downtown making millions or downtown trying to hold on to a $40-a-week job. Men like Liggett—in 1930 you would see them on the roads of Long Island and Westchester, in cap and windbreaker and sport shoes, taking walks on Sunday with their wives, trying to get to know their wives, because they wanted to believe that a wife was one thing they could count on. Of course there was nothing deliberately insulting in this attitude, and as often as not the wife was not conscious of insult, so it was all right. She knew that he always had taken her to football games and the theater, he paid her bills, he bought her Christmas presents, he was generous to her poor relations, he did not interfere with the education and rearing of the children. Sometimes she did not even ask why, when he became more curious, tried to become more companionable. She knew there was a depression, and she saw the magazine articles about the brave wives who were standing shoulder-to-shoulder with their husbands; she read the sermons in the Monday papers in which clergymen told their parishioners (and the press; always the press) that the depression was a good thing because it brought husbands and wives closer to each other.

Liggett was not quite one of these men; Emily certainly was not one of these women. For one thing, Liggett was a Pittsburgher and Emily a Bostonian. That was one thing, not two. Liggett was precisely the sort of person who, if he hadn't married Emily, would be just the perfect person for Emily to snub. All her life she seemed to be saving up for one snub, which would have to be delivered to an upper-class American, since no foreigner and no lower-class American could possibly understand what she had that she felt entitled her to deliver a snub. What she had was a Colonial governor; an unbroken string of studious Harvard men; their women. Immediately and her own was, of course, the Winsor-Vincent Club-Sewing Circle background. She had a few family connections in New York, and they were unassailable socially; they never went out. It came as a surprise which he was a long time understanding for Liggett to learn, after he married Emily, that Emily never had stopped at a hotel in New York. She explained that the only possible reason you went to New York was to visit relations, and then you stopped with them, not at a hotel. Yes, that was true, he agreed—and never told her the fun he had had as a kid, stopping at New York hotels; the time he released a roll of toilet paper upon Fifth Avenue, the time he climbed along the ledge from one window to another. He was a little afraid of her.

But she was better off with him than she might have been with a Boston man. He was rich and handsome, a Yale athlete. Those qualifications were enough to explain his attraction for her. But he was more than that. She was handsome, she was healthy, and therefore she was passionate, and she wanted him from the moment she first met him. In the beginning Liggett himself was all mixed up about her; he was awed by her manner and her accent (he never got over the accent, and only got accustomed to the manner). She was less handsome than other girls he had known, but he had not known anyone like her, not so close. They met at a deb party, on one of her infrequent visits to New York—his last before beginning training for crew. He made a date with her for tea the following day, but had to break it, and thus began a correspondence which on his part was regulated by the necessity of staying in college and rowing at the same time, and on her part by a schedule: never answer more than one letter a week, and never until two days after the letter has been received. Because of her he decided to go to Harvard Business School. This pleased his father, who gave him a Fiat phaeton and anything else he asked for. There was one thing he could not ask his father for, and that was Emily's fair white body. Emily gave that without being asked, one winter's night in Boston. After waiting three miserable weeks to see if anything was going to happen, they decided to be engaged.

She was better off married to Liggett than she might have been with a Boston man because he never took her passion for granted. A Boston man might have, and might not be long looking around for more of the same from someone else. Liggett could not take her for granted. There is something about those good, good words of sleeping together, the language of sleeping together, when spoken in the tones of Commonwealth Avenue, that no man who has been brought up west of the Connecticut River can fail to notice. And when a man is listening for the words, when he teaches them to a woman, when he asks her to say them, he does not take everything all at once. He will want more.

There was that, and there was the secrecy. Their intimate moments were their own, so much so that Liggett did not once mention Emily's pregnancy to anyone, not even to his own sister, while she was carrying their first child. It was nothing they agreed upon; Emily herself told Liggett's sister. But it was part of the way he felt about Emily. Anything that had to do with their intimate life was not to be discussed with a third person, so far as he was concerned.

To a degree this was true of everything else in their relationship. Liggett's impulse was always to talk about Emily, but he had gone that important step above vulgarity: he secretly recognized his own temptation to vulgarity. However valuable an asset this may be, it had one bad effect. A man ought to be able, when it becomes necessary, to discuss his wife with a third person, man or woman. Since it was impossible for him to bring himself to discuss Emily with another man he found himself in a spot where he had to talk to some woman. It had to be someone who knew Emily, someone close to her. He looked around and for the first time became aware that Emily in the years she had lived in New York—at that time, seven; it was in 1920—had not made a single close friend. Her best friend was a Boston girl, Martha Harvey. Martha was a divorcee. She had been married to a young millionaire who was practically illiterate, always drunk, was three inches shorter than she, and never had spoken an uncivil or impolite word to anyone in his life. Martha had grown up with Emily and they saw each other frequently, but when it came time to discuss Emily with her, Liggett saw how impossible it would be. Martha in a way was Emily over again.

The occasion, however, was urgent. Emily's family's money was mostly in cotton mills. Emily's father was a doctor, a pleasant, unimaginative man who studied medicine in a day when surgeons still spoke of "laudable pus." (He never quite got over the surprise of learning that Walter Reed was right.) In fact his presence in medicine is explained by a fondness for the dissection of cats. It was the only cerebral activity he ever had been interested in, so his father and mother steered him into medicine. A merit-badge boy scout would have been as useful in an emergency as Emily's father, but a few friends went to him for colds and sore throat, and they constituted his practice. His practice was his excuse for neglecting his financial responsibilities, but every year or two he would have an idea, and at this time his idea was to get rid of all his cotton holdings and turn the cash into a vague something else. This time the vague something else was German marks. He just knew they were going to be worth something, and as he had traveled in Germany as a young man, he thought it would be pleasant, since his fortune would soon be doubled, to have a castle on the Rhine, where even at that moment you could have a castle, they said, fully staffed and equipped for $100 a month.

Liggett did not care a very great deal what the old man did with his own money, but that money, he felt, was not altogether the old man's to fool with. The doctor had not earned it; he had inherited it, and since he had inherited it, it seemed to Liggett to be a kind of trust which the doctor had no right to violate. At least it was not to be squandered. If the doctor could go on year in, year out without assuming a permanent responsibility for the money, then he ought not to be permitted to risk losing all of it when he had a foolish hunch. Cotton was high that year, and while it was debatable whether it was the height of shrewdness to dump so much stock on a favorable market, Liggett at least conceded that there was a chance the market would absorb the doctor's holdings without strong reaction. No, with the old gentleman's decision to sell Liggett could not seriously quarrel (indeed, it would have been more like the old man to sell at the bottom of the market). But German marks, for Christ's sake!

Liggett wished Emily had a brother, or even the kind of sister some people have. But Emily's sister was a total stranger, and brother she had none. Next was friend, and friend was Martha. He rejected the plan of talking to Martha the moment her name conjured up a picture of her. But the more he thought the more he was convinced that he had to talk to somebody about the situation. Emily and the two little girls were in Hyannisport that summer, and he did not want to speak to Emily if he could help it. She was taking the children very seriously at the time and talk about her father would worry her.

Martha was just going out when he telephoned, going out to dine alone, and she was not surprised or curious at his calling her for dinner. She said yes. He asked her if she would like a drink, and she said she would, very much, and he said he would bring a bottle of gin. He stopped at a place in Lexington Avenue, bought a bottle of the six-dollar gin, had a drink on Matt, the proprietor, and took a taxi, one of those small, low Philadelphia-made un-American-looking Yellows of that period.

Martha lived on Murray Hill between Park and Madison, in an automatic-elevator apartment. They had orange blossom cocktails, which Liggett liked. She asked once, and only once, about Emily.

She said: "How's Emily? She's at Hyannisport, isn't she?" He said she was fine, and was on the verge of correcting himself to say that whether she knew it or not she was not fine at all. Then later, when he saw Martha did not come back to Emily, he was in more real danger of talking about Emily; a girl who had what Martha had, the assurance and poise that gave her courage to accept his wanting to have dinner because she was herself and not merely a trusted friend of his wife's—you could confide in that girl. But at the same time the thing he wanted to talk about began to recede. He began to enjoy himself because he was enjoying Martha's company.

They had two cocktails, and then she told him to take off his coat. Next he thought she would offer him a cigar, because take his coat off was exactly what he wanted to do. It was so comfortable here. "Are you hungry?" he said.

"Not specially. Let's wait. It'll be cool around nine o'clock, if you're in no hurry."

"Gosh, I'm not in a hurry."

"Have some more cocktails, shall we? You know, I like to drink. I never knew I did—gosh, I never even knew about drinking—till I married Tommy, and he used to try to get me drunk, but that was no good. I don't like to have people try to get me drunk. If I want to get drunk. I'll do it."

He took the cocktail shaker to the kitchen and made very strong cocktails, not entirely on purpose, but not entirely accidentally, for what she had just been saying reminded him of a physical, biological, whatever-you-want-to-call-it fact: that Martha had been married and therefore had slept with a man. It meant no more to him for the time being. It was just strange that he had somehow ceased to think of her as a girl with a life of her own. Almost always he had thought of her as someone who, when he knew her better, would become finally a good sport, a sexless friend of Emily's.

"Today is Bastille Day in Paris," he said, when he returned with the cocktails. (It was also the day Sacco and Vanzetti were convicted.)

"So it is. I hope to be there next year on Bastille Day."

"Oh, really?"

"I think so. I couldn't go to the Cape this summer because Tommy finds out where I am and comes calling at all hours."

"Isn't there some way to put a stop to that?" he said.

"Oh, I suppose there is. People are always suggesting things like the police. But why do that? They don't seem to remember that I like Tommy."

"Oh, do you?"

"Very much. I'm not in love with him, but I like him."

"Oh, I didn't know that."

"Well, of course you couldn't be expected to."

"No, that's true. I guess this is the first time you and I've really talked together."

"It is." She had her arm across the back of the sofa. She put down her cigarette and crushed it in the tray and picked up her cocktail. She looked away from him as she raised the glass. "As a matter of fact, I never thought we ever would be like this, the two of us, sitting, talking, having a cocktail together."

"Why?"

"Do you want the truth?" she said.

"Of course."

"Well, all right. The truth is I never liked you."

"You didn't."

"No," she said. "But I do now."

Why? Why? Why? He wanted to ask. Why? Why do you like me now? I like you. How I like you! "But you do now," he repeated.

"Yes. Aren't you interested in knowing why I like you now after not liking you for such a long time?"

"Of course, but if you want to tell me you will and if you don't there's no use my asking."

"Come here," she said. He sat beside her on the sofa and took her hand. "I like the way you smell."

"Is that why you like me now and didn't before?"

"Damn before!" She put her hand on his cheek. "Wait a minute," she said. "Don't get up. I'll do it." She went to one of the two large windows and pulled down the shade. "People across the street."

He had her with her clothes on. And from that moment on he never loved Emily again.

"Do you want to stay here tonight?" she said. "If I'm going to be with child for this we might as well be together all night. If you want to stay?"

"I do, I do."

"Grand. I'll have to phone the maid and tell her not to come in early tomorrow. You'll be out of here before ten, tomorrow I mean, won't you?"

They had a wildly passionate affair that summer. They would have dinner in little French restaurants, drinking bad whiskey out of small coffee cups. She was sailing in September and the night before she sailed she said to him: "I don't care if I die now, do you?"

"No. Except I want to live." All summer he had been doing arithmetic on scratch paper—financial arrangements for getting a divorce from Emily. "Once again, marry me."

"No, darling. We'd be no good married to each other. Me especially. But this I know, that for the rest of our lives, whenever we see each other, if I look into your eyes and you look into mine, and we see the thing that we see now—nothing can stop us, can it?"

"No. Nothing."

The next time he saw her was two years later in Paris. In the meantime he had met and lain with ten other women, and Martha was in the White Russian taxi-driver phase. They didn't even have to give each other up, for there was scarcely recognition, let alone love, when again their eyes met.

It got around that he was on the town, but if some kind friend ever told Emily she never let it make any difference. He was comparatively discreet in that he avoided schemers. Among the women he slept with was an Englishwoman, right out of Burke's Peerage, who gave him gonorrhea, or stomach ulcers as it was then called. To Emily he confided that in addition to the ulcers he had a hernia, and she accepted that, not sure what a hernia was, but knowing that it was not a topic for dinner-table conversation. She was so incurious that he was able to keep at home the paraphernalia for the treatment of his disease.

Dr. Winchester, by the way, did not buy the marks. An honest broker dissuaded him.

LIGGETT addressed his wife: "Are you coming in town tonight or in the morning?"

"Not till Tuesday morning. The girls have a day off tomorrow."

"Why?"

"One of the kids got diphtheria and they're fumigating the school," said Ruth. "Are you staying out?"

"I'd like to. I'd like to really get going on the boat. But I've got to go back to town tonight, so what about you and Bar and Frannie and Miss Rand all getting paint brushes and going to work tomorrow?"

"Pardon me while I die from laughing," said Ruth.

"I will if the others do," said Barbara.

"You're safe and you know it," said Ruth.

"Girls?" said Emily.

"LET's save the Plaza?" said Isabel Stannard.

"Nope. I'm for blowing it up," said Jimmy.

"What?"

"Let it go, dear. It wasn't worth it."

"What wasn't worth what?" she said.

"Please, will you go back to whatever it was you said first? Let's save the Plaza. All right, let's save it. Save it for what? Do you want to go some place else?"

"I think we ought to go there some time when we're feeling more like it."

"Well, I don't exactly see what you mean. I feel like it. I felt like it before I saw you, I felt like it up at your apartment, and you did too—"

"No, not exactly. Remember I was dressed for the country. I thought we were going for a drive."

"Mm. Well, where to, then?" he said.

"Let's keep walking down Fifth—"

"Till we get to Childs Forty-eighth Street."

"All right," she said. "That's all right with me."

"I thought it would be."

"We could go to Twenty-One."

"It's Sunday."

"Aren't they open Sunday? I'm sure I've been there Sunday some time."

"Oh, I know you have, some time. But not at this hour. It's too early, dear. It's too early. They don't open till around five-thirty."

"Are you sure that isn't something new?"

"When the same people were at 42 West Forty-ninth they had the same rule about Sunday. Now that they're at 21 West Fifty-second Street, damned if they haven't the same rule they had at 42 West Forty-ninth. The same people, the same rule, different places."

"Another one of those hats," she said.

"Another one of what hats?"

"Didn't you see it? I think they're rather cute, but I don't know whether to buy one or not. Those hats. Didn't you notice that girl that went by with the foreign-looking man? She was smoking a cigarette."

"She gets paid for that."

"Paid for it?"

"Yes, paid for it. I read that in Winchell's column—"

"The way you wander about from subject to subject, you're like a mountain goat jumping from crag to crag—"

"From precipice to precipice, and back—"

"I know that one, don't say it. Why does she get paid?"

"Why does who get paid, my lamb, my pet?"

"The woman. The one with the hat. The one I just commented on. You said Walter Winchell said she gets money."

"Oh, yes. She gets paid for smoking a cigarette on Fifth Avenue. Winchell ran that in his column after the Easter parade. They're trying to popularize street smoking for women—"

"It'll never go."

"It'll never take the place of the old Welsbach burner, if—hello. Hello." He spoke to two people, girl and man.

"Who are they? See, she has one of those Eugenie hats. She's rather attractive. Who is she?"

"She's a model at Bergdorf Goodman's."

"She's French?"

"She's about as French as you are—"

"That's more French than you think."

"Well, than I am. She's—are you still interested?—a Jewess, and he's a lawyer, a Broadway divorce lawyer. He's the kind you see in the tabloids every Monday morning. He tips off the city editors of the *News* and *Mirror* and gets a free ad on page three. The story's always about his client, of course, but he gets his name printed in the third paragraph, with his address. Winthrop S. Saltonstall, of Fourteen-Something Broadway."

"Huh. Winthrop Saltonstall's hardly a Jewish name."

"That's what *you* think."

"Then I suppose she's getting a divorce—although of course she may just know him anyway."

"That's right. You're catching on."

"I've always wanted to go to a service at St. Patrick's. Will you take me some time?"

"What do you mean, a service? Do you mean Mass?"

"Yes, I guess so."

"All right, I'll take you some time. We'll get married in St. Pat's."

"Is that a threat or a promise?"

He stopped dead. "Listen, Isabel, will you do me a favor? A big favor?"

"Why, I don't know. What is it?"

"Will you just go on being a Bryn Mawr girl, nice, attractive, worried about what Leuba taught you, polite, well-bred—"

"Yes, yes, and what?"

"And leave the vulgarities of the vernacular to me? When you want to be slangy, when you want to make a wisecrack, stifle the impulse."

"But I didn't make any wisecrack."

"Oh-ho-ho, you're telling me."

"But I still don't see what you mean, Jimmy."

"They ought to take those fences down and let the people see what they're doing. I am an old construction-watcher, and I think I will take it up with Ivy Lee."

"What are you talking about?"

"I was just thinking as we passed where they're building Radio City, if they took the fences away I'd be able to check up on the progress and report back to the Rockefellers. Ivy Lee is their public relations counsel."

"Ivy Lee. It sounds like a girl's name."

"You ought to hear the whole name."

"What is it?"

"Ivy Ledbetter Lee. He gets $250,000 a year. Here we are, and we probably won't be able to get a table."

They got a table. They knew exactly what they wanted, including all the coffee you could drink for the price of one cup. On the dinner you could even have all the food you wanted for the prix fixe.

"What are we up to this afternoon?"

"Oh, whatever you like," she said.

"I want to see 'The Public Enemy.' "

"Oh, divine. James Cagney."

"Oh, you like Cagney?"

"Adore him."

"Why?" he said.

"Oh, he's so attractive. So tough. Why—I just thought of something."

"What?"

"He's—I hope you don't mind this—but he's a little like you."

"Uh. Well, I'll phone and see what time the main picture goes on."

"Why?"

"Well, I've seen it and you haven't, and I don't want you to see the ending first."

"Oh, I don't mind."

"I'll remind you of that after you've seen the picture. I'll go downstairs and phone. If King Prajadhipok comes in and tries to pick you up it won't be a compliment, so have him put out."

"Oh, on account of his eyes. See, I got it."

* * *

"WILL you try that number again, please?" said the old man. He held the telephone in a way that was a protest against the hand-set type of phone, a routine protest against something new. He held it with two hands, the one hand where it should be, the other hand cupped under the part he spoke into. "It's Stuyvesant, operator. Are you dialing S, T, U? . . . Well, I thought perhaps you were dialing S, T, Y."

He waited, but after more than five minutes he gave up again.

Joab Ellery Reddington, A.B. (Wesleyan), M.A. (Harvard), Ph.D. (Wesleyan), had come to New York for a special purpose, but the success of his mission depended upon his first completing the telephone call. Without making that connection the trip was futile. Well enough, too well, he knew the address, and the too many taxicabs, the bus systems, the subway and elevated, the street car lines all helped to annihilate space and time for anyone who wanted to present himself in person at the door of the home of Gloria Wandrous. But one of the last things in the world Dr. Reddington wanted to do was to be found in the neighborhood of the home of Gloria Wandrous. The very last thing he wanted to do was to be seen with her, and it went back from there to the other extreme: the thing he wanted most, eventually, was to be so far removed from the company of Gloria Wandrous, from any association with her, that, as he once heard a Mist' Bones say to a Mist' Interlocutor, it would cost twenty dollars to send her a postcard. No, he definitely did not want to go near her home. But he did want to get in touch with her, just this one more time. He wanted to talk with her, he wanted to reason with her, make a deal with her. Failing in making a deal with her, he—he was not prepared to say, even to himself.

But no one answered the telephone. What was the matter with her mother, her uncle? It was no surprise to Dr. Reddington to learn that Gloria was not at home. She was seldom home. But he often had called at her home and been given a number to call. Full well he knew that whether her mother and uncle knew it or not, the number they gave was a speakeasy or a bachelor's apartment; a Harlem beer flat was one number Dr. Reddington had called on occasion (he hated to think of that now, the way those Negroes were not surprised or shocked by the appearance of his kind of man, Phi Beta Kappa key and severely conservative clothes and all, at a beer flat one Saturday noon, calling for a drunken girl who greeted him on terms that too plainly indicated that he was not a stern parent coming to fetch a recalcitrant daughter, but—just what he was).

Dr. Reddington sat on the edge of the bed and (as he expressed it to himself) cursed himself for a blithering idiot for never having written down the numbers he had called. No, that was being unjust to himself. The reason he had not written down those numbers was a good one; he didn't want to be found dead with those numbers on him. He sat on the bed and his finger searched the soft, faintly damp, white skin of his jowls for a hair that had escaped his razor that morning. There was none. There never was. Only when the barber shaved him. He sat in an attitude that is classically pensive, but he could not think. God, wasn't there one name that would come to him? One name in the numbers that he had called?

It was useless to try to think of the names of speakeasies. His personal experience with speakeasies was slight, as he never drank; but he knew from going to them with Gloria that a place would be known familiarly as Jack's or Giuseppe's—and then when the proprietor gave you a card to the place (which you threw away the moment you were safe outside), it would be called Club Aristocrat or something of the sort. So it was no use trying to think of the names of the places, and too much trouble, practically a life work, to try to find them from memory. No telling what a taxi driver would think if you told him to drive up and down all the streets from Sheridan Square to Fourteenth Street in the hope of recognizing a basement entrance through which you had passed one night long ago. No, the thing to do was to recall a name, a person's name, the name of someone Gloria knew.

A. Ab, Ab, Ab, ante, con, de—no, this was no time to be thinking of the Latin prepositions. Thinking of things like that would only rattle him now. Think viciously, that was the thing. A for Abbott. A for Abercrombie. A for Abingdon. A for Abrams. Wonder what ever happened to that Abrams girl that was so good on the piano? He could think kindly of her now and remember her as a girl who had a nice touch at the piano. She was a degenerate at heart, though, and when her father came to him and asked him what was the meaning of this what his daughter had told him, Dr. Reddington had almost felt like telling the girl's father what kind of child he was raising. But instead he had said: "Look here, Abrams, this is a terrible thing you are saying to me, a serious charge. Am I to infer that you are taking an impressionable child's word against mine?" And the little man had said he was only asking, only wanted to know the truth so if it was the truth he could go farther. "Oh, indeed? Go farther, eh? And who might I ask would take your word against mine? I was born in this town, you know, and for five generations my ancestors have been prominent in this town. I myself have spent twenty-two years in the teaching profession, and you have been here how long? Two years? Well, six years. What's six years against hundreds? Do you think even your own people would take your word against mine? Dr. Stein, for instance. Do you think he would believe you rather than me? Mr. Pollack at The Bee. Do you think he would believe you, risk his standing in this community where there are mighty few of your people, to side with you in an attack on me with a story that has no foundation in fact? Mr. Abrams, I could thrash you within an inch of your life for coming to me with this accusation. The only thing that prevents me from doing that is that I am a father myself. I think we've said enough about this. Your daughter is your problem. My job is to see that she is given an education, but my job begins at nine in the morning and ends at three in the afternoon." The Abramses. They probably were in New York, at least they took their daughter out of school and sold out their store shortly after the two fathers had their conversation. Abrams. A lot of Abramses in New York.

B. C. D. E. F. G. H. Think of all the people in this city, the money the telephone company must make. All those people, all with their problems. B. Buckley. Brown. Brown with an e on the end. Barnes. Barnard. Brace. Butterfield. Brunner! Gloria knew someone named Brunner. Dr. Reddington found the number and gave it to the operator.

He heard the signal of the number being rung, and then the practiced voice: "What number did you call, please? . . . I'm sorry, sir, that telephone has been dis-con-nec-ted."

He replaced the transmitter. This was a hunch. He looked up the address and memorized it, and went downstairs and took a taxi to the address. He told the driver to wait at the corner of Hudson Street and the driver gave him a good look and said he would.

Dr. Reddington walked down the street, following a girl with a large package under her arm. Any other time she might have interested him, but not today. She was just the back of a girl with a good figure, from what he could see, carrying a bundle. Then to his dismay she turned in at the number he sought, and he had to walk on without stopping; and he thought of the taxi driver, who would be looking at him and wondering why he had passed the number. All confused he turned around and went back to the taxi and they left the neighborhood and drove back to the hotel in the sunshine.

"THIS is terribly nice of you," said Gloria.

"Oh, that's all right," said Miss Day.

"Thanks a lot, Norma," said Eddie Brunner.

"Oh, I don't mind a bit. I know how it is," said Miss Day. "You'd roast in that mink coat today."

"Eddie, you look out the window a minute," said Gloria.

"Oh! You really did need these," said Miss Day when Gloria took off her coat. "I'm glad I had them. Usually on Sunday my extra things are at the cleaners'. I didn't think to bring a slip."

"I won't need one with this skirt. This is a marvelous suit. Where did you get it?"

"Russek's. Were you playing strip poker?"

"It looks that way, doesn't it? Yes, I was, in a way. That is, we were shooting crap and I was 'way ahead at one time and then my luck changed, and when I offered to bet my dress the men took me up and of course I didn't think they'd hold me to it and it wasn't the men that held me to it, it was the girls on the party. Fine friends I have. It made me very angry and I left."

"Are you going to school in New York?"

"No, I live here, but I couldn't go home looking like this. My family—they won't even allow me to smoke. All right, Eddie."

"Looks better on you than it does on me," said Norma.

"I wouldn't say that," said Eddie.

"I wouldn't either," said Gloria, "but Eddie never says anything to make me get conceited. We've known each other such a long time."

"Eddie, I thought you went on the wagon after Friday," said Norma.

"I did."

"Oh, that. That's mine," said Gloria. "I bought it for Eddie because I wanted to get in his good graces. You see I thought I was going to have to spend the day here and I was going to bribe Eddie to go uptown to one of the Broadway shops, I think there are some open on Sunday night, they always seem to be open. But then he suggested you, and I think you're perfectly darling to do this. I'll hang this up in one of your closets, Eddie, and call for it tomorrow. I've been intending to put it in storage but I keep putting it off and putting it off—"

"I know," said Miss Day.

"—and then last night I was glad I hadn't, because a cousin of mine that goes to Yale, he and a friend arrived in an open car and it was cold. No top. They were frozen, but they insisted on driving out to a house party near Princeton."

"Oh. Weren't your family worried? You didn't go home then?"

"The car broke down on the way back at some ungodly hour this morning. Bob, my cousin's friend, took us to a party when we got back to town and that's where I got in the crap game."

"But what about your cousin? I should think—"

"Passed out cold, and he's not much help anyway. Not that he'd let them make me give up my dress, but he can't drink. None of our family can. I had two drinks of that Scotch and I'm reeling. I suppose you noticed it."

"Oh, no. But I can never tell with other people till they start doing perfectly terrible things," said Miss Day.

"Well, I feel grand. I feel like giving a party. By the way, before I forget it, if you give me your address I'll have these things cleaned and send them to you."

"All right," said Miss Day, and gave her address.

"Let's go to the Brevoort, but my treat."

"I thought you lost all your money," said Miss Day.

"I did, but I cashed a check on the way downtown. A man that works for my uncle cashed it for me. Shall we go?"

THE nose of the Packard convertible went now up, now down. The car behaved like an army tank on a road that ordinarily was used only by trucks. Paul Farley, driving, was chewing on his lower lip, and the man beside him, looking quite pleased with himself and the world at large, was holding his chin up and dropping the ashes of his cigar on the floor of Farley's car.

"Let's stop," said the man. "Just take one more look. See how it looks from here."

Farley stopped, none too pleased, and looked around. It did please him to look at the nearly finished house; it was his work. "Looks pretty swell to me," he said.

"I think so," said Percy Kahan. He was just learning to say things like "I think so" when he meant "You're damn right." People like Farley, you never knew when they were going to say something simple, like "You're damn right," or something sophisticated, restrained, like "I think so." But it was better to err on the side of the restrained than the enthusiastic. Besides, he was the buyer; Farley was still working for him as architect, and it didn't do to let Farley think he was doing too well.

"A swell job. I know when I've done a swell job, and I've done one for you, Mr. Kahan. About the game room, my original estimate won't cover that now. I could have done it earlier in the game, but I don't suppose you're going to quibble over at the most twelve hundred dollars now. You understand what I meant about the game room itself. That could be done for a great deal less, and still can, but if you want it to be in keeping with the rest of the house my best advice is, don't try to save on the little things. I was one of the first architects to go in for game rooms, that is to recognize them as an

important feature of the modern home. Up to that time a game room
—well, I suppose you've seen enough of them to know what most of
them were like. Extra space in the cellar, so they put in a portable
bar, ping-pong table, a few posters from the French Line—"

"Oh, I want those. Can you get them?"

"I think so. I never like to ask them for anything, because I have
my private opinion of the whole French Line crowd, but that's a
mere detail. Anyway, what I want to point out is that I was one of the
first to see what an important adjunct to the home a game room can
be. I'd like to show you some things I've done out in the Manhasset
section. The Whitney neighborhood, you know."

"Oh, did you do the Jock Whitney estate too?"

"No, I didn't do that, but in that section I've—two years ago I had
eleven thousand dollars to spend on one game room out that way."

"But that was two years ago," said Mr. Kahan. "Whose house
was that?"

"Weh-hell, I, uh, it isn't exactly ethical to give names and figures,
Mr. Kahan. You understand that. Anyway, you see my point about
not trying to chisel a few dollars in such an important feature of the
home. For instance, you'll want a large open fireplace, you said.
Well, that's going to cost you money now. You see, not to be too
technical about it, we've gone ahead without making any provision
for fireplaces on that side of the house, the side where it would have
to be if you wanted it in the game room. And, you have the right idea
about it. There *should be* an open fireplace there.

"You see, Mr. Kahan, I want this house to be right. I'll be frank
with you. A lot of us architects just can't take it, and a lot of fellows
I know are pretty darn pessimistic about the future. Naturally we've
been hit pretty hard, some of us, but I personally can't complain. So
far this year I've done well over a half a million dollars' worth of
business—"

"Net?"

"Oh, no. Not net. I'm a residence architect, Mr. Kahan. But that
stacks up pretty well beside what I've been doing the last three
years. I had my best year oddly enough last year, Mr. Kahan."

"No kidding."

"Oh, yes. I had a lot of work in Palm Beach. And so far this year I've had a very good, a very satisfactory year. But next year, I'm a little afraid of next year. Not because people haven't got the money, but because they're afraid to spend it. There's an awful lot of hoarding going on. I know a man who is turning everything he can into gold. Gold notes when he can't get the actual bullion. Well, that isn't so good. The general spirit of alarm and unrest, and next year being a Presidential year, but I've got my overhead, I've got my expenses, Presidential year or no Presidential year. So far I haven't had to lay off a single draftsman and I don't want to have to do it, but great heavens, if people are going to take their money out of industry and let it lie gathering dust in safe deposit vaults, or in secret vaults in their own homes, the general effect is going to be pretty bad.

"Now with a house like this, people will see this house and they can't help being enchanted with it, and it's been my experience that a house like yours, Mr. Kahan, with a page or two of photographs in *Town and Country* and *Country Life* and *Spur,* people who might be tempted to hoard their money—"

"You mean pictures of this house in *Town and Country*?"

"Naturally," said Farley. "You don't suppose I'd let this house go without—unless you'd rather not. Of course if you'd—"

"Oh, no. Not me. I'm in favor of that. Don't tell Mrs. Kahan, though. It'd make a nice surprise for her."

"Certainly. Women like that. And women are mighty important in these things. As I was saying, I'm counting on people seeing this house, and your friends and neighbors coming in—that's one reason why I'd like to see you have a good game room, when you entertain informally, people will see what a really fine house you have, and they'll want to know who did the house. It's good business for me to do a good job for you any time, Mr. Kahan, but especially now."

"Town and Country, eh? Do I send in the pictures or do you?"

"Oh, they'll send for them. They call up and find out my plans in advance, you know, and I tell them what houses I'm doing, or at least my secretary does—it's all routine. I suppose I've had more houses chosen for photographing in those magazines than any architect within ten years of my age. Shall we go back to the club? I imagine the ladies are wondering what's happened."

"Okay, but now listen, Mr. Farley, I don't want you paying for dinner again. Remember last time we were out here I said next time would be my treat?"

"Huh, huh, huh," Farley chuckled. "I'm afraid I cheated, then. I have to sign. Some other time in town I'll hook you for a really big dinner, and I might as well warn you in advance, Mrs. Farley knows wines. I don't know a damn thing about them, but she does."

They drove to the club, where the ladies were waiting; Mrs. Farley fingering her wedding ring and engagement ring and guard in a way she had when she was nervous, Mrs. Kahan painlessly pinching the lobe of her left ear, a thing she did when she was nervous.

"Well," said the four, in unison.

Farley asked the others if they would like cocktails, and they all said they would, and he took Kahan to the locker-room to wash his hands and to supervise the mixing of the drinks. As they were coming in the locker-room a man was on his way out, in such a hurry that he bumped Kahan. "Oh, I beg your pardon, sir," said the man.

"Oh, that's all right, Mr. Liggett," said Kahan.

"Oh—oh, how are you," said Liggett. "Glad to see you."

"You don't know who I am," said Kahan, "but we were class-mates at New Haven."

"Oh, of course."

"Kahan is my name."

"Yes, I remember. Hello, Farley."

"Hello, Liggett, you join us in a cocktail?"

"No, thanks. I've got a whole family waiting in the car. Well, nice to have seen you, Kann. 'By, Farley." He shook hands and hurried away.

"He didn't know me, but I knew him right away."

"I didn't know you went to Yale," said Farley.

"I know. I never talk about it," said Kahan. "Then once in a while I see somebody like Liggett, one of the big Skull and Bones fellows he was, and one day I met old Doctor Hadley on the street and I introduced myself to him. I can't help it. I think what a waste of time, four years at that place, me a little Heeb from Hartford, but last November I had to be in Hollywood when the Yale-Harvard game was played, and God damn it if I don't have a special wire with the play by play. The radio wasn't good enough for me. I had to have the play by play. Yes, I'm a Yale man."

3

"WELL, I CAN see why you didn't want me to see the ending first. I never would have stayed in the theater if I'd seen that ending. And you wanted to see that again? God, I hope if you ever write anything it won't be like that."

"I hope if I ever write anything it affects somebody the way this affected you," said Jimmy.

"I suppose you think that's good. I mean good writing," said Isabel. "Where shall we go?"

"Are you hungry?"

"No, but I'd like a drink. One cocktail. Is that understood?"

"Always. Always one cocktail. That's always understood. I know a place I'd like to take you to, but I'm a little afraid to."

"Why, is it tough?"

"It isn't really tough. I mean it doesn't look tough, and the people —well, you don't think you're in the Racquet Club, but unless you know where you are, I mean unless you're tipped off about what the place has, what its distinction is, it's just another speakeasy, and right now if I told you what its distinguishing characteristic is, you wouldn't want to go there."

"Well, then let's not go there," she said. "What is peculiar about the place?"

"It's where the Chicago mob hangs out in New York."

"Oh, well, then by all means let's go there. That is, if it's safe."

"Of course it's safe. Either it's safe or it isn't. They tell me the local boys approve of this place, that is, they sanction it, allow it to exist and do business, because they figure there has to be one place as a sort of hangout for members of the Chicago mobs. There's only one real danger."

"What's that?"

"Well, if the Chicago mobs start shooting among themselves. So far that hasn't happened, and I don't imagine it will. You'll see why."

They walked down Broadway a few blocks and then turned and walked east. When they came to a highly polished brass sign which advertised a wigmaker, Jimmy steered Isabel into the narrow doorway, back a few steps and rang for the elevator. It grinded its way down, and a sick-eyed little Negro with a uniform cap opened the door. They got in and Jimmy said: "Sixth Avenue Club."

"Yessa," said the Negro. The elevator rose two stories and stopped. They got out and were standing then right in front of a steel door, painted red, and with a tiny door cut out in the middle. Jimmy rang the bell and a face appeared in the tiny door.

"Yes, sir," said the face. "What was the name again?"

"You're new or you'd know me," said Jimmy.

"Yes, sir, and what was the name again?"

"Malloy, for Christ's sake."

"And what was the address, Mr. Malloy?"

"Oh, nuts. Tell Luke Mr. Malloy is here."

There was a sound of chains and locks, and the door was opened. The waiter stood behind the door. "Have to be careful who we let in, sir. You know how it is."

It was a room with a high ceiling, a fairly long bar on one side, and in the corner on the other side was a food bar, filled with really good free lunch and with obviously expensive kitchen equipment behind the bar. Jimmy steered Isabel to the bar.

"Hello, Luke," he said.

"Howdy do, sir," said Luke, a huge man with a misleading pleasant face, not unlike Babe Ruth's.

"Have a whiskey sour, darling. Luke mixes the best whiskey sours you've ever had."

"I think I want a Planter's punch—all right, a whiskey sour."

"Yours, sir?"

"Scotch and soda, please."

Isabel looked around. The usual old rascal looking into a schooner of beer and the usual phony club license hung above the bar mirror. Many bottles, including a bottle of Rock and Rye, another specialty of Luke's, stood on the back bar. Except for the number and variety of the bottles, and the cleanliness of the bar, it was just like any number (up to 20,000) of speakeasies near to and far from Times Square. Then Isabel saw one little article that disturbed her: an "illuminated" calendar, with a pocket for letters or bills or something, with a picture of a voluptuous dame with nothing on above the waist. The calendar still had not only all the months intact, but also a top sheet with "1931" on it. And across the front of the pocket was the invitation. "When in Chicago Visit D'Agostino's Italian Cooking Steaks Chops At Your Service Private Dining Rooms," and the address and the telephone numbers, three of them.

By the time she had studied the calendar and understood the significance of it—what with Jimmy's advance description of the speakeasy—their drinks were served, and she began to lose the feeling that the people in the speakeasy were staring at her back. She looked around, and no one was staring at her. The place was less than half full. At one table there was a party of seven, four men and three women. One of the women was outstandingly pretty, was not a whore, was not the kind of blonde that is cast for gangster's moll in the movies, and was not anything but a very good-looking girl, with a very nice shy smile. Isabel could imagine knowing her, and then she suddenly realized why. "Jimmy," she said, "that girl looks like Caroline English."

He turned. "Yes, she does."

"But the other people, I've seen much worse at Coney Island, or even better places than that. You wouldn't invent a story just to make an ordinary little place seem attractive, would you?"

"In the first place, no, and in the second place, no. In the first place I couldn't be bothered. In the second place I wouldn't have to. People like you make me mad, I mean people like you, people whose families have money and send them to good schools and belong to country clubs and have good cars—the upper crust, the swells. You come to a place like this and you expect to see a Warner Brothers movie, one of those gangster pictures full of old worn-out comedians and heavies that haven't had a job since the two-reel Keystone Comedies. You expect to see shooting the minute you go slumming—"

"I beg your pardon, but why are you talking about you people, you people, your kind of people, people like you. *You* belong to a country club, you went to good schools and your family at least *had* money—"

"I want to tell you something about myself that will help to explain a lot of things about me. You might as well hear it now. First of all, I am a Mick. I wear Brooks clothes and I don't eat salad with a spoon and I probably could play five-goal polo in two years, but I am a Mick. Still a Mick. Now it's taken me a little time to find this out, but I have at last discovered that there are not two kinds of Irishmen. There's only one kind. I've studied enough pictures and known enough Irishmen personally to find that out."

"What do you mean, studied enough pictures?"

"I mean this, I've looked at dozens of pictures of the best Irish families at the Dublin Horse Show and places like that, and I've put my finger over their clothes and pretended I was looking at a Knights of Columbus picnic—and by God you can't tell the difference."

"Well, why should you? They're all Irish."

"Ah, that's exactly my point. Or at least we're getting to it. So, a while ago you say I look like James Cagney—"

"Not look like him. Remind me of him."

"Well, there's a faint resemblance, I happen to know, because I have a brother who looks enough like Cagney to be his brother. Well, Cagney is a Mick, without any pretense of being anything else, and he is America's ideal gangster. America, being a non-Irish, anti-Catholic country, has its own idea of what a real gangster looks like, and along comes a young Mick who looks like my brother, and he fills the bill. He is the typical gangster."

"Well, I don't see what you prove by that. I think—"

"I didn't prove anything yet. Here's the big point. You know about the Society of the Cincinnati? You've heard about them?"

"Certainly."

"Well, if I'm not mistaken I could be a member of that Society. Anyway I could be a Son of the Revolution. Which is nice to know sometimes, but for the present purpose I only mention it to show that I'm pretty God damn American, and therefore my brothers and sisters are, and yet we're not American. We're Micks, we're non-assimilable, we Micks. We've been here, at least some of my family, since before the Revolution—and we produce the perfect gangster type! At least it's you American Americans' idea of a perfect gangster type, and I suppose you're right. Yes, I guess you are. The first real gangsters in this country were Irish. The Mollie Maguires. Anyway, do you see what I mean by all this non-assimilable stuff?"

"Yes. I suppose I do."

"All right. Let me go on just a few sticks more. I show a sociological fact, I prove a sociological fact in one respect at least. I suppose I could walk through Grand Central at the same time President Hoover was arriving on a train, and the Secret Service boys wouldn't collar me on sight as a public enemy. That's because I dress the way I do, and I dress the way I do because I happen to prefer these clothes to Broadway clothes or Babbitt clothes. Also, I have nice manners because my mother was a lady and manners were important to her, also to my father in a curious way, but when I was learning manners I was at an age when my mother had greater influence on me than my father, so she gets whatever credit is due me for my manners. Sober.

"Well, I am often taken for a Yale man, by Yale men. That pleases me a little, because I like Yale best of all the colleges. There's another explanation for it, unfortunately. There was a football player at Yale in 1922 and around that time who looks like me and has a name something like mine. That's not important."

"No, except that it takes away from your point about producing public enemies, your family. You can't look like a gangster *and* a typical Yale man."

"That's true. I have an answer for that. Let me see. Oh, yes. The people who think I am a Yale man aren't very observing about people. I'm not making that up as a smart answer. It's true. In fact, I just thought of something funny."

"What?"

"Most men who think I'm a Yale man went to Princeton themselves."

"Oh, come on," she said. "You just said—"

"All right. I know. Well, that's not important and I'm only confusing the issue. What I want to say, what I started out to explain was why I said 'you people, you members of the upper crust,' and so on, implying that I am not a member of it. Well, I'm *not* a member of it, and now I never will be. If there was any chance of it it disappeared—let me see—two years ago."

"Why two years ago? You can't say that. What happened?"

"I starved. Two years ago I went for two days one time without a thing to eat or drink except water, and part of the time without a cigarette. I was living within two blocks of this place, and I didn't have a job, didn't have any prospect of one, I couldn't write to my family, because I'd written a bad check a while before that and I was in very bad at home. I couldn't borrow from anybody, because I owed everybody money. I'd borrowed from practically everybody I knew even slightly. A dollar here, ten dollars there. I stayed in for two days because I couldn't face the people on the street. Then the nigger woman that cleaned up and made the beds in this place where I lived, she knew what was happening, and the third morning she came to work she brought me a chicken sandwich. I'll never forget it. It was on rye bread, and home-cooked chicken, not flat and white, but chunky and more tan than white. It was wrapped in newspaper. She came in and said, 'Good morning, Mr. Malloy. I brought you a chicken sandwich if you like it.' That's all. She didn't say why she brought it, and then she went out and bought me a container of coffee and pinched a couple of cigarettes—Camels, and I smoke Luckies—from one of the other rooms. She was swell. She knew."

"I should think she was swell enough for you to call her a colored woman instead of a nigger."

"Oh, balls!"

"I'm leaving."

"Go ahead."

"Just a Mick."

"See? The first thing you can think of to insult me with. Go on, beat it. Waiter, will you open the door for this lady, please?"

"Aren't you coming with me?"

"Oh, I guess so. How much, Luke?"

"That'll be one-twenty," said Luke, showing, by showing nothing on his face, that he strongly disapproved the whole thing.

Exits like the one Isabel wanted to make are somewhat less difficult to make since the repeal of Prohibition. In those days you had to wait for the waiter to peer through the small door, see that everything was all right, open at least two locks, and hold the door open for you. The most successful flouncing out in indignation is done through swinging doors.

He had to ring for the elevator and wait for it in silence, they had to ride down together in silence, and find a taxi with a driver in it. There were plenty of taxis, but the hackmen were having their usual argument among themselves over the Tacna-Arica award and a fare was apparently the last thing in the world that interested them. However, a cruising taxi appeared and Isabel and Jimmy got in.

"Home?" said Jimmy.

"Yes, please," said Isabel.

Jimmy began to sing: ". . . How's your uncle? I haven't any uncle. I hope he's fine and dandy too."

Silence.

"Four years ago this time do you know what was going on?"

"No."

"The Snyder-Gray trial."

Silence.

"Remember it?"

"Certainly."

"What was Mr. Snyder's first name?"

"Whose?"

"Mister *Sny*-der's."

"It wasn't Mister Snyder. It was Ruth Snyder. Ruth Snyder, and Judd Gray."

"There was a Mr. Snyder, though. Ah, yes, there was a Mr. Snyder. It was he, dear Isabel, it was he who was assassinated. What was his first name?"

"Oh, how should I know? What do I care what his first name was?"

"Why are you sore at me?"

"Because you humiliated me in public, calling the waiter and asking him to take me to the door, barking at me and saying perfectly vile, vile things."

"Humiliated you in public," he said. "Humiliated you in public. And you don't remember Mr. Snyder's first name."

"If you're going to talk, talk sense. Not that I care whether you talk or not."

"I'm talking a lot of sense. You're sore at me because I humiliated you in public. What the hell does that amount to? Humiliated in public. What about the man that Ruth Snyder and Judd Gray knocked off? I'd say he was humiliated in public, plenty. Every newspaper in the country carried his name for days, column after column of humiliation, all kinds of humiliation. And yet you don't even remember his name. Humiliation my eye."

"It isn't the same thing."

"Yes, it is. It's exactly the same thing. If I got out of the taxi now would that be humiliating you publicly?"

"Oh, don't. It's so unnecessary."

"Please answer my question."

"I'd rather you didn't. Does that answer it?"

"Yes. Driver! Pull over, please, over to the curb, you dope. Here." He gave the driver a dollar and took off his hat. "Good-by, Isabel," he said.

"You're being silly. You know you're being silly, don't you?"

"Not at all. I just remembered I was supposed to be covering a sermon this morning and I haven't put in at the office all day."

"Good heavens, Jimmy! Will you call me?"

"In an hour."

"I'll wait."

*   *   *

LIGGETT took a late afternoon train back to town. He almost enjoyed the ride. It had been a strain, being with the girls. Not so much with Emily; for the time being she was out of this, and she would only be in it if something slipped. So she was not a strain. Not that he expected anything to slip; but there was always the possibility that that fool girl might still be asleep in the apartment, or that she had left something behind, and he wanted to have plenty of time for a thorough search before Emily and the kids got back. Whatever got over him, he asked himself, that he should take that girl to his apartment? He'd never done that before, not even when Emily and the girls were away for the summer, or in Europe. Well . . .

Europe. This had been a tough winter. The things that were supposed to happen this last winter, hadn't happened. He was beginning to think that the things that were promised to happen were not going to happen, either. Privately, secretly, he did not delude himself as to his own importance in his own economic scheme; he was the New York branch manager for the heavy-tool manufacturing plant his grandfather had founded as a tap and reamer plant. Liggett could read a blueprint; he could, with a certain amount of concentration, pass upon estimates with sufficient intelligence to see the difference between cost and eventual purchase price, which was a not inconsiderable part of his job, since one of his best customers was the City of New York. He also had to deal with large utility corporations and he had to have at least a working knowledge of the accounting and valuation systems of these corporations, which make a practice of carrying, say, a $5,000 pneumatic drill outfit as a $5,000 capital investment ten years after the purchase, allowing nothing for depreciation. He had to know the right man to see among all his prospective customers—which did not by any means always turn out to be the purchasing agent. He did not know how to use a slide rule, but he knew enough to call it a slip-stick. He could not use a transit, but among engineers he could talk about "running the gun." Instead of handwriting he always used the Reinhard style of lettering, the slanting style of printing which is the first thing engineers learn. He would disclaim any real knowledge of engineering, frankly and sometimes a little sadly, but this had a disarming effect upon real

engineers: they would think here is a guy who is just like a kid the
way he wants to be an engineer and he might have made a good one.
The superficial touches which he affected—the lettering, the slang,
the knowing the local engineering gossip like who was the $75-a-
week man who did the real work on a certain immense job—all
these things made him a good fellow among engineers, who certainly are no less sentimental than any other group of men. They
liked him, and they did little things for him which they would not
have done for another engineer; he was a non-competing brother.

A crew man, he always had something to talk about to M. I. T.
men. He would talk about the spirit of the M. I. T. navy, taking its
beatings year after year. His own father had gone to Lehigh, so he
always had a word of Lehigh engineers. He would recognize Tau
Beta Pi and Sigma Xi keys a mile away. He was even known to
remark, in the presence of non-Yale men, that he wished he had at
least gone to Sheff and learned something. He never made the mis-
take of saying of Tau Beta Pi and Sigma Xi men, as he once said to a
man he did not like: "I never saw a Phi Beta Kappa wear a wrist
watch."

The "personal-use clause" which required Yale men to sign state-
ments that they hoped their mothers dropped dead this minute if
these football tickets that they were applying for were to be used by
someone else—that was a gift from the gods to Liggett. He would
apply for his tickets, sign the pledge that went with the tickets—and
then when some properly placed Tammany man came to him for a
pair for the Harvard game, Liggett would explain about the pledge
but he would turn over the tickets. Liggett did not think it entirely
necessary to justify this violation of his word of honor, but he had
two justifications ready: the first was that he did not approve of the
pledge; the second, that he had got boils on his ass year after year for
Yale, four years of rowing without missing a race, and he felt that
made him a better judge of what to do with one of the few benefits
he derived from being an old "Y" man than some clerk in the
Athletic Association office. On at least one occasion those tickets
made the difference between getting an equipment contract and not
getting it. And so, looking at it one way, he was a valuable man to

the firm. The plant no longer belonged to the Liggett family, but he was a director, as a teaser for any lingering good will that his father and grandfather might have left. He voted his own and his sister's stock, but he voted the way he was told by the attorney for his father's estate, who was also a director.

It took the whole year 1930 to teach him that he just did not know his way around that stock market. Business was a simple thing, he told himself: it was buying and selling, supply and demand. His grandfather had come over here, a little English mechanic from Birmingham, and supplied a demand. His father had continued the supply and demand part, but had also gone in more extensively for the buying and selling. In 1930 Liggett reasoned with himself: the buying and selling is not up to me the way it was up to my father, and neither is the supplying of the demand up to me the way it was up to Grandfather. I am in the position of participating in the activities of both my grandfather and my father, and yet since I am not right there at the plant, I have something they didn't have. I have a detached point of view. Liggett & Company are supplying—and selling. Now wherever I go I see buildings going up, I see excavations being made. A few common stocks—all right, *all* common stocks—have taken a thumping, but that's because some of them were undoubtedly priced at more than they were worth. All right. Something happens and the whole market goes smacko. Why? Well, who can explain a thing like that; why. But it happened and in the long run it's going to be a good thing, because when those stocks go up there again, this time they're going to be worth it.

On that basis he brought his income down from the $75,000 he earned in 1929 to about $27,000 for 1930. His salary was $25,000 and this was not cut, for his Tammany connections were as good in 1930 as they were in 1929, and he sold. In 1929 his income from Liggett & Company, aside from salary, was $40,000, including commissions. In addition he had an income of about $10,000 from his mother's estate, which was tied up in non-Liggett investments in Pittsburgh. In 1930 his profits from Liggett & Company amounted to $15,000, which went to his brokers, as did the $5,000 he got from his mother's estate. But he and another man did make $2,000 apiece from an unexpected source, and they thought seriously of doing it every year.

Liggett convinced himself he had to go abroad in the Spring of 1930, and a man he had known in college but less well in the after years, came to him with a scheme which took Liggett's breath away. They talked it over in the smoke room, and as part of the scheme they bought out the low field in the ship's pool. The next day shortly after high noon the ship stopped, and was stopped for a good hour. As a result of the delay Liggett and his friend, holding the low field, won the biggest pool of the voyage, and Liggett's end was around $2,000. It was not clear profit, however; $500 of it went to the steward whom they had bribed to fall overboard at noon that day. In Liggett's favor it must be said that he refused at first to go into the scheme, and would not have done so had he not been assured that a financier whom he always had looked up to as a model of righteousness and decorum had once given the bridge an out-and-out bribe, with subtle threats to back it up, to win a pool that didn't even pay his passage. Also, Liggett had to be assured that his fellow-conspirator would choose a steward who could swim. . . .

He hurried from the train to a phone booth and called his home number. No answer. That didn't mean anything, though. It only meant that this Gloria was not answering his telephone. He took the subway to Times Square, but instead of taking the shuttle to Grand Central he went up to the street out of that horrible subway air (it was much better when there were a lot of people in it; you could look at the horrible people and that took your mind off the air) and rode the rest of the way home in a taxi.

He looked for signs of something in the face of the elevator operator, but nothing there, only that six-months-from-Christmas "Good afternoon, sir." He hurriedly inspected the apartment, even opening the kitchen door that opened upon the service hall.

"Well, she's not here," he said aloud, and went back to take a better look at the bathroom. She certainly had made a nice little mess of that. Then he noticed that his toothbrush, which always, always stood in a tumbler, was lying on the lavatory. A tube of toothpaste had been squeezed in the middle and the cap had not been replaced. He held the toothbrush to his nose. Yes, by God, the bitch had brushed her teeth with his brush. He broke it in half and threw it in a trash basket.

In the bedroom he saw her evening gown and evening coat. He picked up the gown and looked at it. He turned it inside out and looked at it at approximately the point where her legs would begin on her body, expecting to find he knew not what, and finding nothing. It was a good job of tearing he had done and he was embarrassed about that. From the way she had behaved when once he got her into bed there was no reason to suspect her of being a teaser, but why had she been so teaser-like when he brought her home? They were both drunk, and he had to admit that she was a little less drunk than he, could drink more was what he was trying not to admit. She had come home with a man she had met only that night, come to his apartment after necking with him in a taxi and allowing him to feel her breasts. She had gone to his bathroom and when she came out and saw him standing there waiting for her with a drink in his hand she accepted the drink but was all for going back to the livingroom. "No, it's much more comfortable here," he remembered saying, and remembered thinking that if he hadn't said anything it would have been better, for as soon as he spoke she said she thought it was more comfortable in the livingroom, and he said all right, it was more comfortable in the livingroom but that they were going to stay here. "Oh, but you're wrong," she said, and looked at him in the face and then slowly down his body, the frankest look anyone ever had given him, the only time he ever was completely sure that he was looking at someone's thoughts. He got up and put his drink on a table and took her in his arms as roughly as possible. He squeezed her body against his until she felt really small to him. She kept her drink in her hand and held it high while she leaned her head back as far as she could, her face away from his face. She stopped speaking, but she did not look angry. Tolerant. She looked tolerant, as though she were dealing with a prep school kid, as though she were suffering but knew this would be over in a little while and she would be there, with her drink in her hand and her dignity unaffected. That finally was what made him release her, but not for the reason she supposed.

She thought he was going to give up, but that dignity was too much for him. He had to break that some way, so he let her go, took his arms from around her, and then snatched the top of the front of her dress and ripped it right down the front. It tore right down the middle.

Instantly there were changes. He had frightened her and she was pitiful and sweet. He didn't even notice that her dignity was at least genuine enough to cause her to hold on to the drink and walk two steps with it to a table. For a minute, two minutes, he was ready to love her with all the tenderness and kindness that seemed to be all of a sudden at his command, somewhere inside him. He followed her to the table and waited for her to put down the drink. He was aware now, the day after, but hadn't been last night, that she looked a little posed, in a trite pose, with her chin almost on her shoulder, her eyes looking away from him, her right arm making a protective V over her chest, her left hand cupped under her right elbow. He put his hands on her biceps and pressed a little. "Kiss me," he said.

"As a reward," she said.

She turned her face toward him, sufficient indication that she would kiss him. He put his hands in back of her again and kissed her tenderly on the mouth, and then she slowly lowered her arms from in front of her and put them around him, and she walked up to him without moving her feet.

Thinking of it now he knew that it went beyond love. It was so completely what it was, so new in its thoroughness and proficiency that for the first time in his life he understood how these guys, these bright young subalterns, betray King and Country for a woman. He even understood how they could do it while knowing that the woman was a spy, that she was not faithful to them; for he did not care how many men Gloria had stayed with since she left this apartment; he wanted her now. He hadn't remembered this all afternoon, so long as he was with Emily and the girls, but right now if he could have Gloria here he would not care if Emily and the kids came in and watched. "God damn it!" he shouted. She couldn't possibly know the things he knew. He was forty-two, and she wasn't less than twenty years younger than he, and—aah, what difference did it make. Wherever she was he'd find her, and he would get her an apartment tonight. This, then, was what happened to men that made people speak of the dangerous age and all that. Well, dangerous age, make a fool of yourself, whatever else was coming to him he would take if he could have that girl. But he would have to have her over and over again, a year of having her. And to make sure of that he would get her an apartment. Tonight. Tomorrow she could have the charge accounts.

He telephoned her at home, not expecting to find her there, but there was always the chance. A timid male voice answered; probably her father, Liggett thought. She was not home and was not expected back till later this evening. That did not discourage Liggett. He thought he knew enough about her to know where to find her. He made a bundle of her evening clothes and took it with him and went downstairs and took a taxi to the Grand Central. He checked the bundle there and was going to throw away the check, but thought she might like to have the dress for some reason, maybe sentimental, maybe to patch something. Women often saved old dresses for reasons like that, and he had no right to throw away the check. Besides, the coat was all right. He hadn't thought of that at first, because all he thought of was the torn dress. It was annoying the way he kept thinking of that. He liked to think of tearing the dress and stripping her, all in one thought, with the memory of how she had looked at just that moment, her body and her terror. But the fact of tearing a girl's dress was embarrassing and he did not like to be left alone with that thought. He went to a speakeasy in East Fifty-third Street, the one in which two men inside of two years shot themselves in the men's toilet. They were taking the last few chairs off the tables, getting ready to open up, but the bar was open and a man in a cutaway and a woman friend were having drinks. The man was a gentleman, in his late forties. The woman was in her early thirties, tall and voluptuous. They were a little drunk and having an argument when Liggett entered the bar, and the man took the woman's arm and steered her away from the bar to a table in the same room but away from Liggett. Obviously the woman was the man's mistress and he was helplessly in love with her.

"Ever since I've known you," she said, very loud, "you've asked me nothing but questions."

Liggett got some nickels and went to the phone booth to call an engineer friend. The engineer did not answer. He tried two other engineer friends because he wanted to go on a tour of the speakeasies where he would be likely to find Gloria, and he wanted to be with a man but not one of his real friends. They would be at home with their wives or out to parties with their wives, and he wanted to go out with a man whose wife did not know Emily. He tried these engineers, but no soap. No answer. He tried a third, a man he did not specially like, and the man was very cordial and tried to insist on Liggett's coming right up and joining a cocktail party where there was a swell bunch. Liggett got out of that. In another minute he was sure he could have had the company of the man in the cutaway, judging by the conversation between the man and his woman. The conversation had taken a renunciatory turn and the woman was any minute now going home and sending back everything he had ever given her, and he knew what he could do with it. Not wishing to be left alone with the man, Liggett drank the rest of his highball, paid his bill and went to another speakeasy, next door.

The first person he saw was Gloria, all dressed up in a very smart little suit. She gave him a blank look. She was with a young man and a pretty young girl. He went over and shooks hands and Gloria introduced him to the other people and finally asked him to sit down for a second, that they were just leaving.

"Oh, I thought we were going to have dinner here," said Miss Day. "I'm really getting hungry."

There was a silence for the benefit of Miss Day, who was being tacitly informed by everyone at the table that she should have known better than to say that. "Are you waiting for someone?" said Liggett.

"Not exactly," said Gloria.

"I really feel like an awful stupid and rude and all when you were so kind to invite us for dinner," said Miss Day, "but really, Miss Wandrous, I'd of rather stayed at the Brevoort and ate there because I was hungry then. I—" Then she shut up.

"I think we ought to go," said Mr. Brunner. "Gloria, we'll take a rain check on that dinner." He had not been drinking, and he had a kind of surly-sober manner that men sometimes get who are temporarily on the wagon but usually good drinkers. Liggett quickly stood up before they changed their minds. Miss Day apparently had postponed her appetite because she got up too.

When they had gone Liggett said: "I've been trying to get you. I phoned all over and I was going to look everywhere in New York till I did find you. What are you drinking?"

"Rye and plain water."

"Rye and plain water, and Scotch and soda for me. Do you want to eat here?"

"Am I having dinner with you?"

"Well, aren't you?"

"I don't know. What do you want that you've been calling me all over, as you put it, although I don't know where you'd be apt to call me except home."

"And the Manger."

"That's not funny. I was drunk last night. That won't happen again."

"Yes. It *must* happen again. It's got to. Listen, I don't know how to begin."

"Then don't, if it's a proposition. Because if it's a proposition I'm not interested." She knew she was lying, for she was interested in almost any proposition; interested in hearing it, at least. But so far she could not tell which way he was headed. He had said nothing to indicate that he had discovered her theft of the coat, but his avoiding that topic might be tactical and only that. She resolved not to say anything about it until he did, but to wait for the first crack that would indicate that he wanted the coat back. She was not at this point prepared to take a stand about the coat. Later, maybe, but not now.

He looked down at his hands, which were making "Here's the Church, here's the steeple, open the door and there's all the people."

"Do you know what I want?" he said.

It was on the tip of her tongue to say yes, the mink coat. She said, "Why, I haven't the faintest idea."

He reached in his pocket and brought out the check for the bundle he had left at Grand Central. "You," he said.

"What's this?" she said, taking the check.

"The rye is for Miss Wandrous. Scotch for me," said Liggett to the waiter who had sneaked up with the drinks. When he went away Liggett went on: "That's for your dress and coat. You got the money I left. Was it enough?"

"Yes. What do you mean you want me?"

"Well, I should think that would be plain enough. I want you. I want to—if I get you an apartment will you live in it?"

"Oh," she said. "Well, I live at home with my family."

"You can tell them you have a job and you want to be uptown."

"But I didn't say I wanted to live uptown. What makes you want me for your mistress? I didn't know you had a mistress, I know that gag, so don't you say it."

"I wasn't going to. I want you, that's why."

"Do you want me to tell you?"

"Well—"

"First you want me because I'm good in bed and your wife isn't. Or if she is—don't bridle. I guess she is, judging by the way you took that. But you're tired of her and you want me because I'm young enough to be your daughter."

"Just about," he said. "I'd have had to have you when I was very young."

"Not so very. I saw pictures of your daughters in your living room, and they're not much younger than I am. But I don't want you to feel too old so we'll pass over that. You want me, and you think because you paid the rent for an apartment that I'd be yours and no one else's. Isn't that true?"

"No. As a matter of fact it isn't. I was thinking not an hour ago, before I knew where you were, Gloria, I discovered something and that is, I didn't care who you were with or in what bed, I still wanted you."

"Oh. Desperate. You *are* getting a little, uh, you're getting worried about how near fifty is, aren't you?"

"Maybe. I don't think so. Men don't get menopause. I may have as many years left as you. I've taken good care of myself."

"I hope."

"I hope you have, too."

"Don't you worry about me. The first thing I do tomorrow is go to my friend on Park Avenue."

"Who's your friend on Park Avenue?"

"My friend on Park Avenue? That's my doctor. I'll be able to tell you this week whether there's anything the matter with you, and me."

"Do you always go to him?"

"Always, without fail. Listen, you, I don't want to sit here and talk about venereal disease. You didn't let me finish what I was saying. You think I'd be faithful to you because you gave me an apartment. My handsome friend, I would be faithful to you only as long as I wanted to be, which might be a year or might be till tomorrow afternoon. No. No apartment for me. If you want to take an apartment where we can go when I want to go with you, or where you can take anyone you please, that's entirely up to you. But after looking around at your apartment and making a guess as to how you live? Not interested. You haven't enough money to own me. Last year, last fall, that is, I got a pretty good idea how much I was worth. Could you pay the upkeep on a hundred and eighty-foot yacht? Diesel yacht?"

"No, frankly."

"Well, this man could and does, and I'll bet he doesn't use it half a dozen times a year. He goes to the boat races in it and takes a big party of young people, and has it down in Florida with him when he goes, and before it was his I saw it at Monte Carlo."

"I guess I know who that is."

"Yes, I guess you do. Well, he wanted me, too."

"Why didn't you take him up if you want money?"

"Do you know why? Because do you know those pictures of

pygmies in the Sunday papers? Little men with legs like match sticks and fat bellies with big umbilicals and wrinkled skin? That's what he looks like. Also I can't say I enjoy his idea of fun. Ugh."

"What?"

"I honestly wouldn't know how to tell you. I'd be embarrassed. Maybe you've heard, if you know who it is."

"You mean he's peculiar?"

"Huh. Peculiar. Listen, darling, do you know why I like you? I do like you. Do you know why? You're just a plain ordinary everyday man. You think you're something pretty hot and sophisticated because you're unfaithful to your wife. Well, I could tell you things about this rotten God damn dirty town that—ugh. I know a man that was almost elected— Well, I guess I better shut up. I know much too much for my age. But I like you, Liggett, because you want me the way I want to be wanted, and not with fancy variations. Let's get out of here, it's too damn effete."

"Where do you want to go?" Liggett said.

"Down to Fortieth Street to my practically favorite place."

They went to the place in Fortieth Street, up a winding staircase. They were admitted after being peered at, it turned out, by a man with a superb case of acne rosacea. "I was afraid you wouldn't remember me," said Gloria.

"What? Fancy me not remembering you, Miss?" said the man, who was the bartender.

"And what will be your pleasure to partake of this Lord's Day?" said the bartender. "Little Irish, perhaps?"

"Yes, fine."

"And you, sir?"

"Scotch and soda."

"Fine. Fine," said the bartender.

It was the longest bar in New York in those days, and the room was bare except for the absolute essentials. One half of it held tables and chairs and a mechanical piano, but there was one half in front of the bar which was bare concrete floor. Liggett and Gloria were getting used to themselves and smiling at each other in the mirror when a voice rose.

"Laddy doo, Laddy doo, Lie die dee. Tom!"

"Please control your exuberation, Eddie," said Tom, the bartender, and smiled broadly at Gloria and Liggett.

"Gimme a couple nickels, Tom, Laddy doo, Laddy doo."

They looked at the man called Eddie, who was down at the other end of the bar, rubbing his fat hands together and sucking his teeth. He had on a uniform cap and a gray woolen undershirt and blue pants, and then they noticed he had a revolver, chain twister, handcuffs and other patrolman's equipment. His tunic lay on a chair. "I beg your pardon, Miss and Mister," he said. "Serve the lady and gentleman first," said Eddie.

"I was doing that very thing," said Tom, "and when I get done I'll be giving you no nickels and stop askin'."

"Laddy doo. Gimme a beer, my Far Doon friend," said Eddie. "After serving the lady and gentleman, of course."

"When I get good and ready I'll give yiz a beer. It's almost time for you to ring in anyway. What about we taxpayers of this great city? When we go to exercise our franchise at the polls we'll change all this."

"Civil Service. Did you never hear of the Civil Service, my laddy-buck? The members of the Finest are Civil Service and what the likes of you repeaters do at the polls affects us not one single iota. A *beer!*"

"Get outa here. Go on out and ring in. It's twenty-five to, time to box in."

"The clock is fast."

"God can strike me dead if it is. I fixed it meself comin' in this evening. Go on or you'll be wrote up again."

"I'll go, and I'll be back with a hatful of nickels," said Eddie. He pulled his equipment belt around and put on his tunic and straightened his cap and as he was leaving he said, "Will I bring you a paper?"

"Go on, don't be trying to soft-soap me now," said Tom.

A party of four young men came in and began to play very seriously a game with matches, for drinks. A man in an undershirt and black trousers, wearing a cap made out of neatly folded newspaper,

came in and waved his hand to the match-game players, but sat
alone. A man with his hat on the back of his head came in and spoke
to the players and to the man with the newspaper cap. He sat alone
and began making faces at himself in the mirror and went into a long
story which Tom showed by nods that he was listening to. During the
story the man never once took his eyes off his reflection in the
mirror. Tom was attentive with the man who looked at himself,
chatted about baseball with the man with the newspaper cap, kidded
with the match-game players, and was courtly with Liggett and Gloria. The cop came back bearing several newspapers and a large paper
bag, from which he took several containers. Out of these he poured
stewed clams into dishes which Tom got out of the bottom of the
free lunch bar. The cop said: "Let the lady have hers first," and then
everyone else was served while the cop looked on, happy; then he
took off his tunic and laid it on the back of a chair, and then he went
over to the piano.

"Get away from that God damn piano," yelled Tom. "Beggin'
your pardon, Miss. Eddie, you lug you, get away from that t'ing, it's
out of order."

"You go to hell," said Eddie. "Beg your most humble pardon,
Lady, I have some rights here." The nickel he had dropped had set
the motor humming, and in a minute the place was filled with the
strains of "Dinah, is there anyone finah?"

"Oh, Jesus, Mary and Joseph, the wrong record," said the cop, in
real pain. "I wanted 'Mother Machree.' "

A SPECIAL delivery letter which arrived at the home of Gloria Wandrous the next morning:

> *Dear Gloria—I see that you have not changed one whit your*
> *deplorable habit of breaking appointments, or did you not*
> *realize that we had an appointment today? I came, at great*
> *inconvenience, to New York today, hoping to see you on the*
> *matter which we are both anxious to settle. I brought with me*
> *the amount you specified, which is a large sum to be carrying*
> *about on one's person, especially in times like these.*

Please try to be at home tomorrow (Monday) between 12 noon and one p.m., when I shall attempt to reach you by long distance telephone. If not, I shall try again at the same hour on Tuesday.

If you realized what inconvenience it costs me to come to New York you would be more considerate.

Hastily,

J. E. R.

Gloria read this letter late Monday afternoon, when she went home after spending the night with Liggett. *"Poor* dear," she said, upon reading the letter. "If I realized what inconvenience, meeyah!"

4

EDDIE BRUNNER WAS one of the plain Californians. He was one of those young men whose height and frame make them look awkward unless they are wearing practical yachting clothes, or a $150 tailcoat. He did not gain much presence from his height, which was six feet two. When he talked standing up he made a gesture, always the same gesture; he put out his hands in the position of holding an imaginary basketball, about to shoot an imaginary foul. He could not talk with animation unless he stood up, but he did not often talk with animation. Like all Californians he made a substantive clause of every statement he made: "It's going to rain today, is what I think . . . Herbert Hoover isn't going to be our next President, is my guess . . . I only have two bucks, is all."

In his two years in New York he had had four good months, or make it five. At Stanford he was what is known as well liked, which tells a different story from popular. Popular men and women in college make a business of being popular. Well-liked people do things without getting disliked for them. Eddie Brunner drew funny pictures. He had a bigger vogue away from Stanford than at it, because the collegiate magazines republished his drawings. He had taken the work of several earlier collegiate comic artists—notably

Taylor, of Dartmouth—and fashioned a distinctive comic type. He drew little men with googly eyes whose heads and bodies looked as though they had been pressed squat. He had a rebus signature: a capital B and a line drawing of a runner. It was a tiny signature. It had to be because the men Eddie drew were so small. In college he drew no women if he could help it; with his technique women would have to have fat legs and squat little bodies. Occasionally he did a female head as illustration for He-She gags, most of which he wrote himself.

The *Stanford Chaparral,* as a result of Eddie's drawings, had a high unofficial rating among college humorous monthlies during the three years Eddie contributed to it. He did nothing in freshman year; he was just barely staying in college, what with his honest laziness, his fondness for certain phonograph records, and a girl.

When he got out of college, with the class of '29, he was secretly envied by a good many classmates. Even the wealthy ones envied him. He had something; back East they knew about Eddie. Hadn't his drawings been in *Judge* and *College Humor* time after time? Eddie's father, a lucky sot who had made the fourth of a series of minor fortunes in miniature golf courses, had become bored with the golf courses and in the nick of time had converted them, wherever the zoning laws would permit, into drive-in car-service eateries, which were doing fabulous business in Eddie's last year in college. Brunner the elder was never so happy as when accompanying a party of "sportsmen" and newspaper writers to a big fight back East. Jack Dempsey was a great friend of his. He himself was an alumnus of the University of Kansas, but he gave huge football parties at Stanford and then at the St. Francis after the games. These did not embarrass Eddie, as Eddie had not joined his father's fraternity, and when the old gent came down to Stanford he called at his own fraternity and otherwise busied himself so that Eddie could follow his own plans. Eddie had for his father the distant tolerance that sometimes compensates for a lack of any other feeling, or, better yet, is a substitute for the contempt Eddie sometimes was in danger of feeling.

Eddie accepted his father's generosity with polite thanks, knowing that Brunner père spent every week in tips at least as much as the $50 allowance he gave his son in senior year. Eddie spent his allowance on collectors' items among old Gennett records, and on his girl. Almost regularly every six months Eddie fell in love with a new girl, and he would be in love with her until some extra-amatory crisis, such as a midyear examination, would occur. That would take his mind off the girl, and he would resume his routine existence to find that he had been thoughtless about breaking dates, and he would have to get a new girl. With a good second-hand Packard phaeton and a seeming inability to get too much to drink, his instinctive good manners and what the girls called his dry sense of humor, he could have just about his choice of the second-flight Stanford girls.

The idea was that the allowance was to continue and he would come to New York and stay until he got a job. So with his records and some Bristol board and the rest of his equipment packed in a seaman's chest, and enough hand luggage to carry his clothes, Eddie and two cronies drove to New York.

His father had arranged with his secretary about the allowance, and so it came regularly. With the cronies he took an apartment in a good building in Greenwich Village, and each of the friends furnished a bedroom and divided the cost of furnishing the common living-room. They bought a bar, a quantity of gin, installed a larger electric icebox and began doing the town. One of Eddie's roommates played pretty fair trombone, the other played a good imitative piano, and Eddie himself was fair on a tenor banjo with ukulele stringing. Eddie also purchased a slightly used mellophone, hoping to duplicate the performance of Dudley—in the Weems record of "Travelin' Blues," which Eddie regarded as about as good a swing number as ever was pressed into a disc. He never learned to play the mellophone, but sometimes on Saturday and Sunday nights the three friends would have a jam session, the three of them playing and drinking gin and ginger ale and playing, complimenting each other on breaks and licks or making pained faces when one or the other would play very corny. One night their doorbell rang and a young man who looked as though he were permanently drunk asked if he could come in and sit down. He brought with him a beautiful little

Jewess. Eddie was a little hesitant about letting them in until the
drunk said he only wanted to sit and listen.

"WELL!" shouted the roommates. "Sit you down, have a drink.
Have two drinks. What would you like to hear?"

" 'Ding Dong Daddy,' " said the stranger. "My name is Malloy.
This is Miss Green. Miss Green lives upstairs. She's my girl."

"That's all right," they said. "Sit down, fellow, and we'll render
one for you." They played, and when they finished Miss Green and
Malloy looked at each other and nodded.

"I have drums," said Malloy.

"Where? Upstairs?" said Eddie.

"Oh, no. Miss Green and I don't live together that much, do we,
Sylvia?"

"Not that much. Almost but not quite," said Sylvia.

"Where are they, the percussions?" said Eddie.

"At home in Pennsylvania, where I come from," said Malloy.
"But I'll get them next week. Now do you mind if Sylvia plays?"

The boy with the trombone offered her his trombone. Eddie
handed up the banjo.

"No," said Malloy. "Piano."

"Oh, p*iano*. That means I mix drinks," said the boy at the piano.

"Yes, I guess it does after you hear Sylvia," said Malloy.

"As good as that?" said the trombone player.

"Go ahead, Sylvia," said Malloy.

"I ought to have another drink first."

"Give her another drink," said Eddie. "Here, have mine."

She gulped his drink and took off her rings and handed them to
Malloy. "Don't forget where they came from," she said. *"And* a
cigarette." Malloy lit a cigarette for her and she took two long drags.

"She better be good," said one roommate to the other.

Then with her two tiny hands she hit three chords, all in the bass,
one, two, three. "Jee-zuzz!" yelled the Californians, and got up and
stood behind her.

She played for an hour. While she played one thing the Californians would be making lists for her to play when she got finished. At

the end of the hour she wanted to stop and they would not let her. "All right," she said. "I'll do my impressions. My first impression is Vincent Lopez playing 'Nola.' "

"All right, you can quit," said Eddie.

"None too soon," she said. "Where is the little girls' room, quick?"

"What does she do? Who is she? What does she do for a living?" the Californians wanted to know.

"She's a comparison shopper at Macy's," said Malloy.

"What is that?"

"A comparison *shopper,*" said Malloy. "She goes around the other stores finding out if they're underselling Macy's, that's all."

"But she ought to— How did *you* ever get to know her?" said the piano player.

"Listen, I don't like your tone, see? She's my girl, and I am a very tough guy."

"Oh, I don't think you're so tough. Big, but not so tough, is my guess."

"No, not so tough, but plenty tough enough for you," said Malloy, and got up and swung at the piano player. The trombone player grabbed Malloy's arms. The piano player had caught the blow on his upraised forearm.

"I'm for letting them fight," said Eddie, but he took hold of Malloy. "Listen, fellow, you're one to three here and we'd just give you a shellacking and throw you downstairs if we had to. But we wouldn't have to. My friend here is a fighter."

"Make them shake hands," said the trombone player.

"What for?" said Eddie. "Why should they shake hands?"

"Let him go," said the piano player.

"All right, let him go," said Eddie to the trombone player. They let him go and Malloy went in after the piano player and stopped suddenly and fell and sat on the floor.

"You shouldn't have done that," said the trombone player.

"Why not?" said the piano player.

"Why not? He asked for it," said Eddie.

"Well, he's plastered," said the trombone player.

"He'll be all right. I'm afraid," said the piano player. He went over and bent down and spoke to Malloy. "How you coming, K.O.?"

"Um all right. You the one that hit me?" said Malloy, gently caressing his jawbone.

"Yes. Here, take my hand. Get up before your girl gets back."

"Who? Oh, Sylvia. Where is she?"

"She's still in the can."

Malloy got up slowly but unassisted. He sat in a deep chair and accepted a drink. "I think I could take you, sober."

"No. No. Get that idea out of your head," said the piano player.

"Don't be patronizing," said Malloy.

"He can afford to be patronizing," said Eddie. "My friend is one of the best amateur lightweights on the Coast. Do you know where the Coast is?"

"Aw, why don't you guys cut it out. Leave him alone," said the trombone player.

Sylvia appeared. "Did you think I got stuck? I couldn't find the bathroom light. Why, Jimmy, what's the matter?"

"I walked into a punch."

"Who? Who hit him? You? You big wall-eyed son of a bitch?"

"No, not me," said the trombone player.

"Then who did? *You!* I can tell, you sorehead, because I showed you how to play piano you had to assert your superiority some way, so you take a sock at a drunk. Come on, Jimmy, let's get out of here. I told you I didn't want to come here in the first place."

"Wait a second, Baby. Don't get the wrong idea. It was my fault."

"Stop being a God damn gentleman. It ill becomes you. Come on, or I'll go alone and I won't let you in, either."

"I'll go, but I was in the wrong and I want to say so. I apologize to you, Whatever Your Name Is—"

"Brunner."

"And you, and you, and thank you for being— Anyway, I apologize."

"All right."

"But I still think I could take you."

"Oh, now wait a minute, listen here," said the piano player. "If you want to settle this right now I'll go outside, or right here—"

"Oh, shut up," said Eddie. "You're as bad as he is. Good night. Good night." When the door closed he turned on the piano player. "He was all right at the end. He apologized, and you can't blame him for wanting to think he could lick you."

"A wrong guy. If I ever see him again I'll punch his face in for him."

"Maybe. Maybe it wouldn't be so easy if he was sober. He had to walk on a loose rug to take that haymaker at you, remember. I don't want to hear any more about it. The hell with it."

"Ah, you give me a pain in the ass."

"You took the very words right out of my mouth. All you tough guys," said Eddie.

"Gee, but that little Mocky could play that piano," said the trombone player.

That was the first of two meetings between Eddie Brunner and Jimmy Malloy. Eddie's life went on as usual for a while. He did a few drawings and sold none. His stuff was too good for a syndicate manager to take a chance on it; too subtle. But it was not the type of thing that belonged in the *New Yorker,* the only other market he could think of at the time. So the three friends would have their jam sessions, and some nights when they did not play they would sit and talk. The names they would talk: Bix Beiderbeck, Frankie Trumbauer, Miff Mole, Steve Brown, Bob MacDonough, Henry Busse, Mike Pingatore, Ross Gorman and Benny Goodman, Louis Armstrong and Arthur Shutt, Roy Bargy and Eddie Gilligan, Harry MacDonald and Eddie Lang and Tommy and Jimmy Dorsey and Fletcher Henderson, Rudy Wiedoeft and Isham Jones, Rube Bloom and Hoagy Carmichael, Sonny Greer and Fats Waller, Husk O'Hare and Duilio Sherbo, and other names like Mannie Kline and Louis Prima, Jenney and Morehouse, Venuti, Signorelli and Cress, Peewee Russell and Larry Binion; and some were for this one and some for that one, and all the names meant something as big as Wallenstein and Flonzaley and Ganz do to some people.

Early in October of that year Eddie got a telegram from his

mother: PAPA DIED OF A STROKE THIS MORNING FUNERAL SATURDAY
PLEASE COME. Eddie counted the words. He knew his mother; she
probably thought the indefinite article did not cost anything in a
telegram. He overdrew at the bank and cashed a check large enough
to take him home, cashed it in an uptown speakeasy where he was
known. He went home, and his maternal uncle told him how his
father had died; in the middle, or the beginning maybe, of a party in
a Hollywood hotel, surrounded by unknown Hollywood characters.
They kept that from Eddie's mother, who had been such a sad,
stupid little woman for so many years that she could have taken it
without shock. All she said, over and over again, as they made plans
for the funeral was: "I don't know, Roy always said he wanted to be
buried with the Shrine band. He wanted them to play some march,
but I can't think of the name of it." They told her not to worry about
it; they couldn't have the Shrine band for a funeral, so don't keep
worrying about it. After the services she said she noticed that Mr.
Farragut was at the funeral. "That just showed, you know," she said.
"I think Roy could have got in the Burlingame Club if he'd of tried
just once more, or why would Mr. Farragut be here today?" Mr.
Farragut was the man Mr. Brunner always had blamed for blackbal-
ling him from membership in the only organization he might have
joined that he did not join.

Roy Brunner was one jump ahead of the sheriff when he keeled
over with his cerebral hemorrhage in his eyes. He had been letting
the drive-in car-service eateries get along without him, as he figured
to do something new with all those lots he had tied up. He had
gained a local reputation for sagaciousness and public-pulse-feeling
as a result of getting out of the miniature golf course business ahead
of time. His new idea was a nickel movie on every available corner;
showing newsreels and short subjects for a nickel. A half-hour show,
and turn them out. That did not give them much for their money, as
it meant only one short and two newsreels, but on the other hand it
was a lot for their money. A nickel? What did they want for a
nickel? It was only a time killer anyway. He was in Hollywood
ostensibly working on this project at the time the grim reaper called.
No papers had been signed, and he hadn't seen the top men, but he

was going to let them know he was in town tomorrow or the day after, and this party was just a little informal get-together with a couple of football coaches and golf professionals and what are known in the headlines as Film Actresses—extra girls. He had all the confidence in the world, and not without some reason. A man who is able to show the motion picture producers one example of how he called the turn of the public fancy can sell them practically anything, so long as he calls it Showmanship. But no papers had been signed.

"Your mother's going to stay with Aunt Ella and me for the present," Eddie's uncle told him, and that settled a problem for Eddie. He did not want to stay around his mother. He loved her because she was his mother and sometimes he felt sorry for her, but all his life (he had realized at a time when he was still too young for such a realization) she was so engrossed in her own life work of observing the carryings-on of her husband that she was like some older person whom Eddie knew but who did not always speak to him on the street. She was a member of a Pioneer Family, which in California means what Mayflower Descendant means in the East. The Mayflower Descendants, however, have had time to rest and recover from the exhausting, cruel trip, and many have done so, although inbreeding did not speed recovery. But the Pioneers had a harder trip and not so long ago, and it is reasonable to suppose that many of their number were so weakened when they got as far as the Pacific littoral that they handed down a legacy of tired bodies. Roy Brunner had come out from Kansas on a train, and his wife became his wife —a little to his surprise—the first time he asked her. She'd never been asked before, and was afraid she never would be again. She would willingly have learned, in married life, the one important thing her husband was able to teach her, but he was tolerantly impatient with her, and went elsewhere for his fun. When it came time to acquaint Eddie with the facts of sexual life, and Roy acquainted him with them, his wife said to him: "How did you tell him?" The reason she asked was that she still had hopes at that time of finding out herself. But Roy's answer was: "Oh, I just told him. He knew a lot already."

Eddie knew that in his mother his uncle was figuring on a profit-

able paying guest. That annoyed him a little, but what was there to
do? She wanted to be there, and it took care of everything satisfacto-
rily. Mrs. Brunner gave Eddie five hundred dollars out of her own
money, and having signed a power of attorney in favor of his uncle,
Eddie returned to New York, believing that his allowance would
continue.

It never came again. His father's estate was tangled enough, and
the Crash fixed everything fine. Eddie's uncle was hit, though not
crippled. He wrote to Eddie, who was a month and a half behind in
the rent with a lease to run exactly a year longer. He told Eddie they
all were comparatively lucky. "You are young," he said, "and can
earn your own living. I hope you will be able to send your mother
something from time to time, as we can give her a roof over her
head, a place to sleep and eat but nothing else. . . ."

Eddie sold his car for $35, he hocked his beautiful mellophone for
$10. He gathered together, early in December, all his money and
found he had not quite $200. His roommates had jobs and they were
more than willing to have him keep his share of the apartment and
owe them his share of the rent, but in January one of them lost his
job in the first Wall Street purge, and in March they all were ousted
from their apartment.

They went their separate ways. One of the roommates had a married sister living somewhere in suburban New Jersey. He went there.
The other, the fighter, died of pneumonia in a room off Avenue A.
Eddie did not even hear about it until long after his friend's body
had been cremated. Eddie went from rooming-house to rooming-
house, in the Village at first, and then in the West Forties, among the
Irish of Tenth Avenue. He stayed uptown because it saved a dime
carfare every day. He tried every place, everyone he knew to get a
job. He was a helper in a restaurant one week, picking dirty plates
off tables and carrying trayfuls of them to the kitchen. He dropped a
tray and was fired, but he paid something on his rent and he had kept
his belly full. He thought of driving a taxi, but he did not know how
to go about it. He knew there had to be licenses and other details,
and he did not have the money for a license. He tried to be an actor,
saying he could play comedy character parts. The only time he was

picked he revealed right away that he had had no experience: he did not know what a side was, nor anything else about the stage. One night, very hungry, he allowed himself to be picked up by a fairy, but he wanted his meal first and the fairy did not trust him, so he punched the fairy one for luck and felt better, but wished he had had the guts to take the fairy's bankroll. He sold twenty-five cent ties in fly-by-night shops and was a shill at two auctions but the auctioneer decided he was too tall; people would remember him. Then, though his landlady, for whose children he sometimes drew funny pictures, he heard of a marvelous opportunity: night man in a hotel which was more of a whore-house. It was through her Tammany connection that she heard about the job. He operated a switchboard and ran the elevator from six in the evening to eight in the morning, for ten dollars a week and room, plus tips. Customers would come in and the password was, "I'm a friend of Mr. Stone's." Then Eddie would look the customer over and ask him whom he wanted to see, and the man would give the name of one of the three women. Eddie then would call the room of the woman named, and say: "There's a friend of Mr. Stone's here for you," and she would say all right, and Eddie would say: "She says she's not sure she remembers you. Will you describe her to me?" And the man would either describe her or say quite frankly that he'd never been there before, and all this was stalling. It gave Eddie a chance to look him over carefully and it gave the woman a chance to prepare to entertain the visitor, or get dressed and get ready to be raided, if Eddie pulled back the switchboard key which rang her room. He was instructed to turn down men who were too drunk, as the place was not paying the kind of protection that had to be paid by clip joints. Eddie never turned anyone down.

On this job he met Gloria. She came in one night, plastered, with a sunburned man, also plastered, who wore in his lapel the bouton-niere of the Legion of Honor. Eddie was a little afraid of him at first, but he guessed it would be too early in the season for a cop to have the kind of tan this man had. And the man said: "Tell Jane it's the major. She'll know." Jane knew and told Eddie to send him right up. The girl, Gloria, went with him. Eddie made the wise guess that this was Gloria's first time here, but not her first experience being a spectator. The major kept smiling to himself in the elevator, humming, and saying to Gloria: "All right, honey?"

The major gave Eddie a dollar when they reached Jane's floor, gave it to him as though that were the custom from time immemorial. Eddie returned to the switchboard. Then in about twenty minutes he heard footsteps, and standing before him was the girl, Gloria.

"Will you lend me that dollar he gave you?" she said. "Come on, I'll give it back to you. You don't want any trouble, do you?"

"No. But how'll I know you'll give it back to me? Honestly, I need that buck."

"You don't have to pimp for your money, I imagine."

"That's where you're wrong, but here, take it."

"I'll bring it back tomorrow. I'll give you two bucks tomorrow," she said. "What are you doing here, anyway?"

"You mean what is a nice girl like me doing in a place like this," said Eddie.

"Good night," she said, "and thanks a million."

He had a feeling she would return the money, and she did, two nights later. She gave him five dollars. She said she didn't have change for it, and he took it. "What happened the other night, anything?" she said.

"Your friend got stinko and Jane had to send out for a bouncer," he said.

"Oh, you're not the bouncer?"

"Do I look like a bouncer?"

"No, but—"

"But I don't look like an elevator boy in a whore-house either, is what you're trying to say."

"Are you from the West?"

"Wisconsin," said Eddie.

"What part of Wisconsin?"

"Duluth," said Eddie.

"Duluth is in Minnesota."

"I know," said Eddie.

"Oh, in other words mind my own business. Okay. Well, I just asked. I'll be seeing you."

"I have something belonging to you, Miss Wandrous."

"What!"

"Your purse, you left it in Jane's room when you left in such a hurry. That's why you had to borrow the buck, remember? I took the liberty of trying to identify the owner, but I couldn't find you in the phone book. I didn't think I would."

"Oh."

"I was going to take a chance that you were still living at the address on your driver's license. You better get a new license, by the way. The 1928 licenses aren't any good any more. This is 1930."

"Did you show this to anybody?"

"No."

"Why not?"

"I just didn't think it was anybody else's business. It wasn't mine, for that matter, but it's better for you to have *me* look at it than turn it over to, well, one of the boys we have around here sometimes."

"You're a good egg. I just happened to think who it is you remind me of."

"I know."

"Do you?"

"I ought to. I've heard it often enough."

"Who?"

"Lindbergh."

"Yes, that's right. I guess you would hear that a lot. When is your night off?"

"The second Tuesday of every week."

"No night off? I thought they had to give you a night off."

"They break a lot of ordinances here, ordinances and laws. Why, what do you want to know about my nights out for?"

"We could have dinner."

"Sure. Do you think I'd be here if I could take girls out to dinner?"

"Who said anything about taking me? I just said we could have dinner. I have no objection to paying for my own dinner under certain circumstances."

"For instance."

"For instance eating with someone I like."

"Now we're getting somewhere," he said, but he could not pro-
long the flippancy. This was the first time in months that anyone had
spoken a kind personal word to him. She understood that.

"Get somebody to work for you, can't you?"

"Why should I? . . . Hell, why shouldn't I? There's a jig-
gaboom had this job before me is working down the street now. He
just runs the elevator at a hotel now, maybe he might work for me if
they said it was all right. I don't want to lose this job, though."

The Negro said he would be glad to take over Eddie's job for a
night, and Mrs. Smith, Eddie's boss, said it would be all right but
not to make a practice of it, as the girls upstairs did not like Negroes
for agents.

Thus began the friendship of Gloria and Eddie.

It would be easy enough to say any one of a lot of things about
Gloria, and many things were said. It could be said that she was a
person who in various ways—some of them peculiar—had the ability to help other people, but lacked the ability to help herself. Someone could write a novel about Gloria without ever going very far
from that thesis. It was, of course, the work of a few minutes for the
1931 editorial writers (who apparently are the very last people to
read the papers) to find in Gloria a symbol of modern youth. She
was no more a symbol of modern youth than Lindbergh was a symbol of modern youth, or Bob Jones the golfer, or Prince George, or
Rudy Vallée, or Linky Mitchell, or DeHart Hubbard or anyone else
who happened to be less than thirty years old up to 1930. There can
be no symbol of modern youth any more than there can be a symbol
of modern middle age, and anyway symbol is a misnomer. The John
Held Jr. caricature of the "flapper" of the 1920's, or the girls and
young men whom Scott Fitzgerald made self-conscious were not
symbols of the youth of that time. As a matter of fact there was no
tie-up between the Scott Fitzgerald people and the John Held people.
The Scott Fitzgerald people were drawn better by two artists named
Lawrence Fellows and Williamson than by John Held. Held drew
caricatures of the boys and girls who went to East Orange High

School and the University of Illinois; the Held drawings were caricatures and popular, and so people associated the Fitzgerald people with the Held drawings. The Fitzgerald people did not go in for decorated yellow slickers, decorated Fords, decorated white duck trousers and stuff like put-and-take tops and fraternity pins and square-toed shoes and Shifter movements and trick dancing and all the things that caught on with the Held people. The Held people *tried* to look like the Held people; the Fitzgerald-Fellows people were copies of the originals.

The average man, Mr. Average Man, Mr. Taxpayer, as drawn by Rollin Kirby *looks* like the average New York man making more than $5,000 a year. He wears Brooks clothes, including a Herbert Johnson hat, which is a pretty foreign-looking article of apparel in Des Moines, Iowa, where J. N. Darling is the cartoonist; but in New York, Kirby's territory, the Kirby taxpayer is typical. He is a man who wears good clothes without ever being a theater-program well-dressed man; it is easy to imagine him going to his dentist, taking his wife to the theater, going back to Amherst for reunion, getting drunk twice a year, having an operation for appendicitis, putting aside the money to send his son to a good prep school, seeing about new spectacles, and looking at, without always being on the side of, the cartoons of Rollin Kirby. But no one would call this man a symbol of middle age or American Taxpayer. If he walked along the streets of Syracuse or Wheeling or Terre Haute he would be known as a stranger. He would be picked out as a stranger from a bigger city, and probably picked as a New Yorker. And a Held flapper would have embarrassed any young snob who took her to a Princeton prom. And a Fellows young man, driving up in his Templar phaeton to the Pi Beta Phi house at a Western Conference University would have been spotted by the sorority girls even before they saw the Connecticut license on his car. There *are* typical men and women, young and old, but only editorial writers would be so sweeping as to pick out a certain girl or a certain boy and call him a symbol of modern youth.

There could be a symbol of modern young womanhood, but the newspapers would not be likely to print her picture. She would have to be naked. The young girl who was about twenty years old in the latter half of the 1920's did conform to a size. She was about five feet five, she weighed about 110. She had a good body. There must be a reason for the fact that so many girls fitted that description, without regard to her social classification. And the reason may well be that between 1905 and 1915 the medical profession used approximately the same system in treating pregnant women and in the feeding and care of infants. Even the children of Sicilian and Ghetto parentage suddenly grew taller, so the system must have been standard; there seems to be no other explanation for this uniformity. It is noticeable in large families: the younger children, born during and after the World War, are almost invariably tall and slender and healthier than their older brothers and sisters.

Gloria missed by ten years being a "flapper"; that is, if she had been born ten years sooner she might have qualified in 1921 as a flapper, being twenty-two years old, and physically attractive. One of the differences between Gloria as she was and as she might have been was that in 1921 she might have been "considered attractive by both sexes," and in 1931 she was considered attractive by both sexes, but with a world of difference in the meaning and inner understanding of it.

It has been hinted before that there was a reason for the recurring mood of despair which afflicted Gloria. When Gloria was eleven years old she was corrupted by a man old enough to be her father. At that time Gloria and her mother and uncle were living in Pittsburgh. Her father, a chemist, had been one of the first people to die of radium poisoning. The word father, spoken with any tenderness or sentimental intent, always evoked a recollection of her father's college class picture. It was the only picture her mother had of her father, as something had happened to their wedding pictures when they were moving from one house to another. The class picture was not much help to a child who wanted to be like other children; she saw her father as a man with a white circle around his head, in the second row of three rows of young men standing on the steps of a stone building. Through her childhood she could not see a haloed saint's picture without thinking of the picture of her father, but she would wonder why the halo did not go around the front and under the chin of the saint, and why the white circle around her father's head did not end at the shoulders the way it did with the saints; and thinking first one thing and then the other she never thought of her father as a saint, and never thought of the saints except as reminders of her father.

Her uncle, a man named William R. Vandamm (R for Robespierre), was the older brother of her mother. He, too, was a chemist and had been a classmate of Gloria's father at Cornell. Vandamm and Gloria's father had gone to Chile after college, and had stayed long enough to hate it jointly and break their contracts together. They came back together and Wandrous married Vandamm's sister. There was a little money on all sides, and both bride and groom brought equal advantages to the union, and it was one of those obscure, respectable marriages that take place every Saturday. When Wandrous died it was Vandamm who went to the radium company and used his Masonic and professional and political connections to see to it that money was provided for the upbringing and education of Gloria. They wanted to give the widow stock in the radium company, but Vandamm was too smart for that and thereby lost close to a million dollars, as it later turned out, but Vandamm was the only one who noticed that, and he did not call his sister's attention to it.

Vandamm was a good enough industrial chemist, and a very good uncle. He lived away most of the time while Gloria was a small child. He would take a job, hold it a year or so, and then take a better job, gaining in money and experience and acquaintance. He would live in men's clubs and Y.M.C.A.'s all over the country, taking half of his annual vacation at Christmas so that he could spend the holidays with his sister and niece. He would bring home beautiful presents, usually picked by one of the succession of nice young women to whom he was attentive. In every town where he worked it was the same. He was clean and respectable and had a good job, and he was unmarried. So he would single out one of the young women he met, and he would be polite to her and take her to nice dances and send her flowers, and tell her all the time what a wonderful thing this

friendship was. Each time he quit his job and moved to another town
he would leave behind a bewildered young woman, who had had him
to her house for Sunday dinner fifty times in a year, but had nothing
to show for it, candy and flowers being the perishable things that
they are. There were two exceptions: one was a young woman who
fell in love with him and did not care how much she showed it. He
had to depart from his Platonic policy in her case, because she was
making what were then known as goo-goo eyes at him every time
she saw him, at parties or alone. At the risk of not being permitted to
finish, he told her that she had made him feel as no other girl had
made him feel, and for that reason he was quitting his job at the
factory. If he stayed on, he said, he would be tempted to ask her
something he had no right to ask her. Why had he no right to ask
her? she wanted to know. Because of his sister and his niece. They
had only what money he could give them, and never would have
more. For that reason he hated to quit this job; he had been able to
do things for them that he never had been able to do before. "I will
never marry," he stated, as though it had national political significance. That fixed her. It also fixed him; instead of making him less
attractive it made him look tall and husky, a philanthropist who gave
millions in secret. It made her feel something she never had felt
before. Before that she and all women like her were a little afraid
that all bachelors were comparing all eligible women. But William,
he wasn't comparing. He had decided on her, even though he could
not, because of his dependents, have her. It turned out to be only a
question of time before he did have her. "Take me," she said, one
moonlight night, and she threw her arms back. He wasn't quite ready
to take her at that moment, but he was in a minute. For the rest of
that year he would take her every Sunday night, after paying a visit
to a drug store in another part of town every Saturday night. In nice
weather they would wander casually in the backyard and dart suddenly into the carriage house. In bad weather they would have to
wait until her father and mother had gone to bed, and then they
would go down cellar. They would leave a scrub-bucket just inside
the cellar door so that if anyone started to come down, whoever it
was would knock the bucket down the steps with a warning racket. It

was better in the carriage house, as she did not get her petticoat so dusty in a barouche as on the cellar floor.

The second exception was the girl in the next town he came to. He fell in love with her and asked her to marry him. She turned him down with such finality that she was sorry for him and suggested that they could still be friends. He snatched at this eagerly, and there was nothing he would not do for her. Years later he read about her. She and a married man, a doctor in the same "set," died together in a Chicago hotel. The doctor shot her through the heart and then turned the revolver on himself. That, after all those years, made Vandamm understand why she would not have him; there was someone else.

The arrival of the World War was propitious for Vandamm, who was getting a little tired of all but the freedom part of his freedom. He was beginning to hate the visits to the drug stores on Saturday night; he hated not being able to go right to sleep; he hated keeping his mind active so that he would not be led into a proposal of marriage. He detested the little university clubs he lived in. He hated American accents. In no town that he ever lived in had he made an impression on the first three families. He could see, when he met them, how they regarded him: an Easterner who wasn't good enough for the East and thought he would be a king among monkeys rather than a monkey among kings. He decided he had had enough experience, and from now on would make money.

He went to Pittsburgh and had no trouble getting a job. In the war years he made excellent salaries and he and his sister bought a house in the East End. It turned out that he had to move again, this time to Wilmington, Delaware, but his visits home—and he thought of it as home—were more frequent than they had been. One of the results of these frequent visits was his discovering that he adored his niece. He never would have put it that way. Even love was a word he had schooled himself against using. But he began to look forward to seeing her every time she was out of his sight. Here was someone he could love without watching what he said and did. It was such a relief after the long cautious years. What started it was the child's beauty, and he took pride in the relationship. She photographed well and he carried snapshots of her in his wallet. He was glad she was not his daughter, because he could love her more. Fathers *have to* love their daughters and sometimes there is nothing else, but an uncle can love his little niece, and they can be friends, and she will listen to him and he can be as extravagant with her as he pleases. His sister was in favor of this obvious enthusiasm on the part of her brother, although she was not unaware that her brother more and more gave to her the status of a privileged governess.

The war, his work, the money it brought him—they were half his life. Gloria was the other half, that he did not talk much about.

He took his sister's money and doubled it for her, not really for her but for Gloria. Then when he saw what he had done, he had what he thought was a brilliant idea. For the first time in his life he indulged the dangerous thrill of planning someone else's life. He wanted to get his sister married off. That would be all for the present. Get her married off, and then see what happened. But he could not stop thinking what might happen, and did not see why he should not enjoy his plans. His sister was young enough to have children, and if she had a child, a new baby, with a living husband, there was no telling what might happen. He reasoned that his sister ought to be glad to let him have Gloria. She would have a child of her own, and he would have Gloria. He would think later on about marriage for himself. If the right woman came along and Gloria liked her, and he liked her for Gloria, he might marry her. In the course of a few months of thinking along these lines Vandamm planned a whole new life for himself. He thought of it only as rearranging his own life, and never as deliberate, planned rearranging of the lives of anyone else, except little Gloria, who was after all, so young. . . .

In Wilmington he had met a man, a major in the Army Ordnance Department. Major Boam was not like most of the men who, without previous military experience, walked into captaincies and majorities in the Ordnance Department and Quartermaster and Medical Corps; he looked well in uniform. He looked fit, healthy, strong. This man worked out of Washington, and spent most of his time in Wilmington, Eddystone, Bethlehem, and Pittsburgh. Vandamm remained a civilian all through the war. He was nearsighted, underweight, flat-footed, and the Army didn't want him. Not that they were rude about it; they wanted him to remain a civilian.

"Next time you're in Pittsburgh stop in and see my sister," Vandamm told Major Boam. The major said he would be glad to, and did, and when next he saw Vandamm he said he had stopped in and had dinner with Mrs. Wandrous, a very nice dinner. Vandamm wanted to know if he had seen Gloria, but the major said he had been so late that Gloria had been asleep, oh, hours, when he got there. To Vandamm that meant that Boam had arrived late and must have enjoyed himself if he stayed, and he found out that Boam had stayed until almost train-time.

Boam was a widower with a grown daughter. Must have married very young, Vandamm decided, to have had a daughter old enough to be married. The daughter lived in Trenton, but Boam never saw her. "She has her own household to look after now," Boam said. "I don't like to go there as a father-in-law." It sounded a little as though Boam were lonely, and that fitted in with Vandamm's plans. A lonely widower, young-middle-aged, well set up, good job probably if they gave him a major's commission right off the bat. "How'd you like Major Boam?" Vandamm asked his sister. She liked him, she said. She judged men by their size. She liked a tall man better than a short man, and a tall husky man better than a tall thin man.

The Armistice interfered with Vandamm's plans. Major Boam took off his Sam Browne belt, his boots and spurs, his uniform with its two silver chevrons on the left sleeve. He stopped in to see Vandamm in Wilmington on his last trip around his circuit, and for the first time in the friendship he relaxed. Leading up to it in the most roundabout way, he finally said to Vandamm: "Well, it's time I went out looking for a job." It developed that Boam was not going back to some highly paid position. He was not going back to any-thing. He told Vandamm that when the United States entered the war he wanted to be a dollar-a-year man, but that he couldn't afford it. He had had expenses in connection with his daughter's marriage, and a lot of other things. The only way he could serve his country was to get a commission. Working for a major's pay was a financial loss, he said, and as much as he could do for his country. And now there was no job waiting for him.

This suited Vandamm. He told the major he would see to it that he got a job. The major thanked him and said he would try to use his own connections first, and if nothing came of them Vandamm was not to be surprised if one fine day Boam turned up in Pittsburgh or Wilmington.

He turned up in 1921, not to ask for a job, but just to pay a social call. He had found a vague job with the political end of the chemical game, he said. The vague job was lobbying. Peace with Germany was about to be signed, and it was his job to see to it that when the German dye factories reopened they did not wreck the American dye industry, such as it was. This was difficult, he pointed out, because many of the German factories were American-owned, or had been until war was declared, and Americans had to move carefully. There were some Americans who wanted their plants back nearly intact, and it was going to be a risky business if the Germans saw that the German dye industry was going to be discriminated against. Official Germany would not dare do anything, but the workers in the German dye factories could not be counted on to keep their sabotaging hands off the factories if they heard that their means of livelihood was being cut off in the American Congress. In other words there were two camps in America; one camp, those who had owned factories in Germany, didn't want Congress to take any tariff action until after they saw what was going to happen about the plants. The other camp consisted of the Americans who had more or less entered the dye industry for the first time when the British navy bottled up German maritime activity. These Americans had spent a lot of money building up our dye industry (under the tremendous handicap that the trade secrets of dye manufacture were kept in Germany), and they didn't want to see their money go to waste just because Germany was licked. What was the use of winning the God damn war if we couldn't get something out of it?

And so Major Boam, who retained his military title partly because the hotel and restaurant people in Washington knew him as Major Boam, and partly because he thought it gave him standing with members of Congress—had been staying in Washington ever since the Harding Administration moved in. He spoke fraternally of Congress: "We're getting a lot of work done down there. You wouldn't believe it the amount of work we're getting done—why, who is this?"

"This is Gloria. Say how do you do to Major Boam," said Mrs. Wandrous.

"How do you do," said Gloria.

"Come here till I have a look at you," said the major. He held out his hands, his big brown fat hands. "Say, this is quite a young lady. How old is she? How old are you, Gloria?"

"I'm almost twelve," she said.

"Come up here," he said. "Sit on my lap."

"Oh, now, Major, she'll be a nuisance," said Mrs. Wandrous.

"Well, if the Major wants her," said Vandamm. "Go on, Gloria, be sociable."

"Shooooor she will," said Major Boam. "Ups!" He picked her up and sat her down on his left leg. He held his left hand on her back and went on talking. As he talked his hands moved, now he would pat and squeeze her bare thighs, now he would pat her little behind. She looked up at him as he did these things, and he went on talking so interestedly and in such a strong easy voice that she relaxed and laid her head on his shoulder. She liked the pressure of his hands, which did not hurt her the way some people's did. She liked the rumble of his voice and the smell of his clean white shirt and the feel of his soft flannel suit.

"Look," said Vandamm, interrupting and indicating with a nod how relaxed Gloria was.

Boam nodded and smiled and continued what he was saying. In a little while Gloria fell asleep—it was past her bedtime. Her mother picked her up off Boam's lap, and Boam immediately jumped up.

He tried to stay away from the Wandrous-Vandamm home after that, but the harder he tried, the more excuses he invented. He would plan to go there after he was sure Gloria would be asleep; but then he would be saying: "How's little Gloria?" and Vandamm would immediately say: "Come up and see her when she's asleep." Boam

had business in Pittsburgh that was supposed to keep him there three
or four days. He stayed a fortnight. All that time he knew what was
happening to him. He did not know what he wanted to do with the
child. He did know that he wanted to take her away, be alone with
her.

Up to that time Gloria had been only another beautiful child, with
a head of dark brown curly hair, and eyes that were startlingly beautiful at first glance, and then the longer you looked at them the more
uninteresting they became. But each time you saw them anew you
would be seeing for the first time how beautiful they were. Their
beauty was in the set and the color, and being dark brown and the
eyes of a child, they did not change much and that was what made
them uninteresting. Gloria was like most female children. She was
cruel to animals, especially to dogs. She was not at all afraid of them
until after they had made friends with her and then she would hit
them with a stick, and after that she would be afraid of them, although for the benefit of her elders she would call nice doggy. A
Negro hired girl named Martha would come out from Wiley Avenue
every afternoon to take Gloria for her walk. The other child's nurses
were white and they did not encourage the colored girl to sit with
them. They did like to have pretty little Gloria with them, and pretty
little Gloria knew this, knew that her company was preferable to
Martha's, so Martha had no control over her. Her mother did not try
to exercise any control over her, except to see that she always looked
nice before she went out. Barring only an occasional enema and trips
to the dentist, Gloria's childhood was lived according to Gloria's
rules. School was easy for her; she was bright, and any little bright-
ness she displayed was rewarded out of proportion to its worth. She
liked all little boys until they played rough, and she would fight any
little boy who was being mean to a little girl, any little girl. There
was one continual paradox all through her childhood: for a child
who frequently heard herself called a little Princess she was very
neglected. She had no one to create or to generate childhood love.

On the way out to Gloria's home Boam did not allow himself to
think of what might happen, of what he hoped would happen. He
had been out to the house every second day while he was in Pitts-

burgh, but this one sunny day he knew was to be the day. He knew he was going to do something. It was after lunch, and he had a hunch Mrs. Wandrous would be out. She was. The maid who answered the door knew him, and when he did not seem disposed to leave when she said Mrs. Wandrous was out, she asked him to come in. "You don't know what time she'll be back?" he said.

"No, sir, but I don't imagine for quite a while. She went all the way downtown shopping. You only missed her by about a half an hour. Can I get you a cup of tea or something?"

"No, thanks, you go ahead with whatever you were doing. I'll just sit down a little while and if Mrs. Wandrous doesn't come along. Little Gloria out playing?"

"No, sir, she's in. The nurse-girl didn't come today. I'll send her in."

"I'd like to say good-by to her. I'm leaving tonight."

The maid was only too glad to get rid of Gloria. She had her own work to do and Mrs. Wandrous did not accept excuses when it wasn't done.

Gloria came running in and then stopped short and looked at him. Then she smiled faintly.

"How's my little girl today?" he said.

"Very well, thank you," she said.

"Come here and I'll read you the funny section," he said, and picked up the paper. He nodded to the maid, who left.

Gloria went to him and stood between his legs while he sat and read comic strips. She had an attitude of attention, but no attention in her eyes. The pressure of her elbow on his leg was becoming unbearable, and he looked into her eyes as he would have looked into a woman's. She showed no fear. Was it possible that this child had—was Vandamm the kind of man—did that explain Vandamm's adoration of this child?

He stopped reading the paper. "Let me feel your muscle," he said. She made a muscle for him. "Mm," he said. "That's quite a muscle for a girl." Then a silence.

"All ready for the summer, aren't you?" he said.

"Yes," she said.

"Not much on," he said. Then panic and fright and the need of haste came on him, and his hands went wild. He kissed her so hard on the mouth that he hurt her and she could not be sure what else was going on, but she knew enough to struggle.

He tried to pass it off with acrobatics. He held her high in the air and spoke to her and tried to laugh. He wanted to get out of this house, but he was afraid. He had not done anything but touch her, but he was afraid of the story she might tell. He could not leave until he was sure she would not run frightened to the kitchen and babble something to the maid. Then he said: "Well, I've kissed you good-by now, so I guess I'll go. All right?"

She did not know what was the polite thing to say.

"You going to miss me?" he said. "I'll bring you a nice present next time I come back. What would you like?"

"I don't know," she said.

"Well, I'll bring you something pretty nice all the way from New York, next time I come here. That's our secret, isn't it?"

"Yes," she said.

"Are you going to say by-by to me?"

"Yes," she said.

"Well."

" 'By," she said.

"Tha-a-at's right. Good-by, Gloria. You tell your mother and uncle I said good-by to them, too." He was tempted to give her money but some kind of hog's caution prevailed. He went away and he never came back, but he was remembered.

Gloria wanted to tell someone what he had done. The minute he left she forgot how he had hurt her with his teeth. She remembered his hand. She went to the kitchen and stood watching the maid, who was polishing silverware. She watched the maid and did not answer when the maid said: "Well, what are you looking at?" She could not tell *her*.

It took a year for her to tell the story, which was doubted word by word by her mother and denied by her uncle. But Vandamm knew something was wrong, because Gloria suddenly did not like him or anything he bought her or did for her. He thought it had something to do with her age. She was twelve years old, and she might be having her menstruation earlier than most girls. Lots of reasons. She was moody. A little depressed always. You couldn't expect her to be a child all the time, though. But the story did come out, little by little, until mother and uncle were able to reconstruct the scene. They took Gloria to their doctor, but Gloria would not let him touch her. They had to take her to a woman physician. Vandamm hired a private detective to look up Boam, and instituted his own campaign to have Boam ousted from his job in Washington. This was not necessary. Boam had gone back to Washington after his maltreatment of the child, quit his job, and left no forwarding address. The private detective ascertained that Boam had got into another similar mess a year or two before the war. His daughter's fiancé found out about it and daughter and fiancé eloped and never saw her father. That was the reason he never went to see his daughter in Trenton.

There was no physical aftermath to the Boam incident, except that her mental state affected Gloria's general health. Vandamm thought it would be a good thing to move away from Pittsburgh. A change of scene. New York.

For three years New York turned out to be a good idea. They put Gloria in a High Church day school where the girls wore uniforms. Thus from the first day she was like all the other girls. Her mother took her to school every day and met her after school. Here Gloria was not the prettiest nor the brightest, and was singled out for no special attention. She made a few friends, and in the summer she went with these friends to a camp in Maine, which was run by two members of the school faculty. There were enough girls at the camp from other schools to keep her from getting tired of the same faces. Then back at school there were always new girls. She improved to such an extent that it was she who asked to be sent away to school. She wanted to go to school in California, but when it came down to giving reasons her only reason was that she loved a tune, "Orange Grove in California," which was popular at the time. At that her uncle almost indulged this fancy, and would have had it not been for the—he trusted—momentarily depleted state of their finances. He tried to get a job in California, and found out for the first time that he was a lucky man; good men were working out there for monthly salaries smaller than the rent of his apartment in New York. And whatever chance there was of Gloria's being sent to California or anywhere west of the Hudson disappeared when two crimes of violence occurred within a week of each other, solidifying for all time Vandamm's inherent prejudice against the West. One crime was the Leopold-Loeb affair, which was too close a reminder of what had happened to Gloria; and the other was the suicide-pact of the woman and the doctor Vandamm had known long ago. A good, not spectacularly fashionable New England school was decided upon for Gloria. She was there almost the whole year before another man, who eventually made Boam seem like a guardian angel, was attracted to her.

WHEN you are a year away from a day that (because of some Thing) was not like other days you are as far away from the day and as far away from the thing, good or bad, as you will ever get. If it is bad, it is far enough away. Its effect may last, but there is no use kidding yourself that you live the thing over again. Something is missing. One thing that is missing in living it in retrospect is the reality; you know when you start that what you are about to recall is only, so far as this moment is concerned, a kind of dreaming. If a year ago you saw yourself cut open, your blood coming out of you, and everything outside was pain coming in you—you still cannot live that over again. Not the day, and not the moment. You can and do live back to the moment when the awful thing, whatever it was, began. Or the good thing (but of course life is not made up of many good things; at least we don't make milestones out of the good things as much as we do the bad). The still beautiful word poignant does not apply to ice cream, medals you won in school, a ride on a roller coaster, something handsome to wear, or "The Star-Spangled Banner"; although "The Star-Spangled Banner" comes closest. It is music, and poor old music, whether it's Bach or Carmichael, it knows when it starts that it is making a forlorn effort to create or recapture something that it of itself does not possess. Music is synthetic, so how can poor, lovely old music, which is the highest art, have by itself a fraction of the poignancy of an important day, an important event that day, in the life of a human being? The answer is it can't. You may shut your eyes for a second while the Maestro is conducting, but you will open them again, and to show how completely wrong you are in thinking that you have been listening to the music he brings out, you will catch yourself noticing that he has shifted the baton from his tired rheumatic right arm to his left. It is nothing to apologize for, however. Only a phony would say that he does not really notice the man Toscanini, but a phony would say it. A phony would think he gained by saying he could overlook the genius because he is a man, a human being. Who the hell wrote the music? A disembodied wraith?

We have had long and uncomfortable periods when we built chairs, forgetting that a chair is meant to be sat in. Music, too, is to be enjoyed, and we might as well face it: it must have human associations if it is to be enjoyed. The same way with love. It can happen to be pure when for one reason or more, two people do not go to bed together; and sometimes it is enough, and better, that they do not go to bed together. Love *can* be as far away from the idea of going to bed together as hate is from the idea of killing. But a chair is meant to be sat in, music is good for what it does to you, love is sleeping together, hate is wanting to kill. . . .

Three years can pass, and for two of them Gloria can be safely away from the ability to live again the time with Major Boam. This is not to say that Boam did her a favor. He was bad for her because he made her different, inside herself, and made her have a secret that was too big for her but was not the kind she could share. But she got bigger and stronger, not in the metaphorical sense, and what she knew—that a man as big as Major Boam, a man that you didn't even know what he looked like undressed, wanted to do the same things to you that little boys did—became final knowledge. It became knowledge that made up for your lack of curiosity, or your willingness to learn. Out of fear you did not want to find out too much when you were thirteen and fourteen, but you could always tell yourself that you knew quite a lot, something the other girls did not know.

The other girls respected Gloria for what they thought was genuine innocence. Children do respect that. All it was was that she did not want to hear talk, to ask questions, to contribute information. But it passed for true innocence. It deceived her mother as well as her contemporaries. When Mrs. Wandrous had to tell Gloria what was going on inside her body she felt two ways about it: one was that it was partly an old story to a girl who had been "violated" by a grown man; the other was that it was awful to have to remind the child that she had a sex. But she told her, and Gloria took the information casually (there was little enough information in what her mother told her) and without questions. Mrs. Wandrous breathed with relief and hiked Gloria off to boarding school.

Coming down from school for the Spring vacation Gloria was with five other girls. It was a bad train and the day was not warm, and every time the train stopped a man who was sitting in a seat that was almost surrounded by the six girls would get up and close the door after the passengers who left the door open. After closing the door he would go back to his seat, the third seat away from the door, and begin to doze. All her life the sound of snoring fascinated and amused Gloria, and this man snored. It made her like this man, and at the next station-stop she got up and closed the door, as she was one seat nearer the door than he was. He smiled and nodded several times, and said thank-you. At Grand Central when her mother met her the man, carrying a brief case and handbag, went to Mrs. Wandrous, who greeted Gloria first off the train, and said: "I want to compliment you on your little girl's manners and consideration. A very polite and well-mannered little girl," he smiled and went away. Mrs. Wandrous wanted to know who he was—he was either a clergyman or schoolteacher she knew that, and thought he must be from Gloria's school. Gloria said she guessed she knew why he had said that, and told her mother. Her mother looked at the man, walking up the ramp, but her instinctive alarm did not last. "There are good people in the world," she told herself. It was easy for her to think thus; Gloria's manners were the personal pride and joy of her mother.

On the way back after the holiday Gloria was with one other girl, but they did not get seats together. She was displeased with the prospect of not talking to anyone all the way back, and very pleased when a man's voice said: "We won't have to worry about the door in this nice weather." It was the man who had snored. He asked her where she was going to school, said he knew two or three girls there, told her who they were, asked her what her studies were, asked her how she liked teachers in general, explained he was one himself if you could call a principal a teacher.

Not altogether by accident he was on the train that brought her back to New York at the end of school. She was with a lot of her friends but she saw him and spoke to him like an old friend. This time in Grand Central her mother was late, and he was lagging behind. She told her friend she would wait for her mother, and the man when he saw she was alone went to her and said he would see that she got a taxi. He could even give her a lift.

It was all too easy. Two days later she called at his hotel in the afternoon, and she was sent upstairs with a bellboy because the man had been a steady patron of the hotel, was known as a respectable schoolteacher, and probably was expecting her but forgot to say so. Within a month he had her sniffing ether and loving it. It, and everything that went on in that room.

She did not see him as often as she wanted to; they could be together only in New York. She stayed two more years in that school but did not finish her college preparatory course there. In May of the second year the house mistress found a bottle of gin in Gloria's room, and she was "asked not to come back." Her mother worried a little about this but attributed it to the fact that Gloria was getting to be very popular with boys, and deep down she was glad; she thought it indicated that the Boam business was a thing of the past. Gloria was immensely popular with boys, and in a less strict school she could have been intercollegiate prom-trotting champion. She went to another school, passed her College Boards for Smith, and then thought better of college. She wanted to study Art. In New York. With her own apartment.

Her uncle enjoyed her popularity because it was the easiest thing for him to do. He never had forgiven himself for bringing Boam into their home, but neither had he ever completely blamed himself. Gloria's current popularity made up for that, and Vandamm was liberal and always on her side in disputes between his sister and his niece.

Neither Mrs. Wandrous nor Vandamm was getting any younger. Gloria won out on her refusal to go to college and on studying art in New York. They said they would see about the apartment. For the present they would move to a house in the Village which was theirs by inheritance, and fix up the top floor as a studio. Vandamm was trading luckily in the market at that time and he seriously thought Gloria had a real talent. She did have a kind of facility; she could copy caricatures by Hugo Gellert, William Auerbach-Levy, Covarrubias, Constantin Alajálov, Ralph Barton—any of the better-known caricaturists. That year she talked a great deal about going to the Art Students' League, but each time a new class would form she would forget to sign up, and so she went on copying caricatures when she had nothing else to do, and she also did some posing, always in the nude. But the thing that about that time became and continued for two or three years to be the most important was drinking. She became one of the world's heaviest drinkers between 1927 and 1930, when the world saw some pretty heavy drinking. The Dizzy Club, the Hotsy-Totsy, Tommy Guinan's Chez Florence, the Type & Print Club, the Basque's, Michel's, Tony's East Fifty-third Street, Tony's West Forty-ninth Street, Forty-two West Forty-nine, the Aquarium, Mario's, the Clamhouse, the Bandbox, the West Forty-fourth Street Club, McDermott's, the Sligo Slasher's, the News-writers', Billy Duffy's, Jack Delaney's, Sam Schwartz's, the Richmond, Frank & Jack's, Frankie & Johnny's, Felix's, Louis', Phyllis's, Twenty-one West Fifty-third, Marlborough House—these were places where she was known by name and sight, where she awed the bartenders by the amount she drank. They knew that before closing she would be stewed, but not without a good fight. There was no thought of going on the wagon. There was no reason to go on the wagon. She drank rye and water all day long. When she remembered that she had not eaten for twenty-four hours she would go to a place where the eggs were to be trusted, order a raw egg, break it in an Old Fashioned cocktail tumbler, shoot Angostura bitters into it, and gulp the result.

That night she would have dinner: fried filet of sole with tartar sauce. Next day, maybe no food, maybe bouillon with a raw egg. Certain cigarettes gave her a headache. She would smoke Chesterfields or Herbert Tareytons, no others. For days at a time she would have no sex life, tying up with a group of young Yale remittance men who in their early twenties were sufficiently advanced alcoholics to make it desirable to their families that they stay in New York. It was understood and agreed that the big thing in life was liquor, and while she was with these young men she believed and they believed that she was—well, like a sister. You did not bother her. Only one disgusting little fat boy, who came on from the Middle West twice a year, ever did bother her, but he stopped when he saw it was not the thing to do. The other young men were in the stock market from noon to closing, by telephone. By three-thirty they knew how they stood: whether to celebrate at Texas Guinan's or to drown their sorrows every other place. There was considerable riding around in automobiles with non-New York license plates, but the cars seldom got out of the state except during football season. The summers were fun in New York. Planters' Punches. Mint Juleps. Tom Collinses. Rickeys. You had two or three of these to usher in the season, and paid a visit or two to the beer places, and then you went back to whiskey and water. What was the use of kidding yourself? Everything was done at a moment's notice. If you wanted to go to a night club to hear Helen Morgan or Libby Holman you made the decision at midnight, you scattered to dress, met an hour later, bought a couple of bottles, and so to the night club. The theater was out. The movies, a little. Private parties, no, unless they were something special. Weddings, by all means. The young men were happiest when they could arrive at "42," stewed and in cutaways, "glad to be back with decent people, not these people that think champagne is something to drink."

"Down with Princeton!" Gloria would say.

"Down with Princeton," the young men would say.

"To hell with Harvard!" Gloria would say.

"The hell with Harvard," the young men would say.

"Hurray for our side!"

"Hurray for our side."

"Bing-go, bing-go, bingo, bingo, bingo that's the ling-go," Gloria would sing, and the young men would smile and join in a little weakly, drinking very hard until they could get like her, except that she could do these things while apparently not drunk. She was not invited to the weddings that they were ushering at, and there were times when she was not exactly a pest, but if she would only understand that a telephone call to a broker was important. On wedding days she would be waiting for them when they finally got away from the sailing of the French ships that in those days were well liked, but when they met her she would have a bill for drinks waiting for them that indicated she had been waiting too—since lunch. Not that she was poor. She always had fifteen or twenty dollars for taxis and things, and if you ran short she would hand it right over. It was just that she was unthinking.

She used to see Weston Liggett sometimes. He would come in, sometimes alone, sometimes with a man, sometimes with women. He would stand at the bar, have his drinks and behave himself. The second or third time she saw him she noticed he was looking at her longer than it was wise to do even in the best-regulated speakeasies. "Who is that man you spoke to?" she said to the Yale boy.

"Oh, a fellow called Liggett. He was in college with my brother."

"Yale?"

"Uh-huh. Yeah. He was one of the atha-letic boys. Crew."

It meant that he could never pick her up, and she would never speak to him until they were properly introduced. He could see her every day of the year after that, but because they had connections in common she would not have anything to do with him; and Liggett understood that and soon became a strange familiar face that Gloria saw unrecognizingly even when she was alone and he was alone. She might never have spoken to him had it not been for one accident: she got pregnant.

One night in the winter of 1929–30 she went home with the surviving two Yale boys. The others had gone back to the provinces to wait out the crash, but these two remained. This night they were prematurely drunk; the liquor was beginning to be harder to take.

Gloria usually got undressed in the bathroom when she stayed at their apartment, and they would lend her pajamas. Up to that point this night was as always. But when she lay down on the sofa Bill said: "Come on over and sleep with me."

"All right," she said.

She picked up her pillow and dragged her comforter after her and got into bed with him. She turned her back and settled herself, but she knew immediately that Bill was not going to be pal Bill tonight. He was holding her too close for any doubt about that. She let him worry for a few minutes, and then she turned around and put her arms around him and kissed him. After all, they had been friends a long time, and she liked Bill.

She also liked Mike, who was in the other bed, and not missing a thing. "How about me, Gloria?" he said.

"All right," she said.

Then they called up another girl, or rather Gloria did. The girls they called would not come over at that hour, but Gloria knew one who would, so long as there was another girl. It was all a lot more than the Yale boys anticipated, and it put an end to the drinking companionship. After that night, which was not unpleasant, Gloria went into another phase of her life; although it was in a way a return to a former phase. The next day, when she and Jane left the boys' apartment, Gloria went with Jane to a date Jane had, and the man got another man and Gloria never went out with the Yale boys again. She meant to, they meant to, but it was time she was moving on.

It was the summer of that year, 1930, when she met Eddie Brunner. She had gone to the place where he worked with "the major" because she had met the major in a speakeasy and had the sudden fear that he might be Major Boam and she might not be recognizing him. In all her life she had met only one other major, and that was Boam, and it became a terribly important thing to find out if this could be he. What if she had forgotten that man's face? It was the first time she had thought of the possibility of having forgotten Boam's face, and when the thought came she had to admit that she might easily have seen Major Boam on the street without recognizing him. This major turned out not to be Boam, but not immediately.

When she asked him his name (it was lost in the mumble of a speakeasy introduction) he told her it didn't make any difference, just call him Major. That was enough to strengthen her fear that it could be Boam without her recognizing him. For the rest of the night she pestered him for his name, and he amiably refused to tell her unless she went to this place and that place with him. His name turned out to be O'Brien or Kelly or some Irish name, but by the time she learned this she had learned too many other things about him.

Many men had the pleasure of sleeping with Gloria in the year 1930, and Eddie was the only one who could have who didn't. He began by being afraid of getting a social disease, and then when Gloria became a friend he thought he saw something in her that he did not want to sleep with. He saw a kid sister. When they were together, going to the movies, having breakfast, having a couple of beers or a highball at his house, he would feel that he was in the presence of the real Gloria. The other part of her life was shut out. They would talk about the things of their childhood (it is always a wonderful thing to discover with someone through memories of childhood how small America is). "When you were a kid did you count out by saying Ibbity-bibbity-sibbity-sab, ibbity-bibbity-ka-nah-ba, or did you just say eenie-meenie?"

"We said ibbity-bibbity."

"When you were a kid did you yell at girls named Marguerite like this: 'Marguerite, go wash your feet, the Board of Health's across the street'?"

"No, we never yelled that."

"Adam and Eve and Pinch-Me went out the river to swim. Adam and Eve were drowned and who was saved?"

"Pinch-Me." Then: "Ouch!"

"Did you go to dancing school?"

"Oh, sure."

"Did your fella used to carry your ballet slippers for you in the fancy bag?"

"I didn't have a fella."

"Brothers and sisters I have none, but this man's—"

"Oh, God, I could never do those."

Or long stories beginning: "Once when I was a kid—" about killing a snake or breaking a finger or almost saving someone's life. They would talk about the stories in *The American Boy,* both of them having been great admirers of Marcus Aurelius Fortunatus Tidd, the stuttering fat boy created by Clarence Budington Kelland; and the Altschuler Indian stories, and the girls of Bradford Hall, and Larry the Bat and Silver Nell—wasn't that her name? In the Jimmie Dale stories? They were for older people, but after reading them Eddie had gone around sticking gray seals all over the neighborhood. What kind of car did Gloria have? No car, until she was twelve or something like that, then her uncle bought a Haines, which he traded in on a National. Oh, but those weren't old cars. Eddie's father had a Lozier, an Abbott-Detroit, a Stutz Bearcat (which he smashed up three weeks after he bought it), a Saxon, an Earl, a King Eight— always buying cars. Of course a lot of Fords, a second-hand Owen Magnetic, and an airplane. He won the airplane as a gambling gain, but he was afraid to learn to fly. Had Gloria played Diabolo? Once, and got knocked on the head. Did you ever sell Easter egg dyes to win a motion picture camera? Did you ever know anyone who won a real Shetland pony by selling subscriptions to some magazine? No, but she had saved bread wrappers and won a pushmobile. What were your words for going to the bathroom? Did you ever really know a boy who robbed birds' nests? No, that was like people making bath-tub gin. Neither of them ever had seen gin made in a bathtub.

"I love you, Eddie darling," she would say.

"I love you, Gloria," he would say, but always wanting to say more than that, like: "No matter what they say about you," or "I wish I'd known you five years sooner," or "Why don't you pull yourself together?"

She knew that and it had a sterilizing effect, which was what they wanted, but no good when they had it. "Eddie," she would say, to change the subject, "why don't you go to a dentist. You're going to lose that tooth and it'll spoil your smile. Go to my dentist tomorrow, now will you promise?"

He would take her home, but they knew she would go right out again, and after these happy evenings that always ended with their knowing they had nothing to look forward to, the next man who had her would say to himself: "Well, I thought I knew everything, but after all the places I've been, all the women, a kid, an American kid. . . ."

Because of the Yale boys she had an abortion, and after that many benders. The night she picked up Weston Liggett for the first time she was coasting along from a bender which had begun after seeing Eddie. She had been home twice during this bender to change her clothes (she long since had had it well understood at home that she did not like to be questioned when she told her mother that she was staying with a friend uptown). A bad thing about days like that was to come out of a speakeasy in the afternoon and find it still daylight, and she would hurry downtown to fill in the remaining daylight with a bath and a change of clothes. The place where she encountered Liggett was a converted carriage house, with no character except for that. It was patronized by kept women and people in moderately good circumstances who lived in the vicinity. Gloria went there when some people she knew telephoned her and said they were all meeting there instead of another place. She went there—it was about nine-thirty in the evening—and discovered she was alone except for a couple, a sort of military grandfather and a young woman out to take him for whatever could be got out of him. Gloria said to the husky Italian who let her in: "I'm meeting Mrs. Voorhees and her party. I'll wait for her at the bar." She had a drink and was smoking and in walked Liggett. He sat at the other end of the bar, munching potato chips and drinking Scotch and soda. When he recognized Gloria he picked up his drink and joined her. "We've never met, but I've seen you so often—"

"Yes, with Billy."

"I went to college with his brother."

"Yes, he told me."

"My name is Liggett."

"He told me that, too. I'm Gloria Wandrous." The bartender relaxed then.

"Wandrous. I'll bet people—it's so much like wondrous."

"Yes, they think I made it up, like Gladys Glad and Hazel Dawn and Leatrice Joy, names like that. I didn't though. It's spelt with an a. W, a, n, d, r, o, u, s, and it's pronounced Wan-drous, pale and wan."

"Not pale and won."

"Mm. Not bad. Not *good,* but not bad."

"Well, I don't make any pretense of being a wit. I'm just a hard-working business man."

"Oh, are business men working again? I hadn't heard."

"Well, not as much as we'd like to. What I was leading up to was, I suppose you have a date."

"You didn't think I came in here every night, the mysterious veiled lady that always sits alone sipping her apéritif?"

"That's exactly what I thought, or hoped. I thought you came here to get away from the usual places—"

"Place, as far as you and I are concerned."

"Right. But now look here, Miss Wandrous, don't dodge the issue. Here is a hard-working business man with Saturday night as free as the air—"

"As free as the air. I have a friend a writer, he'd like to use that some time. As free as the air. That's good."

"You won't go places with me, then?"

"Why go places? Isn't this all right?" she said. "No, Mr.—"

"Liggett."

"Mr. Liggett. No, I'm waiting for some people. It'll probably be all right if you join us. You can sit here till they come and I'll introduce you to those I know."

"Oh, you don't know them. Maybe you won't like them."

"That's possible—here they are, or at least it sounds like. Hello there."

"Gloria darling, you've never been so prompt. Why, Weston *Lee*-gett. I didn't know you knew each other. Weston, why, you dog, you've broken up my party, but it's all right. That means we have an extra man. See now. Gloria, this is Mr. Zoom, and uh, Mr. Zoom, and you know Mary and Esther, and, everybody, this is Weston Liggett, a great friend of Peter Voorhees. Didn't you go to school together or something?"

"Prep school. Look, I don't want to mess up your party. I'll—let me buy you a drink, and—"

"There are four more people coming down from my house," said Mrs. Voorhees. "Elaine and three men, so you really will be an extra man when we all get here. Oh, I wonder what I want to drink. A Stinger, I think. Elaine. If those men knew *you* were going to be here they wouldn't have waited with Elaine."

"They knew," said Gloria.

"Only by name. Isn't she lovely, Weston? She's young enough to be your daughter, Weston. You know that, don't you? You're not pretending otherwise, I hope."

"I'm going to adopt her," said Liggett. "That's what we're here for, a few papers to sign and she's my daughter."

"What do you want with two more daughters I'd like to know?"

"Is anybody hungry?" said one of the Messrs. "Zoom." "I'm gonna order some food. A nice filet mignon."

"That's not very nice after the dinner we had at my house."

"Squop chicken? I never get enough to eat when I eat squop chicken. I told you that when we sat down. You gotta give me that. I told you when we sat down, I said frankly I said this is not my idea of a meal, squop chicken. I'm a big eater. Were you in the Army, Mr. Liggett?"

"Uh-huh."

"Then you know how it is. One thing I said to myself in France. I promised myself if I ever got back home the one thing I was never gonna do was go hungry. When I want to eat I eat."

"Watch this trick," said Mrs. Voorhees. The other Mr. Zoom was doing a trick. You balance a fifty-cent piece on the rim of a glass with a dollar bill between the coin and the glass. You snatched the dollar bill out from under the coin and—if the trick is successful—the coin remains balanced on the glass. "Fascinating," said Mrs. V.

"I can do a better one than that with friction. You get friction in your fingers—"

"Shhhhh. Marvelous! I can't even get it to stay on the glass, let alone make it stay after you pull the bill away. You have a wonderful sense of—I think I do want something to eat, after all. Waiter, have you any uh, that uh, you know, begins with a Z? It's a dessert."

"Zabag—"

"That's it. I'll have some. Nothing for you, Mary?"

"I know one with friction. You get friction in your fingers by rubbing them on the table-cloth. Wait till he puts the table-cloth on the table and I'll show you. And you have to have a fork or a spoon. That's the idea of it. You lift up the spoon with the—"

"Listen, Hoover's all right."

"Will you look at that old fool. Can't he see she's making a fool out of him? I'm glad my father died before he was old enough—"

"I'm sorry, Madame, the chef says—"

"Look at him. Does he get any thrill out of that?"

"It's exactly like the old place. Exactly. The only difference is it's on the uptown side now instead of the downtown side. It used to be on the downtown side but *now* it's on the *up*town. I think they were terribly smart to preserve the same atmosphere. I said to—"

"Did you see that thing they had in *The New Yorker* I think it was the week before last?"

Listening, Gloria and Liggett found themselves holding hands. On her part a tenderness had come over her; at first because she felt responsible for Liggett, and then because she liked him; he was better than these other people. "When the others come we can leave, if you want to," she said.

"Good. Perfect," said Liggett. "Will it be all right with—"

"She won't mind. She just hates to be alone. Two people more or less won't make any difference."

"Good. We'll go some place and dance. I haven't done any volunteer dancing for a long time. That's a compliment, I hope you appreciate it. I haven't done any volunteer dancing since I don't know when. Of course I dance the Turkey Trot. You do the Turkey Trot, of course?"

"Mm-hmm. And the Bunny Hug. And the Maxixe. And the Can-

Can. By the way, what was the Can-Can? Was it worth all the excitement they made about it or that I suppose they made about it?"

"Listen, beautiful Miss Wandrous, I am *not* old enough to remember the Can-Can. The Can-Can was popular around the turn of the
century, and I wasn't. I wasn't at all popular at the turn of the
century."

"I can hardly believe that. At least I can hardly believe my ears
now, hearing you admit that you weren't popular any time in your
life."

"There have been lots of times when I wasn't popular, and I'm
beginning to think this is one of those times."

They went to a lot of speakeasies, especially to the then new kind,
as it was the beginning of the elaborate era. From serving furtive
drinks of bad liquor disguised as demi-tasse the speakeasy had pro-
gressed to whole town houses, with uniformed pages and cigarette
girls, a string orchestra and a four- or five-piece Negro band for
dancing, free hors d'oeuvres, four and five bartenders, silver-plated
keys and other souvenir-admittance tokens to regular patrons, expensive entertainment, Cordon Bleu chefs, engraved announcements in
pretty good taste, intricate accounting systems and business machin-
ery—all a very good, and because of the competition, necessary
front for the picturesque and deadly business of supplying liquor at
huge financial profit—powerful radio stations, powerful speedboats
and other craft not unlike the British "Q" ships, powerful weapons
against highjackers, powerful connections in the right places. And
often very good liquor and enough good wine to set in front of the
people who knew good wine and still cared about it.

Having got thoroughly drunk, picking up couples and dropping
them, joining parties and deserting them, Gloria and Liggett went to
his apartment as the last place to go. He had been wondering all
night how he was going to suggest a hotel. He thought it over and
thought it over, and kept putting it off. At the last place they went to,
which they closed up, they took a taxi, Liggett gave his home address, and it was as easy as that. When Gloria heard the address she
guessed it was no love nest she was going to, and when she saw the
apartment she knew it wasn't.

5

ON MONDAY AFTERNOON AN unidentified man jumped in front of a New Lots express in the Fourteenth Street subway station. Mr. Hoover was on time for the usual meeting of his Cabinet. Robert McDermott, a student at Fordham University, was complimented for his talk on the Blessed Virgin at the morning exercises in her honor. A woman named Plotkin, living in the Brownsville section of Brooklyn, decided to leave her husband for good and all. William K. Fenstermacher, the East 149th Street repair man, went all the way to Tremont Avenue to fix a radio for a Mrs. Jones, but there was no Jones at the address given, so he had to go all the way back to the shop, wasting over an hour and a half. Babe Ruth hit a home run into the bleachers near the right field foul line. Grayce Johnson tried to get a job in the chorus of The Band Wagon, a new revue, but was told the show was already in rehearsal. Patrolman John J. Barry, Shield No. 17858, was still on sick call as a result of being kicked in the groin by a young woman Communist in the Union Square demonstration of the preceding Friday. Jerry, a drunk, did not wake up once during the entire afternoon, which he spent in a chair at a West 49th Street speakeasy. Identical twins were delivered to a Mrs. Lachase at the Lying-In Hospital. A Studebaker sedan bumped the spare tire of a Ford coupe at Broadway and Canal Street, and the man driving the Ford punched the Studebaker driver in the mouth. Both men were arrested. Joseph H. Dilwyn, forty-two years old, had all his teeth out by the same dentist he had gone to for twelve years. A woman who shall be nameless took the money her husband had given her to pay the electric light bill and bought one of the new Eugenie hats with it. Harry W. Blossom, visiting New York for the first time since the War, fell asleep in the Strand Theatre and missed half the picture. At 3:16 P.M. Mr. Francis F. Tearney, conductor on a Jackson Heights No. 15 Fifth Avenue bus, tipped his cap at St. Patrick's Cathedral. James J. Walker, mayor of the City of New York, had a late lunch at the Hardware Club. A girl using an old

111

curling iron caused a short circuit in the Pan-Hellenic Club. An unidentified man jumped in front of a Bronx Park express in the Mott Avenue subway station. After trying for three days Miss Helen Tate, a typist employed by the New York Life, was able to recall the name of a young man she had met two summers before at a party in Red Bank, N. J. Mr. and Mrs. Harvey L. Fox celebrated their thirtieth wedding anniversary with a luncheon in the Hotel Bossert, Brooklyn. Al Astor, an actor at liberty, woke up thinking it was Tuesday. John Lee, a colored boy, pulled the wings out of a fly in Public School 108. The Caswell Realty Company sold a row of taxpayers in Lexington Avenue to Jack W. Levine for a sum in the neighborhood of $125,000. Gloria Wandrous, after taking a warm bath at home, went to sleep while worrying over what she should do about Mrs. Liggett's mink coat. Eddie Brunner spent the afternoon at Norma Day's apartment, playing the phonograph, especially "The Wind in the Willows," the Rudy Vallée record.

Monday afternoon Emily Liggett and her daughters came home by train. They got out of their taxi, carrying their coats and leaving the few bags for the doorman to see to. Emily went straight to her room and of all the things that happened to all the people in New York that day, none was more shocking to any individual than Emily's discovery that her mink coat was not in her closet.

It had been such a good week-end; quiet and peaceful. Saturday was warm, Sunday morning was warm and in the afternoon it turned cool and made Emily think of the coat. It was time, really, to put it away, and she made a note of it as the first thing to do Tuesday morning. This year she would insure it for $3,000, half what it cost in 1928. She would insure it and hope something would happen to it so that she could get the money out of it. There were things she could do with $3,000, and she was getting tired of having a mink coat. She never had been happy with the actual possession of it. Something about the New England conscience; when you added up the maximum number of times you wore the coat in a season, multiplied that by three for three seasons, and divided that into $6,000 you got the cost of the coat each time you had worn it. And it was too much. It was a fair calculation, because she knew she could not get $3,000 for the coat now in any other way than insurance. As for getting $6,000 on it—ridiculous. Well, it had been a good week-end.

She opened the closet door, and the closet might as well have been empty. The coat was not there. She called the cook and the maid and questioned them, but her questioning and her own and their search did not result in finding the coat. Her questioning did not bring about any of the disclosures which the maid was pondering—the inference the maid had taken from certain little things she had noticed about Mr. Liggett's bedroom and bath.

Emily telephoned Liggett, but he was not in the office and his secretary did not expect him back. Emily was going to call his two clubs and a speakeasy or two, because she thought the theft of the coat ought to be reported immediately; but she decided to wait and talk to Weston before notifying the police. When Liggett came home she told him about the coat. He was frightened; he was twice frightened, because he did not know it was gone, but when he learned it had disappeared he knew right away who had it. He told Emily it was best not to notify the police; that losses like that were immediately reported to the insurance company and that it was a bad thing to have to report to the insurance company. "All the insurance companies work together," he said, "and they keep a sort of exchange blacklist. If your car is stolen all the other companies know about it in a week, and it affects your rating with the companies. It makes you a bad risk to lose a thing like that, and when you're a bad risk it's sometimes impossible to get insurance, and the least you get out of it is you have to pay a much higher preminum, not only on, for instance, the coat, if they get it back, but also anything else you decide to insure." Liggett did not believe all this—in fact knew some of it to be inaccurate; but it covered up his confusion. That that girl, that swell kid, could be the same girl he had slept with last night, for whom he was feeling something he never had felt before, and all the time she was a common ordinary little thief—it was beyond him. It was more than beyond him. The more he thought of it the angrier he got, until he wanted to take her by the throat. He told Emily he would have a private detective agency look for the coat before reporting to the insurance company or the police. This was

not the way Emily would have done it, and she said so. Why go to
the expense of a private detective agency when the insurance company assumed that and would be glad to assume it rather than risk
the loss of $3,000 for the coat? No, no, he insisted. Hadn't she been
listening to him? Didn't she pay any attention? Hadn't he just finished telling her that the insurance company kept blacklists, and the
chances were the disappearance of the coat would have some simple
explanation. The detective agency wouldn't charge much—ten dollars, probably. And he would save that much in premiums by not
reporting the loss to the insurance company. "Now please let me
handle this," he told Emily. Well, it seemed pretty irregular to her,
and she didn't like it. What if the private detectives didn't find the
coat? Wouldn't the insurance company be very annoyed when he did
finally report the theft of the coat? Wouldn't they ask why he hadn't
immediately reported to the police? Wouldn't it be better in the long
run to do the regular thing? She thought it was always best to do the
regular thing, the conventional thing. When someone dies, you get
an undertaker; when something is stolen, you tell the police. Liggett
almost said: "Who are you to talk about the conventional thing? You
slept with me before you married me." He was ashamed of that, of
thinking it; but he guessed he always had thought it. It was just
beginning to dawn on him that he never had loved Emily. He was so
flattered by what she felt for him before they were married that he
had been blinded to his true feeling about her. His true feeling was
passion, and that had gone, and since then there had been nothing
but the habit of marriage—he really loved Gloria.

And then he remembered that he did not love Gloria. He could not
love a common thief. She *was* a common thief, too. You could see
that in her face. There was something in her face, some unconven-
tional thing along with the rest of her beauty, her mouth and eyes
and nose—somewhere around the eyes, perhaps, or was it the
mouth?—she did not have the conventional look. Emily, yes. Emily
had it. He could look at Emily dispassionately, impersonally, as
though he did not know her—objectively? wasn't it called? He could
look at her and see how much she looked like dozens of girls who
had been born and brought up as she had been. You saw them at the

theater, at the best cabarets and speakeasies, at the good clubs on Long Island—and then you saw the same girls, the same women, dressed the same, differing only in the accent of their speech, at clubs in other cities, at horse shows and football games and dances, at Junior League conventions. Emily, he decided after eighteen years of marriage, was a type. And he knew why she was a type, or he knew the thing that made the difference in the look of a girl like Emily and the look of a girl like Gloria. Gloria led a certain kind of life, a sordid life; drinking and sleeping with men and God knows what all, and she had seen more of "life" than Emily ever possibly would see. Whereas Emily had been brought up a certain way, always accustomed to money and the good ways of spending it. In other words, all her life Emily had been looking at nice things, nice houses, cars, pictures, grounds, clothes, people. Things that were easy to look at, and people that were easy to look at; with healthy complexions and good teeth, people who had had pasteurized milk to drink and proper food all their lives from the time they were infants; people who lived in houses that were kept clean, and painted when paint was needed, who took care of their cars and their furniture and their bodies, and by so doing their minds were taken care of; and they got the look that Emily and girls—women—like her had. Whereas Gloria—well, take for instance the people she was with the night he saw her two nights ago, the first night he went out with her. The man that liked to eat, for instance. Where did he come from? He might have come from the Ghetto. Liggett happened to know that there were places in the slums where eighty families would use the same outside toilet. A little thing, but imagine what it must look like! Imagine having spent your formative years living like, well, somewhat the way you lived in the Army. Imagine what effect that would have on your mind. And of course a thing like that didn't only affect your mind; it showed in your face, absolutely. Not that it was so obvious in Gloria's case. She had good teeth and a good complexion and a healthy body, but there was something wrong somewhere. She had not gone to the very best schools, for instance. A little thing perhaps, but important. Her family—he didn't know anything about them; just that she lived with her mother and her mother's brother. Maybe she was a bastard. That was possible. She could be a bastard. That can happen in this country. Maybe her mother never was married. Sure, that could happen in this country. He never heard of it except among poor people, and Gloria's family were not poor. But why couldn't it happen in this country? The first time he and Emily ever stayed together they took a chance on having children, and in those days people didn't know as much about not getting caught as they do today. Gloria was even older than Ruth, so maybe her mother had done just what Emily had done, with no luck. Maybe Gloria's father was killed in a railroad accident or something, intending to marry Gloria's mother, but on the night he first stayed with her, maybe on his way home he was killed by an automobile or a hold-up man or something. It could happen. There was a fellow at New Haven that was very mysterious about his family. His mother was on the stage, and nothing was ever said about his father. Liggett wished now that he had known the fellow better. Now he couldn't remember the fellow's name, but some of the fellows in Liggett's crowd had wondered about this What's-His-Name. He drew for the *Record*. An artist. Well, bastards were always talented people. Some of the most famous people in history were bastards. Not bastards in any derogatory sense of the word, but love children. (How awful to be a love child. It'd be better to be a bastard. "If I were a bastard I'd rather be called a bastard than a love child.") Now Gloria, she drew or painted. She was interested in art. And she certainly knew a lot of funny people. She knew that bunch of kids from New Haven, young Billy and those kids. But anybody could meet them, and anybody could meet Gloria. God damn it! That was the worst of it. Anybody could meet Gloria. He thought that all through dinner, looking at his wife, his two daughters, seeing in their faces the thing he had been thinking about a proper upbringing and looking at nice things and what it does to your face. He saw them, and he thought of Gloria, and that anybody could meet Gloria, and Anybody, somebody she picked up in a speakeasy somewhere, probably was with her now, this minute.

"I don't think I'll wait for dessert," he said.

"Strawberries? You won't wait for strawberries?" said Emily.

"Oh, good. Strawberries," said Ruth. "Daddy, you'll surely wait for strawberries. If you go I'll have to eat yours and I'll get straw-berry rash."

"You won't *have* to," said Emily.

"Gotta go. I just thought of a fellow. About the coat."

"Can't you phone him? A detective agency, surely they'd have a phone."

"No. Not this fellow. He isn't a private detective. He's a regular city detective, and if I phoned him he'd have to make a report on it. If I went through the regular channels. I'll get in touch with him through a friend of mine, Casey, down at Tammany Hall."

"Well, where? Can't you phone this Casey and make an appoint-ment?"

"Emily, *must* I explain everything in detail? I just thought of something and I want to do it now. I don't want any strawberries, or if they're that good you can put them in the icebox till I get back."

"Well, all right. I hope this doesn't mean one of your all-night binges with your Tammany Hall friends."

If the girls had not been there he would have given a more blister-ing answer than: "I should have been a doctor."

A taxi took him to a drug store in the Grand Central zone and he tried to get Gloria on the telephone. He tried her home, several speakeasies, and—he did not quite know why—had her paged at two of the Times Square hotels. A woman he guessed was her mother said Gloria was out for dinner and the evening. It sounded so re-spectable, the voice and the words, that he wanted to laugh in the mouthpiece. He could not tell (and he tried) whether he was now angry with Gloria for stealing Emily's coat, or because he had her, in his mind, grappling with some young snot-nose from Princeton. He came out of the telephone booth sweating and uncomfortable, with his hat on the back of his head. He had a Coca-Cola standing up at the fountain, and when he set the glass down on the fountain it made the hollow *cloup* sound those glasses make, but this glass must have been imperfect because it cracked and broke and he cut his finger, ever so slightly, but enough to cause an industrial crisis in the store. The pharmacist and the soda jerker were so solicitous and made him so angry with it that he was rude to them, and away went his resolution not to drink. He had been feeling so respectable and superior up to then, but the cut on his finger, which was minutely painful but enormously annoying, and the store people with their attentions got him upset. "Jesus Christ, why don't you send for a God damn ambulance," he said, and went out in search of a drink.

Fifty-second Street between Fifth and Sixth Avenues was packed solid with automobiles and their sound, never changing. The *eep* sound of the taxis and the *aa-oo-aa* of Lincoln town cars predominated in the chorus. It was like an evening wedding in a small town; with the invited, those who had cards, inside, and the big noise going outside independent of the rest.

He went inside and had a Scotch and soda at the bar. It appeared to be full of people trying to be late for the theater, and out-of-town men in light tan suits, drinking Old Fashioneds and laughing too loud for the humor in anything they could possibly say. Liggett did not want to talk to anyone, not even the bartenders. He drank and smoked and drank and smoked, and when his cigarette was done he ate potato chips and when his drink was done he lit another cigarette and then had more to drink. This way he waited out the people who were going to the theater, and was alone at the bar. By that time the men in the tan suits were kissing the handsome women. Those men were getting drunk much too soon, Liggett decided, getting drunk. He realized he was drinking too much and he put it up to himself squarely, whether to go home now or get really stewed. He decided to get stewed, because he would be uncomfortable if he went home, where he never got drunk; and because if he got drunk here he might think of some crazy thing to do that might lead to his finding Gloria. Where could she be? New York's a big place, but the places Gloria went to were not many. The theater was out; she never went to the theater. The only other place she could be was in any apartment in town. Any other, from the houses that hung over the Harlem River branch of the New York Central to the apartments that hung over the East River, or in a one-room apartment in the Village, or an artist's studio in the West Sixties, or some place on Riverside Drive. Any apartment.

He went home late, having gone to nine speakeasies in one block, having been refused admission to two others. He went home without seeing Gloria.

She was spending the evening with Eddie. She went to his apartment and they had dinner at a restaurant, where Eddie ate a lot of spaghetti, winding it expertly around his fork. They had a bottle of red wine. It was a good little restaurant, with sawdust on the floor and a pool table, where some elderly Italians played a game which Eddie never understood; something to do with shooting the cueball between two tiny bowling pins. A small radio was turned on. They did not change the dial, and the program went from music to speech to adventure story to torch-singer, with no editing on the part of the proprietor of the place. It was probably the only station that came in good, because of the "L," which was only half a block away. Gloria and Eddie were the only Americans in the place, and no one paid any attention to them. When they wanted the waiter they had to call him from his card game with three other patrons.

"What did you do last night?" said Eddie.

"Oh, went to a movie."

"Which one?" Eddie asked.

"The Strand."

"What did you see?"

"Uh, Norma Shearer, in 'Strangers May Kiss.' "

"Oh, did you? How'd you like it? Any good?"

"Not very. I like her, though. I think she's terribly attractive."

"She's a Canadian. From Montreal. You know, Montreal, Nova Scotia," said Eddie.

"Montreal isn't in Nova Scotia," said Gloria.

"I know. And 'Strangers May Kiss' isn't at the Strand, in case you're interested. Of course I'm not. I don't give a damn, only I don't know why you think you have to lie to me."

"Well, I could have got the theater wrong."

"No, you couldn't. You could have got the theater wrong, but not the picture, and 'Strangers May Kiss' isn't playing on Broadway. It was, but it isn't now. So don't lie any more than you have to."

"I'll lie to you if I want to. What I do isn't your affair anyway."

"You won't lie to me often, because I won't be around to listen."

"Why? Are you going away?"

"No. Where would I go? No, it's just that I won't see you. I don't want to see you if you lie to me. I know practically everything about you that there is to know, and I don't mind the kind of life you lead, because that's your business. But just don't go to all the trouble of lying to me. Save your lies for someone you have to lie to."

"Oh—"

He laughed. "Unless of course you want to *practice* on me. You ought to do a little more practicing, by the way. If you think Norma believed that story the other night about you and your imaginary cousin and the crap game where you lost your clothes. What do you think people are? Don't you give them credit for any sense at all? You know it's a form of insult, making up a screwy story to explain something that you don't have to explain. You know, Norma's my girl, and she hasn't any wrong ideas about us."

"Did you tell her?"

"Certainly I told her."

"How? What did you say to her?"

"I told her we weren't having an affair."

"Who brought it up? Did you say it first, or did she ask you? How did you happen to tell her?"

"I don't know," said Eddie, and reflected. "It was when I first knew her. She asked me if I was in love with anybody, and I said no, and she said what about the girl named Gloria that someone said I saw all the time. Someone told her I was seeing you, but all she knew was your first name. So I said you were a platonic friend, and that's all."

"Is it?"

"About all. Nothing else worth repeating."

"Didn't she say that if you and I were platonic friends, you were my only platonic friend?"

"No. Not exactly."

"Not exactly, hah? You know she said something like that, though, don't you?"

"A little like that. Oh, what the hell, Gloria, yes. She didn't put it that way. She wanted to know how I could see a good-looking girl like you and keep up a platonic friendship. I mean keep it platonic."

"And you were peeved because you thought she was laughing at you. It didn't make you look so good to be the one man I didn't sleep with."

"There you're wrong. If I started to resent that now it'd be pretty late in the game."

"Did you ever resent it?"

"No."

"Why not?"

"I don't know."

"Because I'm not attractive to you?"

"No. Not that either."

"Well then, *what?*"

"Well, we didn't start off that way, is the only reason I can give right now. Do you want a psychological reason?"

"Yes."

"Well, I haven't got one for you. Do you want some more wine?"

"Yes, I guess I ought to have some wine from sour grapes."

"Oh, for God's sake," said Eddie. "Am I supposed to infer that you're sour grapes because I like Norma better than you?"

"Why not? Isn't that the truth?"

"No, certainly not."

"You don't like me because you feel superior. You know all about me and that's why you never ask me to sleep with you."

"I've asked you to sleep with me."

"Yes. Sleep with you. Good Samaritan. When I'm tight and you think I'll get the devil if I go home drunk. You ask me if I'll sleep in your apartment. Why, that's the most insulting thing you can do, in a way. It *proves* how you feel about me. You're above my sex appeal. You could sleep with me and not feel a thing."

"Good Lord."

"Yes, good Lord. I'm no good. I'm not fit to touch. You'd be contaminated if you touched me. That's the way you feel about me, isn't it?"

"No."

"It is! You hate me, Eddie Brunner. You can't stand the sight of me. You're so damned superior you—"

"Oh, stop."

"Why should I stop? Because I'm talking too loud. I'm embarrassing you by talking too loud. That's it, isn't it?"

"You *are* talking above a whisper."

"God damn it, why not? Here! You!" She called to one of the elderly Italians.

"Me, Miss?"

"Yes. Come here."

The old man came over and tipped his hat. "Yes," he said.

"Am I talking too loud?"

"Oh, no. Not at all, Miss. You have a good time." He smiled at Eddie.

"I didn't ask you if I could have a good time. I asked you if I were talking too loud."

"Oh, no. We don't mind it," said the Italian.

"Doesn't it disturb your card game to have me talking so loud?"

"No. No. Oh, no."

"All right. You may go."

The old man looked at her and then at Eddie, and smiled at Eddie, and then tipped his hat and went back to the game. He explained in Italian the interruption, and each of the players turned and looked at Gloria before resuming the game.

Eddie went on eating.

"There you sit," she said.

"Uh-huh. Just as though nothing happened. Drink your wine, bad girl, and feel sorry for yourself some more. John!" The waiter came. "Another bottle of wine," said Eddie.

They did not speak while the waiter went to fetch the wine. He opened the bottle and poured some in Gloria's glass.

"That's an insult!" said Gloria.

"Miss?" said the waiter.

"That's an insult. Didn't you see what he did? You know you're supposed to pour it in his glass first."

"I'll take your glass," said Eddie.

"That's not the idea. He's supposed to pour some in your glass first and then fill mine and then fill yours. You know that, so why shouldn't he know it?"

"This wine is just bottled, Miss. It is only when the wine has been in the bottle a long time."

"You don't have to tell me about wine. I know more about wine than you do."

"Yes, Miss. This is home-made wine and it is only bottled this evening."

"I didn't ask you the history of it. I won't drink it. I want a highball."

"Give her a highball. Rye and soda," said Eddie.

"Humor her," said Gloria. "Let her have her own way. Well, I don't want a highball. I want another bottle of wine, and you pour it the right way, whether it was bottled in 1926 or five minutes ago. I've never been so insulted in all my life."

"Are you drunk, by any chance?" said Eddie.

"No, and you know I'm not."

"Well, what are you sore about? All right, John, another bottle of wine. What's the matter with you, Gloria? Did someone do something to you? You're never like this with me. In a minute I'll begin to be sorry for myself. Maybe you hate me and you don't want to tell me."

"No."

"Tell me, what is it?"

"I don't want to talk about it."

"You can talk to me. You always have."

"I don't even know what it is myself. It isn't against you. I love you, Eddie. Oh, I'm so awful."

"Are you in love with someone?"

"Not the way I want to be."

"You mean me?"

"No. Yes. But you're not the one I'm thinking of. No, it's this Liggett."

"You're in love with Liggett?"

"Oh, I think so. I don't know."

"Does he know it?"

"No."

"Really in love with him?"

"I am, yes. He isn't. I know what he thinks. He thinks—well, just a pushover. First night I go out with him I go to bed with him. Even worse than that. He picked me up in a speakeasy."

"Well, being picked up in a speakeasy is better than being picked up in the Grand Central station."

"Why did you say that! Answer me! Why did you say that?"

"Hell's bells, I don't know. Did I say the wrong thing?"

"What made you say the Grand Central station? What do you know about the Grand Central station?"

"Well—it's—a *station.*"

"You said it was better to be picked up in a speakeasy than in Grand Central. Why did you say that? Do you know anything about my being picked up in the Grand Central?"

"No, were you?"

"Oh, God. Oh, Eddie. Take me out of here. Let's go to your apartment."

"Sure. John! Tell John I don't want the wine. Just bring the check."

They went home and she told him about Dr. Reddington. She spent the night there because she was afraid, and Eddie went to sleep in a chair, watching her while pretending to read. He became exhausted by the first experience of the desire to kill a man.

THE next morning, Tuesday, Liggett got awake with an average hangover, the kind that reminded him of mornings after football games and boat races, except that after a night's drinking like last night's he could count on partial recovery within a few minutes after answering the call of nature, and after a day of strenuous athletics nature does not always call, at least not before he was at top form. It always seemed to Liggett that too hard rowing stiffened the muscles of the intestines, resulting in constipation, which resulted in boils. Drinking had for him no such effect. A trip to the bathroom and the worst of this kind of hangover was gone. A shot of tomato juice with a generous dash of Worcestershire sauce, and a cup of black coffee and a plate of cream of tomato soup—that was his breakfast on mornings like this.

Emily came in while he was eating his soup. "Did anything happen about the coat?"

"I couldn't find Casey. I'll get in touch with him today."

"There's some on your vest. Here, I'll get it."

"No, it's all right. I'll do it."

"I'll do it. You'll stain it. Let me." She scraped off the splash of soup with a knife. "There."

"Thanks."

"Let's go to the theater tonight. I want to see Bart Marshall. And you like Zita Johann."

"Bart Marshall? Who is he?"

"Herbert Marshall. I was being funny."

"What are they playing in?"

" 'Tomorrow and Tomorrow.' By Philip Barry."

"Oh, yes. Well, all right if you get the tickets. Who shall we ask?"

"I thought we could ask the Farleys. We'll be going to the country soon and I dislike not having seen her since last summer. What made me think of them was they were at the club Sunday, and Mrs. Farley's a nice woman. I like her."

"Yes, I saw him. He was with a fellow that said he knew me at New Haven. A Jew."

"Oh, ho. You?" Emily laughed.

"What are you laughing at? I have nothing against Jews. I have some good friends Jews. Paul and Jimmy. You know I like them."

"Oh, I know, but not while you were in college."

"Listen, don't you go around saying things like that. This is no time for that kind of snobbishness. Have the Farleys by all means. Her brother is a great friend of Al Smith's. You get the tickets, and what about dressing?"

"I think a black tie."

"Yes. Farley's always very well dressed, and if you don't specify black tie he's liable to come in tails, and I'll be damned if I want to put on tails this late in the season. Is this play any good?"

"Josie liked it."

"What the hell does she know about anything?"

"You *like* Josie. I've heard you *say* you liked her."

"Oh, you mean Josie Wells. I thought you meant Josie Demuth." He wiped his mouth with the napkin lengthwise. He looked at his watch, and then had to look again to see what time it was. "I'll be home as early as I can. I'm going to Philadelphia on the ten o'clock, but I'll be back in plenty of time for dinner, I hope. I'm not going to the office at all, unless I stop in after I get back from Philadelphia. Good-by." He kissed her.

"THIS is Emily Liggett, Mrs. Farley. I tried to wave to you at the club Sunday."

"I saw you, and the *girls*. Was that really Ruth?"

"It was. Isn't she—"

"Oh, she must be such fun. I knew Barbara, but I had to look twice to be sure that was Ruth. She used to be *pretty*, but now she's *handsome.*"

"Oh, thank you. I wish I could tell her that, but I think I'll save it for her. When she needs cheering up. I wondered if you and Mr. Farley could come to dinner tonight on such short notice. I wanted to ask you on Sunday, but it would only be the four of us, you and Mr. Farley and my husband and I. I thought we might go to the theater."

"Tonight? Why, yes, I think so. I'm almost positive."

"Oh, fine. Have you seen 'Tomorrow and Tomorrow'?"

"No, we haven't. Paul said this morning that that was one of the things he wanted to see. I thought it would get the Pulitzer Prize, or at least a lot of people seemed to."

"Oh, have they given the Pulitzer Prize again?"

"Yes, it's in this morning's paper. 'Alison's House,' by Susan Glaspell, won it."

" 'Alison's House.' Oh, yes. That was about Emily Dickinson, but I never did see it. They do so many good things at the Civic Repertory but it's such a nuisance to go all the way down there. Well, I'm so glad you can come. At seven-thirty, and black tie for our husbands."

"Grand, and thank you so much," said Nancy.

She liked Emily Liggett, and she was pleased because she knew Mrs. Liggett had not tried to wave to her on Sunday. That lie was one of the amenities. Nancy Farley knew that what had happened was that Mrs. Liggett had seen her at the club, had thought of her some time, perhaps several times, on Monday, and had decided probably last night to invite her to dinner. Nancy had no hope of being or desire to be an intimate friend of Emily Liggett's. Emily Liggett was one of a few women whom Nancy always spoke to, addressing them as Mrs., seeing them a lot around the club in the summer and over the heads of people at the theater. She knew Emily liked her—which meant little more than liking her looks, but that was quite all right—and that the liking had in it such qualities as mutual respect and approval. They never would be close friends, because they never would have to be. Nancy knew that if she ever happened to be taking a boat trip or a long train ride with Emily Liggett they would find they had friends in common other than the same general group they knew in New York; but Nancy was satisfied to take that for granted, along with probable tastes in common. There was warmth now in her admiration for Mrs. Liggett; it took a kind of courage for Mrs. Liggett to invite the Farleys to dinner, and it was that which Nancy admired. She called Paul's office and left word with his secretary that they were going to the Liggetts' for dinner. Then she went to Paul's room to see that one of his two dinner jackets was pressed and ready to wear, and she made a routine inspection of his shirts and collars and ties.

The Farley boys were long since at school and Nancy had nothing to do until five o'clock. Every day at five, unless Paul had other plans, Nancy would drive down Lexington Avenue to the neighborhood of the Graybar Building, where Paul had his offices. She had been doing this for four years. It began accidentally. She happened one afternoon to be in the neighborhood of his offices, which were then at 247 Park Avenue, and she waited for him and caught him coming out. It was such a good idea, they agreed, that it would be fun to do it every day she could. It did have its points; there were many afternoon parties in those days, and she would stop and pick

him up and they would go to the parties together. Although they
never happened to say so to each other or to anyone else, both Nancy
and Paul hated to enter a room alone. But together they put up a
good united front, and they were two people who in the minds of
their friends were thought of always as husband and wife. Only to
his draftsmen and to the employees of his clubs and a few business
acquaintances did Paul have an identity of his own. After working
hours everyone thought of him as the one in masculine attire of the
inseparable Mr. and Mrs. Paul Farley. It was almost true of Nancy,
too; as true as it could be of a woman, who, if she has anything at all
—beauty, ugliness, charm, bad taste, good taste, sex appeal—begins
with a quicker identity and holds it longer than a man does. And so
they would go to parties together, or simply go home together. Every
day she would meet him.

After a while it began to be a habit that to Nancy was not an
unmixed blessing. At first occasionally, and then every day, Paul
would come up in back of the car and gently pinch the back of
Nancy's neck. In the beginning it was cute, she thought. Then she
found that she was expecting it. Then she found she was setting
herself against it, tightening her nerves and sitting in the very middle
of the front seat, hoping he would not be able to take her by surprise.
But he always did. It became a game with him, and she could count
on the fingers of one hand the number of times when luck was with
her and she was quicker than he. They had a phaeton then, a Packard. When they were buying a convertible one thing she had in mind
was that she would be able to raise the window on her side and he
would not be able to touch her neck. This was no good, though; he
would get the same surprise effect by rapping hard with his ring on
the raised window. Little by little the custom of meeting Paul every
day became a nuisance, then almost a horror. It made her jittery, and
all because he was doing something she at first thought was cute,
sweet. After they would get in the car it would take her a few minutes to get her mind on what he was saying. A few times, on days
when the weather was fine and he had reason to expect her to meet
him, she just could not bring herself to face it—although face it was
precisely not the word—and she would find excuses not to turn up.

At such times he would be so hurt that she would tell herself she was a little beast; Paul was so kind and considerate and sweet in everything else, what on earth was the matter with her that she couldn't pass over such a slight fault? But this self-reproach did not have any lasting effect. It was a form of self-indulgence that certainly did not solve the problem.

As for coming right out and telling Paul she objected to his pinching the back of her neck—that was out of the question. From conversations with her friends, and from her own observations, Nancy knew that in every marriage (which after all boils down to two human beings living together) the wife has to keep her mouth shut about at least one small thing her husband does that disgusts her. She knew of a case where the marriage was ruined because of the husband's habit of allowing just a little of the white of egg to hang from the spoon when he ate soft-boiled eggs. In that case the disgusting thing occurred every morning. She knew of another case where the husband walked out on his wife because he said she was unclean; it took one of those psychoanalytical quacks a month to get the man to reveal that the woman never went to the bathroom without leaving toilet paper floating in the bowl of the toilet. Things like these that you kept quiet about, they were worse than the things you could quarrel about; your husband's behavior in bed, or your wife's; his taste in clothes, or hers; cheating at games, flirtatiousness, bad manners, differences of opinion, repetitiousness, bragging and humility and punctuality and the lack of it and all the other things that people can quarrel openly about. Then there was always the hope that please God he might stop. But, no; he probably did it because he thought it was expected of him.

Now this Tuesday Nancy Farley, with nothing to do all day, began thinking of Paul's little trick early in the day. It was going to be a fine day. There wasn't a cloud in the sky and no chance of any legitimate excuse not to meet Paul. This same day, this idleness gave her plenty of chance to think from time to time of John Watterson, the homely actor who everyone said had more charm than—well, everyone said he had more charm than anyone they ever knew. Watterson came of an awfully good Boston family and he had gone to

Harvard, and he usually played hardboiled parts, although he looked well in tails. He reminded some people of Lincoln; he was tall and homely like Lincoln, and Lincoln must have had a marvelous voice too. Watterson had. What with one play and another, Watterson had reached that point where he could be identified by his first name: "Are you going to John's opening?" meant Watterson as surely as Kit and Alfred and Lynn and Helen and Oggie and Jane and Zita and Bart and Blanche and Eva and Hopie and Leslie meant the people that those names meant. Watterson certainly had arrived, and having arrived he had quietly settled down to the practice of his profession, on and off the stage.

The first thing Nancy said about him when she first laid eyes on him was that there was an honest man, which she amended to there is a man with honesty. He had hair like an Indian's, straight and black and it fell over his forehead—never with any attempt on his part to keep it from falling. He had big thick lips and out of them came the sounds of this hard strong voice of his in a Chicago accent which he never tried to change, except when he played the captain of an English minesweeper and in his one try at the films, when he played an Indian. He was used to being told he had beautiful hands. They were big, and on the little finger of each hand he wore a signet ring which had had to have more gold put in to fit his fingers. He liked women whose buttocks just fit his spread hands, and although Nancy did not quite qualify, she was still on the small side. He wanted Nancy.

She had seen him probably a dozen times offstage. This was extremely painful to him, as he was every bit as aware of the number of times he had seen her as Nancy was of the number of times she had seen him. But it had always been Mr. Watterson and Mrs. Farley. The last three times she had seen him he had asked her to come in some afternoon, any afternoon, when she was in the neighborhood and had a minute. That was as far as he would go. If she came it would be with the understanding, et cetera. She knew that. And he knew as well as the next one what his reputation was, and all the women he knew also knew his reputation. "I have no etchings," he would say, "but I'll bet I can get you tight." Yes, he had honesty, and he was in the phone book.

It was Spring and Nancy had nothing to do all day until the daily ordeal with Paul, and last week she had seen Watterson and that time he had said: "You haven't come in for a drink, Mrs. Farley. What about that?"

"I haven't been thirsty."

"Thirsty? What has thirsty got to do with it? I'm going away for the week-end, but I'll be back Tuesday and I'm in the phone book, so I think you'll need a drink Tuesday. Or Thursday. Thirsty on Thursday. Or Wednesday. Or any other day. But beginning Tuesday." Then he had laughed to take the curse off it a little and also to let her know that of course he didn't think for one minute she'd come.

Once in her life with Paul, Nancy had let herself go in a kiss with another man, a hard kiss, standing up, with her mouth open and her legs apart. Now that she thought of it, that had been an actor too. A young actor, a practically unknown juvenile. This day, thinking about Watterson, and then about the juvenile, she went back to a truth which she had discovered for herself. It was something she discovered watching the progress of the extra-marital love life of her friends—while pretending not to watch at all. The truth was that there is a certain kind of man, attractive and famous in his way and sought after by women, whom sound women, women like Nancy herself, can conceivably have an affair with, but would not marry if he were the last man on earth. Once Nancy had heard the French wisecrack: that you can walk in the Bois without buying it. (It sounded better than the American: why keep a cow when milk is so cheap?) She would use the Bois remark to justify the behavior of some men whom she liked without liking their behavior. Only in the past three or four years had she even attempted to apply it woman to man. Well, she would not marry a man like Watterson, but since there were men like Watterson, why not find out about them? Why not find out about at least one other man? She knew every hair on Paul's body; they knew everything about each other that they might be likely to learn. A new man would be all strange, and Nancy wondered about herself, too. Maybe she was all strange, to herself as much as to any new man. And this was a good time to find out. As coolly as that she made up her mind to have an affair with John Watterson the actor.

She was sitting down with *The Good Earth* in front of her. She put it aside the moment she made her decision, got up and went to the closet where her hats were perched on things that looked like huge wooden collar-buttons. She took two hats, tried on both of them, and went back to the closet and took out a third, which she kept on. Gloves, purse, cigarette extinguished, and she was ready to go.

The car was parked outside. She got in and drove the few blocks to the block in which Watterson lived. When she came to his house she drove right past without changing her speed. Somehow—not today. She had a hunch. "If my foot had eased its pressure on the accelerator I'd have gone in. But it didn't, so, not today." She went to the movies—dear George Arliss, in "The Millionaire." "I suppose that's passing up an opportunity," she said to herself, thinking of Watterson, and enjoyed it over and over again.

"Do you want some coffee? I made some coffee if you can stand it," said Eddie.

"Huh?" said Gloria. "Oh. Eddie. Hello, Eddie darling."

"Hello, sweet. How about some coffee?"

"I'll make it. Just give me a minute to wake up."

"You don't have to make it. It's made. All you have to do is drink it."

"Oh, thank you." She sat up in bed and reached with both hands for the cup and saucer. She drank some. "Good," she said. "You make this?"

"Yes, ma'am," said Eddie.

He sat down easy on the bed so he would not jounce it and cause her to spill the coffee. "Did you have a good sleep?"

"Mm. But marvelous," she said. Then: "What about you? Where did you sleep? My beamish boy."

"Right here."

"Where 'right here'?" she repeated.

"There. On the chair."

"There, there, under the chair. Run, run, get the gun," she said. "No, where did you sleep, Baby?"

"The chair, I told you."

"You couldn't. With those legs? You couldn't sleep in any chair with those legs. What did you do with your legs?"

"I didn't do anything with them. I just put my fanny deep in the chair, and my legs—I don't know. Extended. They extended in a, uh, southwesterly direction and I went to sleep and my legs went to sleep."

"Ooh, you must feel like the wrath of God. Are you stiff?"

"No, as a matter of fact I feel fine. I was so tired when I went to sleep. I read a while after you dropped off, and I went to sleep with the light on. I woke up I guess around three or four and doused the light and got up and got an overcoat. Reminds me. You know that fur coat you came here in Sunday. It's still in my closet. You better haul off and do something about it. Take it back where you got it, will you?"

She seemed to think about it.

"Will you?" he said. "It's none of my business, Gloria, and what you do is—as I just said, it's none of my business, only I wish you'd return that coat. That's the kind of a fast one that—maybe you had every reason in the world to take it at the time, but you can't keep a coat like that, that cost four or five hundred dollars or more."

"Four or five *thousand.*"

"Jesus! All the more reason. My God, Baby, a coat like that, that kind of money, they insure those things. The first thing you know they'll have detectives parked on our doorstep."

"I doubt it. I imagine I could keep that coat as long as I wanted to."

Eddie looked at her but not long. He stood up. "Do you want some more coffee? There is more if you want it."

"You don't like that, do you?"

"What difference does it make whether I like it or not? I told you what I thought. I have no say over you."

"You could have. Come here," she said. She held up her hands. He sat on the bed again. She put her arms around his head and held him to her bosom. "Oh, you don't know what I'd do for you, my precious darling. You're all I have, Eddie. Eddie, you're afraid of me. I'm no good, Eddie. I know I'm no good, but I could be good for you, Eddie, Eddie, my darling. Oh. Here. One second, darling. One second. My baby. My baby that needs a haircut. Ah, my— *What's that!"*

"Phone," he said.

"Answer it. It's bad luck not to answer it."

"I never heard that."

"It is. Go on, darling, answer it."

"Hello," he said into the telephone. "What? Yes. Speaking." Pause.

"Why, you son of a—," he slammed the phone into its cradle. "The Bush Brothers Hand Laundry. The bastards."

"Is that the laundry you owe the money to?"

"Oh, God. Maybe it is. I forgot the name of that one. I don't think I ever did know it. No, it couldn't be the same one. The Bush Brothers were soliciting new work, so that's not the laundry that has my stuff. *They* don't want any new work. I want you."

"Do you? Here I am. Can anybody see us from those windows over there?"

"They might. I'll get it. I'll do it."

"I ought to get up."

"No, don't."

"I'll have a child."

"Don't you want a child?"

"Yes, very much. But, all right."

He sat up again and looked away. He made his gesture of shooting a foul in basketball, but with his fists clenched. "No," he said.

"It's all right, Eddie," she said. "It's all right, darling."

"No," he said. "No, it isn't. It's anything *but* all right."

"I'm clean. You needn't worry about that, if that's what's worrying you."

"Oh, I know. I wasn't thinking that."

"You used to think it. Didn't you?"

"A long time ago. Before I knew you."

"I'd never do that to you."

"I know. I don't think that any more. That's not what I'm thinking now."

"Don't you love me? Do you love Norma?"

"Nope."

"Have you told her you love her?"

"Once or twice."

"Does she love you?"

"No. I don't think so. Maybe."

"You're not sure."

"Oh, I'm sure. She doesn't love me. No, it hasn't anything to do with Norma. I love you."

She touched his shoulder. "I know. And I love you. The only one I ever did love, and the only one that ever loved me."

"I doubt that. Aw, you're *crazy.*"

"No. I know. I know what it is even if you don't. Or maybe you do know and won't say it. It's because I've stayed with so many men that you think—"

"Don't talk. Don't say anything."

"All right," she said, and was silent, as was Eddie. Then she went on: "If you didn't know I'd stayed with so many men would you love me?"

"I do love you."

"But it would be different, wouldn't it? Of course. It's stupid of me to ask you that. But will you answer this truthfully? If you had just met me, without knowing a thing about me, what would you think of me?"

"How do you mean? There isn't a better-looking girl in this town, is my honest opinion. Your face, and you have a beautiful build." He stopped. She was staring ahead, not listening to him.

Despair.

"What are you thinking?" he said.

"Mm?"

"What are you thinking about so seriously?"

"It's all right with you now, isn't it? You'll be all right if I get up now, won't you? I mean and get dressed. Will you be all right?"

"I'll be all right."

"Because I know about men when they get excited and nothing happens. I wouldn't do that, either. If it's just a question of—oh, I don't know. I don't know how to talk to you now, Eddie. If you're going to be uncomfortable the rest of the day because we started something and didn't finish it, then let's finish it."

"Not that way I won't. I don't even feel like it now."

"No, neither do I, but I don't want you to feel as if you'd been pulled through a wringer."

"I won't. Don't worry about me."

"Then I guess I'll get up and take a shower."

"I'll get you a clean towel. I have one."

"All right."

"Here, I'll get you my bathrobe," he said, and stopped on his way to the closet. "The melancholy Dane has come, the saddest of the year." He smiled at her.

"What made you say that?"

"Damned if I know."

"What was it? 'The melancholy *Dane* has come, the saddest of the year.' Did that have any special meaning?"

"No, not a bit. I just thought of myself as melancholy, and you as melancholy, and melancholy made me think of the melancholy Dane, and then I got melancholy Dane mixed up. The melancholy Dane has come, the saddest of the year. It's nothing. I get rhythms and words mixed. The melancholy Dane has come, the saddest of the year. You used to come at nine o'clock but now you come at ten. I'll get you the bathrobe."

"And the towel. The towel's more important."

"No, it isn't. Not in my present state."

"Oh—do you really feel—"

"No, no. Not seriously."

She got out of bed and put on his bathrobe with her arms folded in front of her and her shoulders slightly hunched. She smiled at him and he smiled back. "I guess—I guess I never felt worse. Not sad. It isn't sadness the way I and you think of sadness and everybody else thinks of it. It's just this, that the one thing we have—nope. I won't say it."

"Oh, you've got to finish it now."

"Must I? Yes, I guess I must. Well, it's awful when you think that you've stayed with so many men and made such a mess of your life, and then someone you really want to stay with because you love him, that person is the one person you mustn't stay with because if you do he immediately becomes like the rest, and you don't want him to become like the rest. The thing he has that the rest haven't is that you haven't stayed with him."

"No, that's wrong. I don't want you to think that. It isn't true. Maybe it is, but I don't think so."

"No, I guess not, but—I don't know. The hell with it. You go on out for a walk. Ten minutes, and when you get back I'll be dressed."

"I'll buy a coffee ring."

She stood at the bathroom door, watching him put on his coat. "I'm a real bitch, Eddie. Do you know why?"

"Why?"

"Because I know what's right, but I'm so strongly tempted. You've never seen me without any clothes on, have you?"

"I'll get the coffee ring."

"That's right," she said.

When he did not return in fifteen minutes she began to worry, but he did return in ten minutes more, and they had more breakfast. He brought also a container of orange juice for her and a morning paper. "Mm. Legs Diamond's arrested," she said. "I met him once."

"Who didn't?" said Eddie. "What did they arrest him for? Parking near a fire plug, I'll bet."

"No. The Sullivan Law. That's uh, buzz buzz buzz buzz. Weapons. Deadly weapons in his possession. By Joel Sayre. This is an interesting article. Yes, I met Legs Diamond. What did you say? Who didn't? Lots of people didn't. I met him and the boy I was with didn't know him, even by reputation, and he kept making cracks. Governor Roosevelt's mother is sick and he's going to Paris where she is. She's in the hospital. Did you know that he has infantile paralysis? I never knew that till about a month or two ago. It never shows in his pictures, but he's always holding on to a state policeman's arm. Mm. As an aftermath of the. It says here as an aftermath of the airplane crash in which Knute Rockne lost his life the Fokker 29's are being given the air by the Department of Commerce. I can use Fokker in a sentence."

"I can use identification in a sentence. I'm not going away this summer because identification till October."

"Mine was dirty. Oh, the Pulitzer Prize. '*Alison's* House'? Now for God's sake. 'Alison's House.' And *The Collected Poems of Robert Frost.* Well, I suppose that's all right. Edmund Duffy. Have you read *The Glass Key?*"

"No."

"It's by the same man who wrote *Maltese Falcon,* but it's not nearly as good. Oh, here's one for you. Listen to this. This is old Coolidge. 'Collins H. Gere, buzz buzz buzz buzz belongs to a generation of strong character and high purposes. Their passing marks the end of an era.' Whose passing? Does he mean strong character and high purposes' passing? Maybe he does. Maybe he's right. Do you know anybody with strong character and high purposes?"

"You."

"No, that's insulting. Think of someone. It has to be our generation, not older people, because Coolidge says their passing marks the end of an era, I guess he means the era that had strong character and high purposes. You, now. Let me see. Have you a strong character, darling?"

"No character."

"I'd say yes. About the high purposes, I'm not so sure. How are you on high purposes?"

"Low."

"No character and low purposes."

"Not low purposes," he said. "I just said I was low on *high* purposes. It isn't exactly the same thing."

"No, you're right. Well, I can't think of anyone I like that has strong character and high purposes. The Giants beat Brooklyn, if you're interested. Six to three was the score. Terry tripled, scoring

when the Giants worked their squeeze play, Vergez laid down a
perfect bunt. That shouldn't sound dirty, but when you have a mind
like mine. I must look at Bethlehem Steel. My uncle has some of
that. Closed at 44⅝. That's enough of that. Oh, here *is* sad news.
Clayton, Jackson and Durante are splitting up. Schnozzle is going to
Hollywood and they're breaking up. Oh, that's sad. That's the
world's worst. Why did you have to show me this paper? No more
wood number? No more hats? No more telegrams like the one he
sent: 'Opening at Les Ambassadeurs as soon as I learn how to pro-
nounce it.' Ah. That makes me sad, really sad. I hope he divides his
salary with the others. Do you like this hat? On the right hand page.
. . . On me."

"No. It hides the eyes."

"All right. I must go home to the bosom of my family. A flat
chest if I ever saw one. Shall I call you tomorrow?"

"Yes. Oh, how about that fur coat?"

"I don't know. I'll call you tomorrow."

"Well, aren't you going to give it back to this fellow?"

"Well, I can't just take the coat to him, can I?"

"I don't see why not," said Eddie. "If you want to return the coat,
you can. The way you do it is up to you."

"All right, I will then, if it'll make you feel any better. I'll call
him up right now." She telephoned Liggett. "He's out of town, his
office said."

"Well, phone him tomorrow."

She went home and there was a telegram there from Liggett,
asking her to meet him at their favorite speakeasy at four. They had
told her at his office that he was out of town, but her life was full of
inconsistencies like that.

She was there before four, and took a small table by herself and
watched the world come in. That afternoon the speakeasy was vis-
ited by a fairly representative crowd. On their lips soon would be her
name, with varying opinions as to her character. Most of these people were famous in a way, although in most cases their fame did not
extend more than twenty blocks to the north, forty blocks to the
south, seven blocks to the east and four blocks to the west. There

were others who were not famous, but were prominent in Harrisburg, Denver, Albany, Nashville, St. Paul-Minneapolis, Atlanta, Houston, Portland, Me., Dayton and Hartford. Among these was Mrs. Dunbar Vicks, of Cleveland, in town on one of her three or four visits a year to see a friend's private collection of dirty movies and to go to bed with a young man who formerly worked for Finchley. Mrs. Vicks was standing at the bar, with her back to Walter R. Loskind, the Hollywood supervisor, who was talking to Percy Luffberry, the director. Percy owed a great deal to Walter. When Percy was directing "War of Wars" he had small charges of explosive buried here and there in the ground, not enough to hurt anyone, but enough so that when the charge was set off the extras in German uniforms would be lifted off the ground. The extras had been warned about that and were being paid a bonus for this realism. It went all right until Percy decided he wanted to have one extra crawling along the ground instead of walking. When the charge was set off the extra lost both eyes, and if Walter hadn't stood by Percy, Percy would have been in a hell of a fix. Seated directly across the room was Mrs. Noel Lincoln, wife of the famous sportsman-financier, who had had four miscarriages before she found out (or before her doctor dared tell her) that a bit of bad luck on the part of her husband was responsible for these misfortunes. Mrs. Lincoln was sitting with pretty little Alicia Lincoln, her niece by marriage, who was the source of cocaine supply for a very intimate group of her friends in society, the theater, and the arts. Alicia was waiting for a boy named Gerald, whom she took to places where girls could not go unescorted. Bruce Wix, the artists' representative, came in and tried to get the eye of Walter R. Loskind, but Walter did not look. Bruce stood alone at the bar. Henry White, the writer, was told he was wanted on the telephone—the first move, although he did not know it, in the house technique of getting rid of a drunk. On the way out he bowed to Dr. (D.D.S.) Jack Fry, who was arriving with one of his beautiful companions. It was afternoon, so the companion was not wearing the Fry pearls, which Dr. Fry always loaned to show girls and actresses while they were out with him. Mr. and Mrs. Whitney Hofman, of Gibbsville, Pennsylvania, arrived at this time, wishing they had been better friends so they could find something to talk about without self-consciousness. They were joined by Whitney's cousin Scott Hofman, a cross-eyed fellow who at the age of thirty did not have to shave more than once a week. Mike Romanoff came in, looked around the room, and went out again. A party of six young people, Mr. and Mrs. Mortimer House, Mr. and Mrs. Jack Whitehall, and Miss Sylvia House and Mr. Irving Ruskin, were told at the door that they could not come in because they had not made reservations. They had to make way for a Latin-American diplomat whose appointment to Washington showed what his country thought of this. He had had malaria *before* he caught *siflis,* which is the wrong order for an automatic cure. Inside again, banging on his table for a waiter, sat Ludovici, the artist, who had several unretouched nude photographs of Gloria which she wished she had back. He was with June Blake, show girl and model, who after four days was still cheerful over winning nearly a thousand dollars on Twenty Grand. The bet had not been made through a bookmaker, and involved no cash outlay on her part. It was a slightly intricate arrangement between herself and Archie Jelliffe, the axle man, who told June he would place the bet for her if she would agree to bring to his country place a certain virgin he wanted to know better. Was it June's fault that the former virgin was at this minute in a private hospital? Robert Emerson, the magazine publisher, came in with his vice-president, Jerry Watlington. Emerson was trying to make life pleasanter for Watlington, who had just been blackballed at a good club which Emerson belonged to. Emerson sincerely regretted the blackball, now that he had put it in. Mad Horace H. Tuttle, who had been kicked out of two famous prep schools for incendiarism, was there with Mrs. Denis Johnstone Humphries (whose three names seldom were spelled right), of Sewickley Heights, near Pittsburgh. Mrs. Humphries was telling Horace how she had to drive around in a station wagon because strikers stoned her Rolls. The worst of it was she was riding in the Rolls at the time, personally holding her entry for the Flower Show, and when the stones began to beat against the car she had presence of mind enough to lie on the floor, but forgot about the roses and crushed them. Her story was not interrupted when Horace nodded to Billy Jones, the gentleman jockey, who walked quickly to the bar with two dollars in his hand, had a quick double whiskey-soda, and walked out, with the two dollars in his hand. The bartender simply entered it against Billy's account—Billy was supposed to be a little screwy from knocks on the head. Kitty Meredith, the movie actress, came in with her adopted son, four years old, and everybody said how cute he was, what poise, as he took a sip of her drink.

"I'm sorry I'm late," said Liggett.

Gloria looked up. "It's all right," she said. "In five more minutes I'd have gone, or at least I wouldn't have been alone."

"Who? That one that's looking at you now?"

"I won't tell you," she said.

"Uh, what are you drinking?"

"Ale."

"One ale, and a brandy and soda."

"Well, what's it all about?" said Gloria. "I went home and your telegram was there. I phoned you at your office, but they said you'd gone away."

"Where were you last night?"

"Oh, no. Not in that tone. Who do you think you are?"

"All right, I'm sorry." He went through the business of getting a cigarette lit, then he remembered and offered her one. That doubled the delay before he said: "If what I want to ask you makes you very angry will you try not to hold it against me? First of all—please let me talk—first of all, I think you know I'm crazy about you. You know that, don't you?"

No answer.

He repeated: "You know that, don't you?"

"You said not to interrupt."

"Well, you do know that, don't you?"

"I'm not so sure. Crazy about me doesn't mean anything."

"Well, I am. In the worst way. Don't make a joke about it. I am crazy about you. I can't think of anything but you. I can't make sense for thinking about how long it's going to be before I see you again. When I don't know where you are, like last night. I was here and all over, trying to find you." He saw she was not paying much attention.

"You're right," he went on. "That's not what I want to talk about. At least not now. Or I mean I want to talk about it, now, but there is another matter."

"That's what I thought."

"That's what you thought. Well—Jesus, I wish we were some place else. Drink your drink and we'll get out of here. What I want to say I don't want to say in this madhouse, all these people yelling their heads off."

She gulped some beer and left some in the glass. "That's all I want."

He left two dollar bills and a quarter on the table and they went out. He refused the taxi at the door, but walked down the block towards Fifth Avenue and took a taxi that was moving. "Fortieth Street and Seventh Avenue," he told the driver.

"Where are we going?"

"That place you took me to the other night. The newspaper place." He took off his hat and held it on his knee. "You know, Gloria, I'm in a bad way about you. The thing that's happened to me usually happens to men I know who have been good husbands. I don't mean that I've been an especially bad husband. I've been good to my wife in most ways. I've always kept things from her that would hurt her—"

"You're the kind of man that would have a mistress and insult her in front of your wife because you thought that would mislead her."

"You're wrong. No, you're right. The only time I had a mistress that my wife knew I did say disparaging things about her, the mistress. How do you know these things? You're not more than I'd say twenty-two. How do you know these things?"

"How do I know them? What else has there been in my life but finding out things like that? But go on, tell me about what happens to men of your age."

"What happens to men of my age. What happens to men of my age is this, if they've been good husbands. They go along being good husbands, working hard and having a good time, playing golf, making a little money, going to parties with the same crowd, and then sometimes it's a woman they've known all their lives, and sometimes it's a filing clerk in the office, and sometimes it's a singer in a night club. I know of one case where it was a man and his sister. Not that they ever did anything about it, except that the man committed suicide, that's all. He'd been happily married—oh, what the hell am I talking about, happily married. Is anybody happily married? I often wonder whether anybody is." He stopped talking.

"What made you stop all of a sudden? You were going great."

"Was I?"

"I'll say."

"I just discovered something, or almost did. Wondering whether anyone was happily married. I wondered if I was, and then I wondered if I wasn't. God, I'm in a worse spot than anyone. I don't even know if I'm unhappily married. I don't know anything about myself. I must be happy, because whenever I've looked back and remembered times when I was happy, I always find that I didn't know I was happy when I was. Well, if I'm happy now it's because of you. Let me rave. I'm thinking out loud."

"A little too loud for the taxi driver, or else maybe not loud enough."

"Well, that's all he's going to hear. This is the end of the line."

This time they were not greeted by the voluble bartender, but by a tall sad man who looked as though he ought to be a Texas Ranger. They went to the small room off the bar where there were booths, and when the bartender brought their drinks Liggett began: "I didn't feel like talking about this in the taxi. Now I have to talk and get it over with. Gloria, did you take a fur coat out of my apartment Sunday?"

Silence.

"Did you? Are you not answering because you're angry, or what?"

"What do you think?"

"I'm asking you."

"Yes, I took it."

"Well,—will you give it back? It's my wife's coat, and I've had a hard time keeping her from telling the police."

"Why don't you let her tell the police?"

"Do you really want the coat that much?"

"I could have it, couldn't I?"

"Yes. You could, but not very easily. Uh, naturally it would break up my home. The first thing the detectives would do would be to question the employees of the apartment house, and the elevator operator would remember your leaving with the coat on Sunday. Then they'd tell my wife there was a girl in the apartment Saturday night, and while my wife might possibly forgive my being unfaithful, for the sake of the children, I don't think she'd forgive my bringing anyone into her home. It's her home, you know, even more than it is mine, or as much. Well, so that would break up the home, but that wouldn't be all. When the police are notified in a thing like that they like to make an arrest, so they'd probably find out who you were."

"From you?"

"No. Not from me. They could arrest me, I suppose, but I wouldn't tell them who it was. But from—did you take a taxi? You must have. Well, they'd find out where you went, and so on. They have ways of finding out, without any help from me. So you wouldn't have the coat long. And what if my wife told the insurance people? That would fix me in a business way. Not that there's much left to be fixed, but at least I have a good job. Well, if my wife became vindictive and told the insurance people to, uh, proceed just as though I were a stranger, they would arrest me for compounding a felony or accessory before the fact or something like that, and the tabloids would get hold of it. No, you can't win."

"Crime does not pay, eh?"

"I don't know whether it does or not, but I do know this, you won't gain anything by keeping the coat."

"Except the coat."

"Not even the coat. They'll take it away from you. Oh, come on, don't be unreasonable. I'll buy you a coat just like it."

"It's an expensive coat."

"It's insured for I think four thousand dollars. That's quite an

item for an insurance company to have to make good on. What are
you doing, having fun?"

"A little. You have fun with me Saturday night. Big stuff, tearing
my dress and all that old cave-man act."

"I'm sorry about that. I've told you before I was sorry."

"It didn't sound very convincing before, but now that you're in a
jam—"

"Listen, God damn it—"

"Don't swear at me. I'm going."

"Oh, no, you're not."

"Oh, yes, I *am,* and don't you try to stop me, if you know what's
good for you."

"Listen, you little bitch, I'll go to jail before I let you get away
with this, and you will too. Sit down." He reached for her hand, but
she ran out to the barroom.

"Let me out of here," she said to the bartender.

"Don't open that door," said Liggett.

"Out of the way, Mister," said the bartender.

"What is it, Joe?" said a man at the bar, who Liggett saw was in
uniform. The man turned, and it was a patrolman's uniform. The cop
put on his cap and came over.

"Don't hurt him. Just let me out," said Gloria.

"Is he molesting you, lady?" said the cop.

"I just want to get out," said Gloria.

"Listen, officer—"

"Out of the way, wise guy," said the cop, and in some manner
which Liggett did not understand the cop put his hand inside Liggett's coat and held him by the vest high up. He could not move.
They let Gloria out and the cop still held Liggett.

"Wuddle we do with him, Joe?" said the cop. "You know him?"

"I never seen him before. Who are you, anyway?"

"I can identify myself."

"Well, identify yourself," said the cop.

"If you let me, I will," said Liggett.

"Stand in back of him, Joe, just in case."

"Oh, I won't do anything."

"Huh, you're telling me. You picked the wrong spot to try anything, fellow, didn't he, Joe?"

"Just leave him try something, he'll find out."

"I happen to be a very good friend of Pat Casey, if you're interested," said Liggett.

"A friend of Pat Casey's," said the cop. "He says he's a friend of Pat Casey's, Joe."

"Wuddia know about that," said Joe.

Whereupon the cop slapped Liggett back and forth on the face with the palm and the back of his hand. "A friend . . . of Pat . . . Casey. Don't give me that, you son of a bitch. I don't care if you're a friend of the Pope of Rome, any . . . son . . . of a bitch . . . that tries to . . . skeer me . . . with who he knows. Now get outa here. Pat Casey!"

"Go on. Get out," said Joe.

Liggett could hardly see. There were tears in his eyes from the cop's slaps on his nose. "Like hell I will," he said, ready to fight. The cop reached out and pushed him hard and quick, and he went down on his back. Joe, who had been standing in back of him, had knelt down back of his legs and all the cop had to do was push and down he went. He fell outside the speakeasy on the stair landing, and the two men began kicking him and kicked him until he crawled away and went down the stairs.

He had no hat, he could hardly see, his clothes were a mess of dirt and phlegmy spit that he had picked up on the floor, he was badly shaken by hitting his coccyx when the cop pushed him, his nose was bleeding, his body was full of sharp pains where they had kicked him.

To be deprived of the right to fight back when you have nothing left to lose is awful, and that made Liggett feel weak. They had beaten him in a few minutes worse than he ever had been beaten before, and he knew he could have gone on fighting now till they killed him, but they would not give him the chance, the bastards. Outside the world was disinterested or perhaps even friendly, but there was no fighting outside. It was inside, upstairs, where there was fighting, and he wanted to go back and fight those two; no rules, but kick and punch and swing and butt and bite. The only thing was, he was facing the street now, and it was too damn much trouble to turn around, and inside of him he knew he did not have the strength to climb the stairs. If he could be transported up the stairs and inside he could fight, but the stairs were too much. He heard the door upstairs being opened, then closing as his hat landed at his feet. He reached down painfully and picked it up and put it on his aching head, and walked out to the street. He stumbled along into a taxi. The driver didn't want him to get in, but was afraid to take a chance on crossing him. Then as the driver said: "Where to?" Gloria opened the door of the cab.

"It's all right, I know him," she said.

"Okay, Miss Wandrous," said the driver.

"Out. Get out. Get outa my tax'cab," said Liggett.

"Go to 274 Horatio Street," Gloria told the driver.

"Okay," said the driver, and reached back to close the door, which had clicked only once.

Liggett got up and opened the door, mumbling: "I'm not going anywhere with you." She tried to stop him but not very hard. It wasn't much use trying and the streets were full of people, little people coming up from the fur center to pile into the southernmost entrance to the Times Square subway station. She saw Liggett get into another cab.

"Will I folly him?" said her driver.

"Yes, will you please?" she said.

Her taxi followed his to within a block of his home. She stopped and watched him get out, saw the doorman at his apartment pay the cab driver. "Go to the Horatio Street number," she said.

Eddie did not answer his bell, though she rang for five minutes. She left a note for him and went home.

6

You could still read a newspaper in the street when Nancy and Paul Farley arrived at the Liggetts'. Nancy was wearing a printed chiffon frock, Farley was wearing a dinner jacket with shawl collar, a soft shirt, a cummerbund instead of a waistcoat, and pumps. The pumps were old and a little cracked, and in his hand he had a gray felt hat that certainly did not look new. Emily wondered where she had got the idea Farley would be dressed like something out of the theater programs. Where? From Weston, of course. Where, where was Weston? What had happened in Philadelphia?

"Good evening, Mrs. Farley, Mr. Farley. Let's go in here, I think it's cooler."

"It is cool, isn't it?" said Nancy.

"Bobbie did this building," said Paul.

"A friend of ours," Nancy explained. "Robert Scott? The architect? Do you know him, by any chance?"

"No, I don't believe I do," said Emily. "All right, Mary. The cocktail things. Mr. Farley, do you mind if I pass that job on to you? My husband hasn't arrived! He went to Philadelphia this morning and I expected him home at four, but I could have been mistaken. Perhaps he meant the four o'clock train, which arrives at six I think. He may have stopped at the office on the way uptown. It must be important, because it isn't a bit like him not to phone."

"Well, one thing, it isn't his health," said Paul. "I mean lack of it. When I saw him on Sunday I said to Nancy how well he looked."

"Yes, I only got a fleeting glimpse of him but I noticed too how well he looked," said Nancy. "He always gives the impression of strength."

"Yes, not like most men that were athletes in college," said Paul. "They usually . . ." he made a gesture of big-belly.

"Oh, he *was* an athlete?" said Nancy.

"He was on the Yale crew," said Emily. "I think he keeps well. He played some court tennis this past winter."

"Oh, really?" said Paul. "That must be a swell game. I've never played it. I've gone back and forth from squash to squash rackets and this winter I played a little handball, but never court tennis."

"I never know one from the other," said Nancy.

"Neither do I," said Emily. "Mr. Farley, would you like to mix a cocktail? If you have anything in mind. There's gin and French and Italian vermouth, but we could just as easily have something else."

"I like a Martini and so does Nancy."

"I think a Martini," said Emily.

"Tell Mrs. Liggett what you told me about shaking Martinis," said Nancy.

"Oh, yes," said Farley. "You know, like everyone else, I suppose, I've been going for years on the theory that a Martini ought to be stirred and not shaken?"

"Yes, that's what I've always heard," said Emily.

"Well, in London last year I talked with an English bartender who told me that theory's all wrong. American, he said."

"Scornfully," said Nancy.

"Very scornfully," said Paul.

"I can imagine very scornfully," said Emily.

"Well, we've always been taught that if you shake a Martini you bruise the cocktail. I've always taken a holy delight in not bruising a poor little cocktail until this English barkeep explained the right way, or his way, and I must say it sounds plausible. He told me a Martini ought to be shaken very hard, briskly, a few vigorous shakes up and down, so that the gin and vermouth would be cracked into a proper *foamy* mixture. He said Americans, especially in these dark ages—I mean Prohibition, not the depression. We have a tendency to drink a cocktail in two gulps, for the effect, whereas if you shake the cocktail the various ingredients go into solution more completely, and the result is a foamy drink—not very noticeably foamy, but more foamy than not—and you have a cocktail that you can sip, almost like champagne."

"Oh, I never heard that," said Emily. "It does sound like a plausible theory, as you say."

"You see, our cocktails, stirred, are syrupy and very strong. Two

Martinis out of a stirred batch have much more effect than two shaken ones. Stirred cocktails are little more than straight gin and vermouth. So we've followed his advice and I must say I think he's right."

"Let's do it that way, then. I'll get the other shaker. This one has only the stirring kind of top."

"Oh, no, not if it means—"

"Not at all," said Emily. "I want to try your way." She went to the dining-room and came back with a shaker.

"I noticed you have new cocktail shakers too," said Nancy. "You know, we have newer cocktail shakers and things like that than a cousin of Paul's. She was married five years ago, and by actual count she was given twenty-two cocktail shakers for wedding presents. All sorts. And those she kept look positively obsolete compared with ours. Ours are all new, within the last two years."

"When Weston and I were married no one would have thought of giving a cocktail shaker."

"We didn't get a single one," said Nancy.

"There," said Paul. "I hope you like this after all my build-up, Mrs. Liggett."

She tasted her cocktail. "Oh, yes, by all means. Oh, even I can see the difference right away."

"Isn't it a lot better?" said Nancy.

"Yes. Weston will like it too, I know. His favorite drink is whiskey and soda. He'd almost rather not drink cocktails for that reason, that they're too syrupy. This ought to be the solution of the cocktail problem for him. Speaking of Weston, I think we'll wait five more minutes and if he hasn't arrived we'll begin without him. He's usually so punctual about meals, and I know he was especially anxious to be on time for the Farleys. I hate being late for the theater, so we'll give him five more minutes. I'm so glad you hadn't seen 'Tomorrow and Tomorrow.' Herbert Marshall has *such* charm, don't you think so, Mrs. Farley?"

"Just about the most charming man I know. Not that I know him. I did meet him."

"I don't see how he gets around with that leg of his," said Paul.

"I can't even tell which one it is, and I watch every time," said Nancy.

"He lost it in the war, didn't he?" said Emily.

"I believe so," said Nancy.

"Yes, he did. He was in the British Army," said Paul.

"Not in the Austrian Army, dear?" said Nancy.

Everyone laughed politely. "As a matter of fact he was in the Austrian Army," said Paul. "He was a spy."

"No, no. That's not getting out of it," said Nancy. "Besides, that's not original. Who was it said that first? You read it in the *New Yorker.*"

"What was that?" asked Emily.

"Oh, you must have seen it. I think it was in the Talk of the Town column. George S. Kaufman, you know, he wrote 'Once In a Lifetime' and a hundred other plays."

"Yes," said Emily.

"Well, he and some of the Algonquin literati were together one night and there was a stranger in their midst who kept bragging about his ancestry, and finally Kaufman, who is a Jew, spoke up and said: 'I had an ancestor a Crusader.' The stranger looked askance and Kaufman went on: 'Yes, his name was Sir Reginald Kaufman. He was a spy.' "

"All right, except that it was Sir Roderick Kaufman," said Nancy.

Emily laughed. In one more minute she would have taken her guests in to dinner, but before the minute was up the doorbell rang and then the door was opened and Liggett came in, supported by the elevator operator and the doorman, who Emily noticed first was trying to take off his cap.

"Oh, God," said Emily.

"Good Lord," said Paul.

Nancy sucked in her breath.

"What in God's name happened, darling?" said Emily, going to him.

"I'll take this arm," said Paul to the doorman.

"Please let me walk by myself," said Liggett, and shook off his helpers. "I'm terribly sorry, Mrs. Farley, but you'll have to excuse me tonight."

"Oh, well, of course," said Nancy.

"Can't I give you a hand, old man?" said Paul.

"No, thanks," said Liggett. "Emily—will you—I think Mrs. Farley, Mr. Farley."

"Let me help you to your room," said Farley. "I think I ought to do this, Mrs. Liggett."

"I'd rather you didn't, Farley. Thanks just the same, but I'd really rather you didn't," said Liggett. "Apologize to you, Emily, before the Farleys."

"Oh, they understand I'm sure," said Emily. "Mrs. Farley, Mr. Farley, you will excuse us I know?"

"Of course," said Farley. "If you want me to do anything?"

"No, thank you. I'll manage. I'm sorry."

"Come on, darling," said Nancy. "Anything at all, Mrs. Liggett. Please call us."

"Thank you both," said Emily.

The Farleys left. Nancy could hardly wait till they got inside a taxi where only Paul could see her crying. "Oh, what a terrible thing. What an awful sight." She put her arms around Paul and wept. "That poor unhappy woman. To have that happen to her. Ugh. Disgusting beast. No wonder, no wonder she has such sad eyes."

"Yes, and the son of a bitch was no more in Philadelphia than I was. I saw him getting tanked up at the Yale Club at lunch time. He didn't see me, but I saw him." He waited. "But it's nothing for you to be upset about, darling. They aren't even close friends of ours."

"I'll stop," said Nancy.

"We'll go to Longchamps."

"No, let's go where we can drink," said Nancy.

WHEN Gloria came home in time for dinner her uncle told her he would like to have a talk with her before dinner, or after dinner, if there wasn't time before dinner. She said they might as well talk now, before dinner.

"Well," he began, "I don't think you've been looking at all well lately. I think you ought to get out of New York for a month or two. I really do, Gloria."

Yes, she had been thinking that too, but she wondered how often he had had a chance to see her to decide she wasn't looking well. "I haven't saved anything out of my allowance," she said, "and as for work—well, you know."

"This would be a birthday present. It's a little early for a birthday present, but does it make any difference what time of the year it is when you get your present? I'll send you a penny postcard when your birthday comes, and remind you that you've had your present. That is, providing you want to take a trip."

"But can you afford it?"

"Yes, I can afford it. We don't live on our income any more, Baby"—he often called her that—"we've been selling bonds and preferred stocks, your mother and I."

"Oh. On account of me? Do I cost that much?"

He laughed. "No-ho-ho. You don't seem to realize. Don't you know what's been going on in this country, Baby? We're in the midst of a *depression*. The worst depression in history. You know something about the stock market situation, don't you?"

"I looked up your Bethlehem Steel this morning or yesterday. I forget when it was."

"Oh, that's all gone, long since, my Steel. And it was U. S. Steel, not Bethlehem."

"Oh, then I was wrong."

"I'm glad you took an interest. No, what I've been doing, I've been getting rid of everything I can and do you know what I've been doing? Buying gold."

"Gold? You mean real gold, the what do they call it—bullion?"

"The real article. Coins, when I can get them, and gold bars, and a few gold certificates, but I haven't much faith in *them*. You know, I don't like to frighten you, but it's going to be a lot worse before it's any better, as the fellow says."

"How do you mean?"

"Well, I'll tell you. A man I know slightly, he was one of the

smartest traders in Wall Street. You wouldn't know his name, because I don't think I ever had occasion to mention it except perhaps
to your mother and it wouldn't have interested you. He was a *real*
plunger, that fellow. The stories they told downtown about this man,
they were sensational. A Jew, naturally. Why, say, that fellow
couldn't lose. *And,* he was shrewd, the way all Jews are. Well, as I
say, he's always been a pretty smart trader. They say he was the only
one that called the turn in 1929. He got out of the market in August
1929, at the peak. Everybody told him, why, you're crazy, they all
said. Passing up millions. Millions, they told him. Sure, he said.
Well, I'm willing to pass them up and keep what I have, he told
them, and of course they all laughed when he told them he was
going to retire and sit back and watch the ticker from a café in Paris.
Retire and only thirty-eight years of age? Huh. They never heard
such talk, the wisenheimers downtown. Him retire? No. It was in his
blood, they said. He'd be back. He'd go to France and make a little
whoopee, but he'd be back and in the market just as deeply as ever.
But he fooled them. He went to France, all right, and I suppose he
made whoopee because I happen to know he has quite a reputation
that way. And they were right saying he'd be back, but not the way
they thought. He came back first week in November, two years ago,
right after the crash. Know what he did? He bought a Rolls-Royce
Phantom that originally cost over eighteen thousand dollars, he
bought that for a thousand-dollar bill. He bought a big place out on
Long Island. I don't know exactly what he paid for it, but one fellow
told me he got it for not a cent more than the owner paid for one of
those big indoor tennis courts they have out there. For that he got the
whole estate, the land, the house proper, stables, garages, everything.
Yacht landing. Oh, almost forgot. A hundred and eighty-foot yacht
for eighteen thousand dollars. That figure I do know because I remember hearing he said a hundred dollars a foot was enough for any
yacht. And mind you, the estate was with all the furniture. And all
because he got out in time and had the cash. Everything he had was
cash. Wouldn't lend a cent. Not one red cent, for any kind of interest. Not even a hundred per cent interest. Just wasn't interested, he
said. Buy, yes. He bought cars, houses, big estates, yachts, paintings

worth their weight in radium, practically. But lend money? no. He
said it was his way of getting even with the wisenheimers that
laughed at him the summer before when he said he was going to
retire."

"Uncle, did you say you *knew* this man?" said Gloria.

"Oh, yes. Used to see him around. *I* knew him to say *hello* to."

"Where is he now? I mean whatever became of him?"

"Ah, that's what I was going to tell you," said Vandamm. "I was
inquiring about him, whatever became of him, about a month or two
ago, and fellow I see every once in a while, a professional bridge
player now. I mean makes his living that way, but he used to be a
customer's man. I ran into him a short time ago at the New York
A. C. and we had a glass of beer together, just friendly because he
knows I don't go in for playing bridge for high stakes. We got to
talking and in the course of the conversation Jack Wiston's name—
that was his name, Jack Wiston, if you want to know his name. His
name came up and I asked this friend of mine whatever became of
Jack? 'Didn't you hear?' my friend said. Very surprised. He thought
everybody knew about Wiston. Seems Wiston had the yacht recondi-
tioned and started out on a trip around the world. I understand he
had a couple of Follies girls with him and one or two friends. When
they got to one of the South Sea Islands, Wiston said that was as far
as he was going, and sent everybody on home in the yacht. Bought
himself a big copra plantation—"

"I've always wanted to ask that, what's a copra plantation?"

"Uh, copra? It's what they get cocoanut oil from. So—"

"I've often wondered when I read stories in the *Cosmopolitan*—"

"Well, that's what Wiston must have done too, because it was one
of those Dutch islands. The story that got back was that Wiston
didn't believe in big nations any more. Large countries, doomed to
failure, he said. The trend was the other way. There wasn't a single
major power in the world that wasn't in sorry straits, but take any
little country like Holland or Belgium and Denmark, they were
weathering the depression better than *any* large country, irregardless
of which one it was. The way I heard, he said he was thirty-eight,
thirty-nine then, years of age, he had his good health and a reason-

able expectation of at least twenty more years of an active life, and he didn't want to be beaten to death or shot next year, 1932."

"What?"

"That's his theory. Next year, according to Wiston, is a presidential year, and we're going to have a revolution."

"Oh, hooey."

"Well, I don't know. A lot of fellows are taking that seriously. A lot of people think there's going to be a change. Looks like Al Smith might get in or Owen D. Young. Some Democrat. But will things be any better? I doubt it. Hoover must have something up his sleeve or things would be a lot worse than they are right now."

"But you said a revolution. What kind of a revolution? You mean radicals? I know they talk all the time, but I'd rather have Hoover— well, not Hoover, but I wouldn't want to be governed by some of those people. I've met some of them on parties and they're awful."

"Yes, but what about the farmers? They're dissatisfied. What about in Pittsburgh, all those big factories closed down? I don't know where it's all going to end up. All I can do is do the best I can for you and your mother, so every chance I get I'm turning everything into gold."

"You're not a chemist. You're an alchemist," said Gloria.

"Ah ha ha ha ha. Very good. Quite a sense of humor, Baby."

"Dinner, you two," said Gloria's mother.

"I'm ready," said Vandamm. He whispered to Gloria: "I'll talk to you later about the vacation."

LIGGETT's story to Emily that night was that he and his friend Casey had gone the rounds of Hell's Kitchen speakeasies, trying to do their own detective work. An old enemy of Casey's turned up, Liggett said, and there was a free for all.

The next day he told her the truth, keeping back only the name of the girl.

He awoke that day stiff with pain and with an early realization that there was something ahead that he had to face. It was totally unlike the feeling he had in the war, when he would know each night that the next morning there would be a bombardment and the danger of

an attack; it was less unlike the nervous fear in the days when he first
began to row in college; the race day would be long until the race
started in the late afternoon, and full of things to worry about, but
then the boring alumni and muscle-feelers and door-openers would
start coming around noon and by starting time the race was almost a
pleasant escape. No, this was more like the time he had gonorrhea
and had to force himself to the doctor's office, horribly in ignorance
of what the treatment was going to be. He had known men with it, of
course, but he was sure his was a special case and he could not talk
to anyone about it. This morning was like that and like a time when
he stayed away from the dentist for two and a half years. It was the
knowledge that the unpleasant thing ahead was something that he
himself had to force himself to do, that it was in his own hands, no
one else could make him do it.

He thought he was awake very early and long before Emily, but
when he groaned a little in a way that was like a sigh, she was
standing at his bed before his eyes were fully open. She had been
sleeping in a chaise-longue which she had moved into his room. His
first angry thought was that she had done that to try to catch what he
might say in his sleep, but her manner and her words changed this:
"What is it, darling?"

He looked up at her, taking a good look at her for a change.

"Go on back to sleep, darling. It's ten minutes of six. Or shall I
get you something? A bedpan?"

"No. I don't want anything."

"Does it hurt? Is it painful where they hit you?"

"Who hit me?"

"The men, the friends of Casey's that beat you up. Oh, you poor
dear. You haven't tried to move. You don't know yet that you're hurt.
Well, don't try to move. You've been badly beaten up, darling. Do
you want me to get in bed with you? I'll keep you warm and I won't
bump you. You don't want me to close the window, do you? Get
some more sleep if you can."

"I think I will," he said. Then: "What about you?"

"Oh, don't worry about me. It's almost my regular time to be up anyway. The girls will be awake in another half or three quarters of an hour."

"I don't want to see them."

"I know. I won't let them come in. You go on back to sleep. I'll connect the buzzer." She referred to the line which ran from the button beside his bed to the kitchen, a line which had not been used since it was installed.

She had made the offer to get in bed with him and followed it up quickly with more talk because it meant something to her, and he had not taken up the offer immediately. She would not ask him again. Whatever he wanted she would do, and he did not want her to lie beside him.

She went to her own room. It was too early for the mail, too early for the *Times* and the *Tribune*. There was something wrong about reading a book so early in the day, like ice cream for breakfast. She thought she might have a bath, but it was too early for that too; that is, there was so much power behind the wide-mouthed faucet in her tub that it would be inconsiderate of the girls' sleep to run a tub now. It had been a source of unexpressed complaint; Emily meant to have something done about it, but it was one of those things that made her accuse herself of being a far from perfect housewife; one of the things she did not do because it was good enough, in satisfactory working condition, and only once in a while she would be reminded that there was room for improvement. Thinking of the girls she went to their room.

Barbara was actively at sleep, lying on her right side with her left arm almost straight up on the pillow. Compared with Ruth she was lying in a twisted position. Ruth was lying on her back with her mouth open just a little and her arms stretched out, at first reminding Emily of the Crucifixion, but then almost immediately of a Red Cross poster. Ruth was the daughter she would watch and be proud of; Barbara would be the one she would guard and protect and make sacrifices for if they became necessary. But it was Ruth who interested her now, because Ruth was closer to Weston, and it was Weston who was all on Emily's mind at present.

She might be dead, might Ruth, lying there so still, so quietly asleep with one leg bent a little but not enough to take away from the illusion of death which—knowing it to be an illusion—Emily created for the moment.

Ruth opened her eyes without moving any other part of her body, without moving so much as a muscle. She had that close but superior look of one who comes awake completely and effortlessly. "Mummy," she said.

"Shh."

"Is it time for school?"

"No." Emily whispered.

"Good." Ruth smiled and closed her eyes again, then opened them again to say: "Why are you up so early?"

"I don't want you to make any noise. Daddy isn't feeling well and we mustn't make any noise."

"What's the matter with Daddy?"

"He was beaten up in a fight last night." Emily did not know what she was saying until she had said it. It had not occurred to her to lie to this child of hers. The words were out, and Emily looked for a reason for the frankness. She could find none.

"Oh." Ruth said it and said it again: "Oh."

Emily could see what was going on in her mind, could tell it from the two ohs. The first was pain and the quick sympathy that you would expect from Ruth. The second was wanting to ask how, where, when, by whom, how badly—and a firm control of her tongue.

"He wasn't *badly* hurt," said Emily, "but they hurt him. When Barbara wakes up don't say anything about it to her, dear."

"She'll be noisy, though. You know how she always is."

"Tell her Daddy has a headache and not to make any noise."

"Is there anything I can do? I don't want to go back to sleep now."

"The best thing is to keep quiet, not to make a sound that will disturb Daddy."

"How did they hurt him?"

"In the ribs mostly, and punched him in the face. Don't worry about him, Ruthie. Try to sleep again."

She smoothed her daughter's hair, as though Ruth had a fever, and ended with a few little pats on the forehead. She went to the kitchen and started the coffee percolator. She sat down and waited, staring straight ahead and thinking about Ruth with her lovely intelligent innocent eyes, and her sing-song voice when she said: "What's the matter with Daddy?" All the innocent things about her eyes and her face and her ruffled hair and her voice—then she thought of the form outlined under the bed-clothes. At this minute, probably in New Haven or in Cambridge, some young man who would one day . . . No, it would be all right. It would be love with Ruth, one love. Barbara was the one to worry about, with one love after another, and many pains and the need for watching. Emily thought she knew for the first time why she thought oftener of Ruth. The reason was that Ruth and she understood each other; Ruth understood about Barbara, and she understood about herself. That was good—but it was too neat. No; if Ruth understood so much then she must be unhappy about something else. What? She went back to the thoughts of Ruth's little-woman's body. It was all there, ready to move in on life; the breasts were small, but they were there; the hips were not large, but they were there; and part of the intelligence, or part of the information behind the intelligent look of the eyes was the knowledge Emily had imparted to Ruth nearly two years ago. Ruth knew the mechanics of the female, as much as could be told in words. No, no. The look of those eyes, it wasn't an intelligent look; it was just that they were intelligent eyes. There was a difference. But Emily made up her mind that she would watch Ruth with boys, *because of* love.

She poured the coffee and took a cup in to Weston's room. "I brought you some coffee," she said.

What she did not know was that he had meanwhile manufactured the antagonism that was necessary before he could tell her the truth. Also he wanted to tell her because he felt that if he told her the truth as it was up to this minute, he would not be so much to blame if something else was going to happen—and he was not by any means sure that nothing else was going to happen. He had to see Gloria again, he knew that, and he knew that even though he didn't want Gloria now, the next thing he would want would be Gloria.

"Will you get me a cigarette out of my coat pocket, please?" he said. "Thanks. Emily, I want to tell you something. That's probably the last favor I'll ask you to do for me, and when I tell you what I'm going to tell you you won't want to do any more."

"Do you have to tell me now?"

"Right now. I won't go through the day wanting to tell you. I'll go crazy if I do."

"Well, in that case."

"You sound almost as though you knew what it was I want to tell you."

"I can guess. It's about a woman."

"Yes."

"Well, then I don't want to hear it now. I know you've been unfaithful. You've stayed with another woman. I don't want to hear the rest of it at this hour of the morning."

"Well, you'll have to hear it. If you don't mind, please, I want to tell you now."

"Why?"

"Emily, for Christ's sake."

"All right."

"I want to tell you the truth about this because it's a very special thing. Can you look at it this way? Can you, uh, think of me as someone you know that has nothing to do with you, not married to you, but someone you know? Please try to. Well, this man, me, last Saturday night . . ."

From the time he reached the point where he told about bringing Gloria to this apartment Emily did not try to follow his words. He told the story in chronological order up to that point, and she got a kind of excitement out of listening and wondering how he would reach what was for her the climax of the story; the awful climax, but the climax. She knew what was coming, but she never expected to hear the words: "So I brought her here." The words were not separate; they were part of a sentence: ". . . got in a taxi and I didn't have any baggage so I brought her here and we had a few drinks and . . ." But the last words that she paid attention to were: "So I brought her here." After that he went on and on. She knew his throat was dry because his voice broke a little but she did not offer to get him a glass of water. Every once in a while he would ask if she was listening and she would nod and he would say she didn't seem to be, and then continue. She had been sitting on the bed when he began. Once she changed her position so that she sat in a chair beside the head of the bed and she would not have to look at him. "Go on," she would say. Let him talk himself out. She didn't care how long he talked. She was back from Reno, back in Boston, it was 1932, the girls were at Winsor School, she was avoiding her father and his well-meaning solicitousness. Mrs. Winchester Liggett. Mrs. Emily W. Liggett.

What did people generally do with furniture? What did they do for immediate cash? Wasn't it a good thing that it was so near the close of the school year? Wasn't it a good thing New York meant living in an apartment? How awful if it had been in a house, a real home? Ah, but if it had been anywhere else he wouldn't have brought that girl here, to an apartment. No, it wasn't so good that New York meant living in an apartment. That was only a consoling thought and not a matter for congratulation. Let him talk.

". . . tried to swing at him, the policeman, but . . ."

Who cared? Now he was describing the fight. Why hadn't he been killed? He looked so foolish and unrelated to her, with his bandages and bruises. She knew he wasn't asking for sympathy, but she couldn't help denying it to him. What he had asked in the beginning and what she thought would be so hard—to think of him as someone she knew who had nothing to do with her, not married to her, but someone she knew—that was what she felt. Telling the end of the story, or the second half of it, or the latter two thirds, or whatever it was that remained after "So I brought her here," he was like someone who had nothing to do with her, someone not married to her, someone she knew and did not even like, did not even hate. Here was a man whom she could not escape, who was telling a long and

pretty dull story about an amour and how he came to be beaten up.
Come to think of it, she once knew a man like that, a man who got
you in a corner and told you long dull stories about his love life,
what a boy he was with the ladies, and how he got into fights. The
man's name was Weston Liggett.

"Oh, no," she said.

"What?" he said.

The fool thought she was protesting at something he had said,
when she only meant to pull herself together. "Oh, no. I mustn't
think hysterically," was what she meant to say, but the Oh-no part
had come out in spoken words.

"Well, and that's all," he said. "I wanted to tell you because I
didn't—I couldn't stand lying here and letting you wait on me—
what are you, what on earth are you laughing at?"

"You can't stand lying here. I just thought it was obvious that you
can't stand and lie down at the same time."

"Oh, it's funny."

"No, not funny," she said, "but I don't know what you expect me
to do. I won't congratulate you."

"Well, at least I've been honest with you. Now you can do as you
please."

"What do you suppose I please?"

"How should I know. I'll give you a divorce. I mean, if you want
a divorce in New York I'll give you grounds."

"You have. But I don't want to talk about that now."

"You haven't one word of understanding. Not a single instinct of
understanding."

"Oh, now really."

"Yes, now really. You didn't even try to understand. The only
thing that interested you was that I was unfaithful. You didn't care
about anything else."

"I'm not going to quarrel with you. I'm not going to let you turn
this into a little spat. I don't want to talk about it."

"You've got to talk about it. You've got to tell me what you're
going to do. I was honest with you, I told you the truth when I didn't
have to. You believed the story I made up."

"I beg your pardon, but I didn't believe the story you made up. I did at first, but not when I thought it over. I knew there was more to it than that. And don't tell me I've *got* to tell you what I'm going to do, or that I *have* to talk about it. There aren't any more have-to's as far as you and I are concerned."

"We'll see."

"All right, we'll see."

"Emily," he said.

She walked out.

He dressed and had breakfast after the girls had gone to school. He knocked on Emily's door and she called: "Yes?"

"May I see you a minute, please?"

"What about?"

"I'm leaving."

She opened the door.

"You can stay."

"Thanks, but I'm not going to. I just want to tell you, first of all, I'm going to a hotel. I'll let you know which one when I've decided. Probably the Biltmore. In the second place, I'll deposit some money for you some time today, five hundred now, and as much more than that as I can, later in the week. I'm going because I don't want you to take the girls out to the country at least for the time being."

"Why not?"

"Because they're looking for that Two-Gun Crowley, the fellow that murdered a policeman. He's somewhere on Long Island and there's a big reward out for him. Long Island will be full of crazy people with guns and policemen wanting to shoot this Crowley and it won't be safe. Now please take my advice on this. Stay here till they've captured him or at least till the excitement blows over."

"What else?"

"That's all, I guess. If you want a lawyer, Harry Draper's good. He isn't a divorce lawyer, but if you were planning to go to Reno, for instance, you won't need a divorce lawyer here. The New York lawyer will have a correspondent in Reno. That's the way they always do it, unless the divorce is contested, then sometimes they—"

"If you don't mind I'd rather not go into details now." She shut the door quickly, because she suddenly knew by his face that he wanted her, and much as she loathed him, this would be one of the times when he could have her. That was disgusting.

He knew some of that, too.

7

THAT SAME DAY, Wednesday, a coincidence occurred: Gloria decided she didn't want to see Eddie for a couple of days, and Eddie decided he didn't want to see Gloria for a couple of days.

Gloria went shopping with her mother, purchasing a beach hat with a flowered linen band, for $8.50; a suit of beach pajamas with horizontal striped top to the trousers, which cost her mother $29.50. She bought a surf suit that tied at both shoulders for $10.95. A one-piece bouclette frock cost $29.50 and a stitched wool hat with a feather cost $3.95. Also a linen suit, navy jacket and white skirt, for the incredible price of $7.95, a woolen sports coat for $29.50, a tricot turban with a halo twist was $12.50, and two pique tennis dresses (with crocheted belt) for $10.75 apiece. Her uncle had given her mother $150 to spend and the purchases were practically on the dot of that sum. Gloria made the purchases with practically no inter-ference from her mother and she felt good and went home for the express purpose of sending Norma Day's suit to the dry cleaners'.

She was wrapping the suit in newspaper but she could not resist reading the paper. It was Monday's *Mirror*, and she was surprised to discover that she had missed reading Walter Winchell's column. She skimmed through it for a possible mention of her name (you never could tell) and then she read more carefully, learning that Barbara Hutton was being sent to Europe to forget Phil Plant, that the Connie Bennett-Marquis de la Falaise thing was finished, "Joel McRae be-ing the new heart." She read a few lines from that day's installment of "Grand Hotel," which was running in the *Mirror*, and then she turned to "What Your Stars Foretell": "Today in particular," it said, "should bring encouragement to correspondents, typists, writers and advertisers. Tuesday may be a nervous and upsetting day in many ways, but Tuesday evening as well as Wednesday evening are very satisfactory for pleasure and dealings with the other sex on a friendship basis. Do not expect too much of Wednesday. It is not a good day for anything outside of the regular routine, and Thursday will be a discouraging day for those with tempers. Beware of disagreements and quarrels in business and with your sweetheart. Saturday should be a very encouraging day from almost any angle; you may act with confidence in either social or business matters. This week is favorable for those born Jan. 29 to Feb. 10, Mar. 3–11, April 1–10, May 5–12, June 2–9, July 7–12, Aug. 1–8, Nov. 15–20, Nov. 29–Dec. 5, Dec. 7–11, Dec. 24–28." Well, her birthday was December 5, so taking it altogether, by and large, if she would be careful today and keep her temper tomorrow—not that she had a really bad temper, but sometimes she did fly off the handle—she ought to have a good week, because Saturday was going to be a very encouraging day from almost any angle, the stars foretold. It might be a good time to plan a trip, and immediately she thought of Liggett. All these clothes, they were for the summer and the trip her uncle was going to give her, but if the weather was nice—but what was she thinking about? Had she gone completely screwy that she was planning anything with Liggett, when for all she knew he had a fractured skull? What if he had a fractured skull? It would be a nice mess and it wouldn't take the police long to get her mixed up in it. Why, there was a policeman right there in the speakeasy when she ran out. All he had to do was ask the bartender her name, and she'd be mixed up in it. She was frightened and she read over again what it said about Tuesday: ". . . may be a nervous and upsetting day in many ways." It certainly had been. It said Tuesday evening was satisfactory for pleasure and dealings with the other sex on a friendship basis, but her relations with Liggett had not been on a friendship basis, not by a whole hell of a lot, as Eddie would say. No, this stuff was right; ordinarily she didn't put much stock in it, but it was like superstitions; maybe there was something to them so it didn't do any harm to be careful. Besides, it was right enough about Tuesday being nervous and upsetting, and when you considered daylight saving time, then all that mess in the speakeasy was part of Tuesday the day, and not the evening. Do not expect too much of Wednesday . . . routine. Well, she would have Eddie's girl Miss Day's suit cleaned, and return the fur coat, those ought to be routine things. Tomorrow was Thursday, the day to be careful about disagreements and quarrels in business (that ought to cover the coat, so she would forestall any trouble tomorrow by returning the coat today), and she would guard against a quarrel with her sweetheart by returning the coat. How to do it would have to be figured out later. But she did not ignore the ease with which she was thinking of Liggett as her sweetheart. Whatever he was, she loved him. *"Don't* I?" she asked.

When he was alone in his apartment Eddie smoked a pipe. It was one of the few gifts his father had given him that was not cash outright. It had a "2S9" in silver on the front of the bowl, which was the way his father had ordered it, but it happened to be a good pipe and Eddie liked it in spite of the adornment. It was cheaper than cigarettes, and when he had money Eddie usually bought a half-pound or a pound tin of tobacco and laid in a supply of cigarette papers. Thus he almost always had something to smoke.

It was a furnished apartment, and probably had a history, but the only part of its history that interested Eddie was that it had come down in price from $65 to $50 a month. Something undoubtedly had taken place in the apartment to account for the lowering of the rental. As Eddie well knew, the depression did not result in decreases in rents of apartments that took in $100 a month or less. One-room and two-room apartments cost just as much as they always had, and renting agents could even be a little choosy, for people who formerly had paid $200 and more now were leasing the cheaper apartments, and paying their rent. So there must have been a reason why this apartment could be held for fairly regular payments of $50 a month. It must not be inferred that Eddie never had any interest at all in the processes that brought about the reduction. At first he wondered about it a little; the furniture was not the kind that is bought for a furnished apartment and the hell with it. No, this was hand-picked stuff, obviously left there by a previous tenant. Eddie thought it possible that the previous tenant had been slain, perhaps decapitated with a razor. He resolved some day to suggest as a magazine article the idea of going around to various apartments in New York where famous crimes had occurred. The apartment where Elwell, the bridge player, was killed; the Dot King apartment; the room in the Park Central where Arnold Rothstein was killed. Find out who lived in the apartment now, whether the present occupant knew Elwell, for instance, had lived there; what kind of person would live in an apartment where there had been a murder; how it affected the present tenant's sleep; whether any concession was made in the rent; whether the real estate people told the prospective tenant that the apartment had a past. It was one of the ideas that Eddie had and rejected for himself because he did not know how to write, but would have passed on to a writer friend if he had had any.

It was hard to tell whether this apartment had been a man's or a woman's. The distinguishing small things had been taken away. There was a bed that could be disguised in the daytime with a large solid red cover; a cheap (it was all cheap) modern armchair; a small fireplace that did not look too practical; a folding bridge table; three modern lamps; a straight-back chair like a "5" with the horizontal bar cut off. Over the fireplace was a colored map of New York with cute legends, and there was a map of Paris, apparently executed by the same cartographer, on the inside of the bathroom door. The pictures that remained were an amateur's replica of a Georgia O'Keeffe orchid, and a Modigliani print. There were a few ash trays from Brass Town via Woolworth.

Whenever he shaved Eddie would hum "I Got Rhythm." The reason for this was that he once had used the words in a sentence: "I had crabs but I got rhythm." He had first thought it up in the bathroom, while shaving, and he would always recall it, at least until something else took its place. Eddie never told anyone he could use the title in a sentence; it was not his kind of humor. Some day he would hear someone else say it and then he would stop thinking of it. That, exactly that, often happened to Eddie. He would make up puns, keep them to himself, and then he would hear them from someone else and they would cease to be his property. It made him wonder; he thought it was indicative of a great lack in himself; not that he cared about the puns, but it was just as true of his own work, his drawing. Once he had an idea that he turned into something; the drawings he did in college. But he also had thought and worked out a technique that was very much like that of James Thurber. In his case he knew it to be reminiscent of the technique employed in a 1917 book called *Dere Mabel,* by Ed Streeter, drawings by Bill Breck, but still he had done nothing with his idea, and then along came Thurber with his idea, and look what he did: everybody knew who Thurber was—and the people who knew who Brunner was were making a pretty good job of forgetting it.

All these things ran through Eddie's mind, which was like blood running through Siamese twins; there was a whole other half of his mind.

Then he began to consider the other half of his mind, and gave himself up a little to the pleasure of the day, the first pleasure of its kind since he had come to New York. For this day, not two hours before he had come here to this apartment and lit this pipe and looked at this furniture and wondered about this lack in himself— two hours ago he had been promised work, and given a half promise of a job. "I won't say yes and I won't say no," the man had said. "All I'll tell you positively now is we can use your drawings."

The work was for a movie company, in the advertising department, the art room of the advertising department. Eddie had gone there for a job several times two years ago, because he knew there was a Stanford man, a couple of classes ahead of him, working in the department. But the Stanford man at that time had been terrified at the idea of being responsible for increasing the company's payroll by another salary. He knew that the officials of the company were worried about their own nepotism and the cousins of cousins were being laid off. And so Eddie had said well, he would leave a few drawings just in case, and never heard any more.

Then this morning he had gone to that office for the first time in nearly two years. He had asked for his old friend and had been told that the friend was in Hollywood. Then could he see someone in the department? Yes, he could see the man in charge of the art room. The man in charge of the art room listened with a mystifying respect to Eddie's account of his experience of two years ago. The man said: "Oh, I see. You were a personal friend of Mr. De Paolo's?"

"Yes, I knew him in college. That's what I was saying."

"Have you heard from him lately?"

"Well, no, not lately. I understand he's in Hollywood," said Eddie.

"Yes, but we expect him back in a day or two. Thursday or Friday."

"Well, then I'll come in and see him then. Will you tell him Eddie Brunner was in? Tell him I have some ideas for him."

"For Benny the Beetle?" the man said.

"No."

"He needs some for Benny."

"No, these are just some of my own drawings I thought he could use."

"Oh, do you draw?"

"Yes."

"Mm," said the man, and put on his thinking look. "Just a minute, Mr. Brunner." The man left the office and was gone five minutes. He came back with a batch of rough advertising lay-outs. "Could you do something with these?"

"Jesus, yes. That's just my stuff," said Eddie. The lay-outs were for a campaign advertising a college picture. "Do you want me to try?"

"Sure do. I think these are lousy, and the boys in the department just don't seem to get the right angle. No yoomer. They can draw tits till I want to chew the paper, but these girls are not supposed to have that kind of tits, you know what I mean. What I want is more on the order of John Held Jr. You know. Comedy girls. I want them female, but I don't want to stress the sex angle." He smiled and shook his head. "We did a campaign, God damn, boy, we had everything but the old thing in every paper in town. The picture was a terrible turkey, 'Strange Virgin,' but they almost held it over the second week it did such business, and every other company in town was bellyaching to the Hays office about our ads, so we got the credit for whatever business the picture did. Maybe you saw the campaign?"

"I sure did."

"The one where she's lying with her legs out like this, and the guy! I did that one my*self*. We even had squawks from Andre Jacinto on that. He happened to be in town making personal appearances when the ads came out and oh, he called up and he blew the house down, he was that sore. 'Listen,' he said, 'maybe I am like that and maybe I'm not, but you got no God damn license to put something in the ads that ain't in the picture.' That gave me a laugh, because when you take into consideration what that ad looked like he was doing, it'll take a long time before they put that in any picture they make in Hollywood. Maybe over West Forty-six Street, that kind of a picture. But for the time being. Well, anyway, that was some campaign. The other companies squawked to the Hays office, but I don't mind telling you I got myself two very nice offers from the companies that squawked the loudest. But with such a college picture we require an altogether different technique. You know? Dames, but cute, and comedy. Stress the comedy angle. I tell you what I'll do, Mr. Brunner. I'll take the responsibility on my own head. You go on in and sit down and just give me all you got on a couple roughs like what I have in mind, and if I like them I'll give you twenty-fy dollars top price for all we use, then if I like them maybe we can come to some kind of an arrangement about more work in the future."

Eddie did some drawings and the man said they were sensational. He'd take one anyway. Mr. De Paolo would be proud, he said. He made out a voucher for $25 and told Eddie to come back next Friday. "Oh, of course if you were going to see Mr. De Paolo maybe I'll see you before that." There was just a chance that there might possibly be a regular job there for Eddie.

Before he left the place Eddie of course had found out that his old friend De Paolo had struck it rich; he was in charge of the work on Benny the Beetle, the company's own plagiarism of Mickey Mouse. . . .

On twenty-five a week Eddie figured he could even go to a movie now and then and get a load of Benny the Beetle. It was too much to hope for a steady job in an art department, where they certainly would pay more than twenty-five a week, but if the friendship with

De Paolo had got him this far, no telling how far he would get when Polly—De Paolo—came to town, always providing Polly hadn't gone high-hat and wouldn't pass him up. But he didn't think Polly would go high-hat. High-powered, maybe, but not high-hat.

And so Eddie breathed in streams of tobacco smoke, tobacco that he had dug out of the luxurious bottom of the can, where it was still faintly moist and had a flavor. He had $23 and some change, he didn't know how much, in his kick right now. Five dollars for canned goods would leave $18 plus, and would assure him of food for at least a week. Take Norma to a show, tickets at Joe Leblang's. Explain the situation to Norma, whom he had permitted to pay his rent on a loan basis, in return for which he put up her kid brother, a junior at the University of Pennsylvania, who came to town every other week-end to see a girl friend of Norma's. Norma had her own money, left her by a grandmother, and she also had a job as secretary to an assistant professor at N. Y. U. She and her brother were orphans and her brother had his own money too, but in trust until he was twenty-one years old.

What about Norma, anyway? Eddie now asked himself. He had the feeling that his troubles were over, temporarily, and he wondered if it wouldn't be a good idea to marry Norma. He thought back over the years, and it might as well have been Norma all along. His succession of girls always had been about the same general type; smallish, usually with breasts rather large for the girl's height; sometimes the girl would be chunky. They had to have a feeling for jazz that was as good as you can expect in a girl. They had to be cute rather than blasé, a little on the slangy side, and come to think of it, all of them including Norma had to go to bed for one day out of every twenty-eight. They were all fundamentally the same, and probably they were all fundamentally Norma.

About love Eddie was not so sure. The thing that he supposed existed, that kept together a man and woman all their lives and made them bring up children and have a home and that kept them faithful to each other unquestioningly and apparently without temptation—he had not seen that in his own home and so he was not personally acquainted with it. He was not sure that he ever had seen it, either.

He knew, for instance, that he saw the parents of his friends in a way
that was totally unlike the way his friends saw them. All through his
adolescence he practically took for granted that Mr. Latham and Mr.
O'Neill and Mr. Dominick and Mr. Girardot, fathers of his closest
friends of that period, were unfaithful to Mrs. Latham and Mrs.
O'Neill and Mrs. Dominick and Mrs. Girardot. He never spoke of it,
because his friends never did, but if they had he was sure he would
have come right out and said what he thought. He had it thought out
beyond that: he believed that those fathers were human, and subject
to desire, a thing which did not have to be forgiven except in the case
of his own father. His own father had inadvertently taught him to
accept infidelity in all other fathers but himself. On the other hand
Eddie liked absolute faithfulness in a wife, not so much because his
own mother practiced it, but because as a result of her practicing it
she became finally a much better person in his eyes than his father.
The years of being constant were a lot like years of careful saving,
compared with years of being a spendthrift. It was just that it was
easier to be a spendthrift than to save. Of course sometimes you
saved for nothing better than a bank crash, but even though you lost
everything that was in the bank, you still had something around the
eyes, something in the chin, that showed you had been a saver.
Sometimes he would say to himself: "Yes, but your mother was
pretty stupid." All right, what if she was? She had kept her promise,
which was more than his father had done. Eddie had no liking for
the fellows in college who thought it would be swell to have a father
who was more like an older brother. If his father had been an older
brother Eddie would have been likely to give him a punch in the
nose. Not that he idealized any other father he knew, but because he
never met a father whom he regarded as the ideal did not mean that
none such existed. Psychology and the lines of thought it indicated
mildly fascinated Eddie, and he approved some of it; but he was not
willing to ascribe, say, fidelity to a weakness or a dishonesty. Maybe
it all did come down to the value of a promise. You gave your word
that you would not sleep with another woman; in either case it was a
promise, and if you couldn't depend on a promise then nothing was
any good.

He was always telling himself that when he got older and knew more he would take up the subject of promises. But he hoped the day never would come when he did not believe a promise—just a promise, and not all the surrounding stuff about Gentleman and Honor—was a good and civilized thing.

He was lying on his bed, thinking these things, and he suddenly felt disgust with himself. For only yesterday he had come within inches of laying Gloria, and months ago he had promised Norma that he would not stay with anyone else. All his self-satisfied introspection went away and he could not find anything anywhere in his thoughts that would justify what he had all but done. It was not his fault that it had not been done. There it was, the first time his promise to Norma had been put to a test, and right away, without even thinking about it, he was ready for Gloria, very God damn ready; and it was worse because he had come so close without thinking about it. It was possible that if he had thought it out he would have found a reason, if no other reason than that he would stay with Gloria and stop staying with Norma. Then next he was thinking the thing he always thought when he was getting out of one romance and beginning another: the self-reproach that he was no better than his father; that he was his father's son. Maybe the psychoanalysts would tell him that that helped to explain how he would be faithful to a girl for months, then get another girl and be faithful to her until he was unfaithful. That's the way it had been, and almost the way it was this minute, with Norma and Gloria. But he had not stayed with Gloria; for that break he thanked his luck. If he had he would have had to tell Norma. But he hadn't. That seemed to him an important thing, one of the most important things in his life, and at that moment he decided he had found the girl he wanted to marry. A laundry called him on the telephone, and that prevented his having an affair with Gloria. Good. Something beyond his understanding had intervened, he was sure of that; maybe it was only his luck. Well, he wasn't going to fool with his luck. When he saw Norma tonight he would ask her to marry him. No money, no job, no nothing. But he knew she was the one he wanted to marry. He laughed a little. He was pretty proud of Norma, and he loved her very much. He was already loyal to her, too; in the sense that in his mind he could defend her against the kind of thing Gloria might say about her: he could hear Gloria calling Norma a mouse-like little creature (although Norma was the same size girl as Gloria, and, speaking of mice, it was not hard to imagine someone saying Norma had a mind like a steel trap). Eddie let his loyalty go to Norma and did not try to deny to himself that this probably was at the expense of his loyalty to Gloria.

It was strange about Gloria, how he always had had this feeling of loyalty to her. Offhand he could not recall a time when there had been any need for it; yet he knew that with the life Gloria led there probably were dozens of people who said things about her that, if he heard them, would evoke a loyal response and some kind of protective action on his part. He had been ready to defend Gloria at any time when he might meet someone who said things about her or did things to her. By God it was an instinctive thing: that first night he saw her he lent her money when money was life to him. It saddened him to think of the things implicit in his decision to marry Norma. One of these things was the giving up part. Maybe he was wrong (he admitted) but always it seemed to him as though he and Gloria were many many times on the verge of a great romance, one for the ages, or at least a match for the love and anguish of Amory and Rosalind in "This Side of Paradise" and Frederick and Catherine in "A Farewell to Arms." He nodded to an undefined thought: that yes, to marry Norma was a sensible thing and if out of the hundred pounds of the relationship between himself and Norma there was one ounce sensible thing, that one ounce was an imperfect, unromantic thing. All right; what of it? There never had been much romance in his past romances, and he distrusted romance for his own self; in a sort of Elks-tooth way his father had been a romantic guy, and he was not going to have any of that. He was in no danger of it, either, he was sure; his mother had not been like Norma. Disconnectedly he found himself off on a tangent, realizing how awful parturition must have been for his mother, all that stuff about getting up on a table and having a doctor look her over, and her realization that "the little one" she talked about and thought about and felt, also was a hideous little thing called a foetus. (He was able to think of this without any identification of the foetus as himself. You may say, "That was me," but you cannot imagine yourself as being no bigger than the present size of your foot.) No, it wasn't so disconnected as he called it; Norma never would speak of "the little one." If she were pregnant she would know beforehand what was going on inside her, and she would know about the placenta and all that. He hoped Norma would not have much pain. But what stuff this was! this thinking about Norma deliberately having a baby when he had not yet seriously asked her to marry him. She might fool him and say no; there was that chance. "A celluloid cat's in hell," he assured himself, but a chance.

He was already as married as though he were half of Mr. and Mrs. Eddie Brunner. Did babies sometimes come out upside down because that was the position of their parents when the baby was conceived? Could parents tell which lay had made the baby? How long did the husband and wife have to stop sleeping together when the wife was pregnant? (He had heard the story about an artist who tried to stay with his wife when she was being wheeled into the delivery room.) What if Norma had a dwarf: would the doctors let it live? What if they had a baby and it turned out to be an hermaphrodite? Would Norma's beautiful breasts get so painfully sensitive that he would not be able to touch them while she was pregnant? Did they always lose their firmness after pregnancy? What was this stuff about tearing? Did it mean *literally* tearing? ripping open when she did not stretch enough? Could doctors keep the size of the baby down so it would not endanger the mother's life? How much did a baby cost?

Well, it cost more than he would be able to pay for a long time, so he might as well stop thinking about it. He ought to be glad he had enough money to take Norma to a show tonight, that's what he ought to be.

8

WEDNESDAY PASSED FOR all those living in the world at that time, and it was Thursday. It was for instance payday for James Malloy, who had been living since Monday on borrowed dollars. For Gloria Wandrous it was all of a sudden the day on which she would give up Liggett. She had had a good night's sleep. Wednesday evening she had spent in the bosom of her family, after trying without success to talk to Eddie on the telephone. She had a good dinner at home, of things she liked: her mother's cream of tomato soup with just a touch of sherry in it; roast beef, scalloped potatoes, succotash, lettuce and mayonnaise (homemade), ice cream with strawberries, coffee and a lick of Curaçao. Her uncle had to go uptown after dinner and Gloria was left with her mother. Her mother had not been so bad. They talked about the clothes she had bought that day, and Mrs. Wandrous, who knew something about women's clothes, reaffirmed her trust in Gloria's taste. She said Gloria had clothes sense. "That's one thing about you I never had to teach you even as a little girl. You always had good sense about clothes. Oh, so few girls have it these days. Sunday before last, you know when I went for a drive with Mrs. Lackland, we drove past Vassar College. Now you'd think those girls would know how to dress, at least have sense enough to put on something decent on Sunday. But no. Sweater and skirt, sweater and skirt, all the way up and down the street from Poughkeepsie proper to the college. And the same sweater, and the same skirt. I said to Mrs. Lackland, if those girls were told they *had* to wear a uniform the way girls have to in preparatory school, why, they'd yell and scream and have school strikes and everything. But there they were, just the same, wearing a uniform. And it isn't as though they dressed any better when they came to New York. But I suppose they have no style. *You have.* You have style. I noticed those things you bought today. I was afraid for a minute when you asked to try on that one dress at Altman's. I knew it was wrong for you but I didn't want to say anything till after you tried it on."

"Oh, I wouldn't have bought it."

"I know."

"I just wanted to try it on. They're handy."

"Well, I don't think so, Gloria. When I'm tempted to buy a dress because I think it's going to be handy, I think twice about it. Those handy dresses, so-called, I should say a woman won't get as much out of one of those as she will out of a really frivolous dress. I mean in actual number of hours that they're worn. Take your black satin . . ."

Clothes, and cooking, and curiously enough the way to handle men, were matters in which Gloria had respect for her mother's opinions. Packing, housecleaning, how to handle servants, what to do for blotches in the complexion, kitchen chemistry, the peculiarities of various fabrics—Mrs. Wandrous knew a lot about such matters. It occurred to Gloria that her mother was a perfect wife. The fact that her husband was dead did nothing to change that. In fact that was part of it. And any time anybody had any doubt about how well her mother could manage a house, all they had to do was count up the number of times Gloria's uncle had had to complain. No, her mother was a fine housekeeper, and she knew how to handle men. Gloria often would hear her mother say that if So-and-So did such and such she'd be happier with her husband. What Gloria meant was that her mother, dealing with her kind of man in her kind of life, was just as capable as she was with baking soda in the kitchen. Mrs. Wandrous knew what baking soda could be made to do, and she knew what the kind of man she would be likely to have dealings with (who bored Gloria to death) would do. It was almost a good life, Gloria decided. Without regret she recognized the impossibility of it for her; but a pretty good life for someone like her mother.

That Wednesday night after she went to bed she lay there trying, not very hard, to read, and thinking about her mother. Now there was a woman who had known (Gloria was sure) only one man in her entire life. Known meaning slept with. And that had not lasted very long. Yet after twenty years her mother was able to recall every detail of sleeping with a man, almost as though it had happened last night. She had not discussed it at any length with her mother, but now and then a thing would be said that showed how well her mother remembered. Think of living that way! Going to bed these nights, so many nights through so many years; some nights dropping off to sleep, but surely some nights lying there and saddened by the waste of shapely breasts and the excitement in oneself with a man, and the excitement of a man's excitement. And then nothing to do about it but lie there, almost afraid to touch one's breasts, probably, or anything else; and remembering one man long ago. There was only one possible explanation for being able to live in memory like that, and Gloria felt tears in her eyes at the thought of her father's and mother's love.

It showed, too. It showed in her mother's face. It worried Gloria a little to come around again to a theory she sometimes had that a woman ought to have one man and quit. It made for a complete life no matter how short a time it lasted. Gloria resolved to be a better girl, and after a long but not unpleasant time she fell asleep, preferring her own face but thinking well of her mother's.

She had breakfast in her room. It was too warm a day for breakfast in bed. To have breakfast in bed ought to be a luxury and not a nuisance, and it was a nuisance when covering over the legs was a nuisance, as it was this day. She drank the double orange juice and wanted more, but Elsie, the maid, had gone back to the kitchen out of call. Gloria drank her coffee and ate her toast and poured another cup of coffee. Then a cigarette. While having breakfast she was busy with her hands. With no one to look at her she swung her butter knife like a bandmaster's baton, not humming or singing, but occasionally letting her throat release a note. She felt good.

What, if anything, she had decided the night before had not been changed by the morning and the good night's sleep, principally because she had not fixed upon a new mode of life. The good night's sleep she knew had a lot to do with the absence of her usual morning despair, but it wasn't that she was happy, exactly. It came close to the feeling that she was ready for anything today, whereas if she had come to a solemn decision the night before to be an angel thenceforward, she would now be having a special kind of gayety—not removed from the despair—that was cap-over-the-windmill stuff. No;

today she felt good. The big problem of Liggett would be settled somehow, not without an awful scene and maybe not right away, but it would probably be all right—and that concession was a step in the right direction, she thought. She felt good, and she felt strong.

She looked at the advertisements in the paper while smoking her second cigarette. She had a patronizing, superior feeling toward the advertisements: she had bought practically all the clothes she wanted and certainly all she would need. She had her usual quick visit to the bathroom, and then she had a lukewarm bath and she was dressing when her mother called to her that Ann Paul was on the phone and wanted to speak to her, and should she take the message? Yes, take the message, Gloria told her mother. The message was that Ann wanted to have lunch with her. Gloria said she would come to the phone. She didn't want to have lunch with Ann, but she had known Ann in school and did want to see her, so she asked Ann to come downtown if she could, and Ann said she could.

Ann lived in Greenwich where she lived an athletic life; sailing her own Star, hunting and showing at the minor league horse shows and in such ways using up the energy which no man had seemed able to get to for his personal use. In school Ann, who was very tall for a girl, was suspect because of a couple of crushes which now, a few years later, her former schoolmates were too free about calling Lesbian, but Gloria did not think so, and Ann must have known that Gloria did not think so. She called Gloria every time she came to New York, which was about twice a month, and the last two times Gloria had not been home for the calls.

Ann came downtown, parked her Ford across the street from Gloria's house, and went right upstairs to Gloria's room. Ann was in the Social Register, which fact impressed Gloria's mother as much as Gloria's indifference to it. Ann was always made to feel at home in Gloria's house.

"I had to see you," said Ann. "I have big news."

"Ah-hah."

"What?"

"Go ahead."

"Why did you say ah-hah as if you knew it? Does it show?"

"No. I knew there was something. You've never looked better."

"Look," said Ann, and extended her left hand.

"Oh, you *girl!* Ann! Who is it? When? I mean do I know him or anything?"

"Tell you everything. His name is Bill Henderson and you don't know him and he's at P. and S. and gets out next year and he went to Dartmouth before that and he's even taller than I am, and I haven't the faintest idea when we're going to be married."

"How long have you known him? What's he *like?*"

"Since Christmas. He's from Seattle and he spent Christmas with friends of mine in Greenwich which is how I happened to meet him. I sat next to him at dinner the night after Christmas, and he was the quiet type, I thought. He looked to be the quiet type. So I found out what he did and I began talking about gastroenterostomies and stuff and he just sat there and I thought, What is this man? He just sat there and nodded all the time I was talking. You know, when I was going to be a nurse year before last. Finally I said something to him. I asked him if by any chance he was listening to what I was saying, or bored, or what? 'No, not bored,' he said. 'Just cockeyed.' And he was. Cockeyed. It seems so long ago and so hard to believe we were ever strangers like that, but that's how I met him, or my first conversation with him. Actually he's very good. His family have loads of money from the lumber business and I've never seen anything like the way he spends money. But only when it doesn't interfere with his work at P. and S. He has a Packard that he keeps in Greenwich and hardly ever uses except when he comes to see me. He was a marvelous basketball player at Dartmouth and two weeks ago when he came up to our house he hadn't had a golf stick in his hands since last summer and he went out and shot an eighty-seven. He's very homely, but he has this dry sense of humor that at first you don't quite know whether he's even listening to you, but the things he says. Sometimes I think—oh, not really, but a stranger overhearing him might suggest sending him to an alienist."

"He sounds wonderful! Oh, I'm so glad, darling. When did he go for the ring and all?"

"Well—New Year's Eve he asked me to marry him. If you could call it that. Sometimes even now I can't always tell when he's tight. New Year's Eve he was dancing with me and he stopped right in the middle of the floor, stopped dancing and stood away from me and said: 'Remind me to marry you this summer.' "

"I like that. This summer."

"No, I guess not this summer. But I don't know. Oh, all I care about is I guess this is it, I hope."

"It sounds like it to me. The real McCoy, whatever that is. So what are you going to do this summer? Where is—what's his name? Bill?"

"Bill Henderson. Well, he wants to go home for a little while just to see his family and then come back. I—I'm sort of embarrassed, Gloria. I don't really know. When he gets ready to tell me something, he tells me, and I never ask him. But what I wanted to see you about, can you come up for the week-end tomorrow? Bill's coming, and I forget whether he's just getting ready for examinations or just finishing them. See? I don't know anything. I just sit and wait."

"That's good preparation for a doctor's wife."

"So everyone tells me. But what about it, can you come?"

"I'd love to," said Gloria. Then, thinking of Liggett: "I have a half date for the week-end, but I think I can get out of it. Anyway, can I take a rain check if I can't make it this week?"

"Of course. Do try to get out of the other thing. Is this other thing —would you like me to invite someone for you? I mean is there someone that—I could ask your other date."

"No. It was a big party, a lot of people, not anyone in particular."

"Then I won't ask anyone for you till I hear from you. Will you call me? Call me tomorrow at home, or else call this afternoon and leave word. Just say you're coming. And of course if you think you can't come and then change your mind at the last minute and decide you can, that's all right too."

"All right. I'll most likely call you tonight." Gloria noticed that Ann seemed to have something else to say. "What, Ann? What are you thinking?"

"I can tell *you,* Gloria," said Ann. "Darling, I've had an affair. Bill and I. We've had an affair. Almost from the very beginning. Do you think any the less of me?"

"Oh, certainly not, darling. *Me?"*

"I never knew about you. I've always thought you had, but I could never be sure. It's only in the last six months I found out why you can't be sure. It doesn't show on you. You know? You think the next day you're going to be a marked woman and everybody on the street will know. But they don't. And men. Men are so funny. Mothers tell us all our lives that boys lose respect for girls that they go all the way with. But they must have changed a lot since my mother was our age. At first I was so frightened, and then I saw that Bill was the one that really was frightened, not I. I don't mean about children only. But they're so helpless. When we're with people I'm quiet as a mouse and sit there listening to the great man, or when we're dancing I think how marvelously witty he is, with his sense of humor. But when we're really alone it all changes. He's entirely different. At first I used to think he was so gentle, terribly gentle, and it almost killed me. But then I realized something—and this isn't taking anything away from him. He *is* gentle, but the things about him that I used to think were gentle, they aren't gentle. The really gentle things he does aren't the same things I thought were. What I mistook for being gentle was his own helplessness, or practically helplessness. Yes, helplessness. He *knows* everything, being a medical student, and I don't suppose I'm the first for him, but—Lord! I don't know how to explain it. Do you see what I mean at all?"

"I think so. I think something else, too. I think you two ought to get married, right away. Don't lose any of the fun. Right away, Ann. He has his own money, and you have some I know. There's no reason why you should miss anything. Get married."

"I want to, and he's crazy to, but I'm afraid of interfering with his studies."

"It won't interfere with his studies. He might have to neglect *you* a little, but he'll be able to study much better with you than he would being in New York and wishing you were here or he was in Greenwich. No, by all means get married. Just look at all the young marriages there are today. People getting married as soon as the boy gets out of college. The hell with the depression. Not that that's a factor in your getting married, but look at all the young couples, read the society pages and see, and there must be a lot of them that are really poor and without jobs. If you got married now and he goes back to P. and S. next year you'd have the fun of living together and all that, and then he'll probably want to go abroad to Vienna or some place to continue his studies, and that will be like a honeymoon. Your family aren't going to insist on a big wedding, are they?"

"Well, Father thinks it's a good thing to keep up appearances. Mother doesn't like the idea as much as she used to. She'd rather use the money for charity, but Father says he's giving more to charity than ever before and with less money to do it on. He's very serious about it. You see he knows Mr. Coolidge, and I think he thinks if we invited Mr. Coolidge to the wedding he'd come, and that would do a lot toward sort of taking people's minds off the depression."

"I don't agree with your father."

"Neither do I. Of course I wouldn't dare say so, but I think Coolidge got us into this depression and he ought to keep out of the papers."

"That's what I think, too."

"Well, you've given me something to think about. Not that I hadn't thought of it myself, but whenever I broach the subject people say oh, there's plenty of time. But you're the only one that knows we're practically married right now."

"Oh, no, you're not," said Gloria. "Where do you go?"

"Usually to an apartment of a friend of Bill's."

"Well, then you've—have you ever spent the whole night?"

"Once."

"That's not enough. *You're* not practically married."

"How do *you* know so much? Gloria, don't tell me you're married?"

"No, but I know how it is to wake up with a man you love and have breakfast and all that. It takes time before you get accustomed to each other. Who's going to use the bathroom first, and things like that. Intimacies. Ann, I can tell you a lot."

"I wish you would."

"I will. God! I know everything!"

"Why, Gloria."

"Yes, everything. I know how good it can be and how awful, and you're lucky. You marry Bill right away and hold on to him."

"I've never seen you like this. Why does it mean so much to you? Is the man you love married?"

"You've guessed it."

"And his wife won't give him a divorce?"

"Yes," said Gloria. "That's it."

"But couldn't you both go to her and tell her you love each other? Is she a nice woman? How old is she?"

"Oh, we've had it out. Not she and I, but Jack and I."

"Jack. Do I know him?"

"No." She was on the verge of confessing that his name was not Jack, but she did not want to tell Ann too much. "Look, darling, I'll call you tonight for sure and if you're not there I'll leave word that I'm coming or not."

"All right, my pet," said Ann, getting up. She kissed Gloria's cheek. "Good luck, and I'll see you, if not this week, perhaps a week from tomorrow."

"Mm-hmm. And thanks loads."

"Oh, I'm the one to thank you," said Ann, and left.

Gloria thought a long time about how uncontagious love was. According to the book she ought to be wanting to telephone Liggett, and she did want to telephone Liggett in a way, but talking to Ann, virginal Ann with her one man and her happiness and innocence and her awkward love affair (she was sure Bill Henderson wore glasses and had to take them off and put them in a metal case before necking Ann)—it all made her angry with love, which struck in the strangest places. It didn't seem to be any part of her own experience with love, and it depressed her. What possible problems could they have, Ann and Bill? A man from the Pacific Coast, comes all the way from the Pacific Coast and finds right here in the East the perfect girl for him. What possible problems could they have? What made them hesitate about getting married? She felt like pushing them, and pushing them roughly and impatiently. They would get married and after a couple of years Bill would have an affair with a nurse or somebody, and for him the excitement would die down. But by that time Ann would have had children, beautiful children with brown bodies in skimpy bathing suits. Ann would sit on the beach with them, looking up now and then from her magazine and calling them by name and answering their foolish questions and teaching them to swim. She would have enormous breasts but she would not get very fat. Her arms would fill out and look fine and brown in evening dress. And, Gloria knew, Ann would slowly get to disliking her. No; that wouldn't be like Ann. But Gloria would be the only person like herself whom Ann could tolerate. Every Ann probably has one Gloria to whom she is loyal. And the girls they had gone to school with, who had made the cracks about Ann's being Lesbian—they would turn out to be her friends, and she would ride with them and play bridge and go to the club dances. They would meet sometimes in the afternoons, parked in their station wagons, waiting for their husbands, and their husbands would get off the train, all wearing blue or gray flannel suits and club or fraternity hatbands on their stiff straw hats, with their newspapers folded the same way all of them. And she, Gloria, would visit Ann and Bill once each summer for the first few summers, and the men with the hatbands would make dates for New York. Oh, she knew it all.

She tried to laugh it off when she thought of the motion picture she had thought up for Ann's future, but laughing it off was not easy. It was unsuccessful. Laughing it off was unsuccessful because the picture was accurate, and she knew it. Well, every Gloria, she reminded herself, also had an Ann whom she tolerated and to whom she was loyal. Ann's was not her way of living, but it was all right for Ann. The only possible way for Ann, or rather the only good way. Hell, here she was in a bad humor, and for no apparent reason. You couldn't call Ann's happiness a reason.

IN the rear of the second floor of the house in which Gloria lived there was a room which Mrs. Wandrous and the rest of the household called Mrs. Wandrous' sewing-room. It was small and none of the furniture made you want to stay in it very long. Mrs. Wandrous kept needles and spools of thread and darning paraphernalia and sewing baskets in the room, but she did her sewing elsewhere. Occasionally Gloria went to that room to look out the window, and for no other reason.

The sewing-room looked out on the yard of Gloria's house, and across the yard and across the contiguous yard was the rear of an old house which had been cut up into furnished apartments. It was nothing to look at. A woman in that house had a grand piano with a good tone, but her musical taste was precisely that of Roxy, the theater fellow. In fact Gloria had a theory that this woman closely followed the Roxy program, except when the program called for Ravel's "Bolero" and the César Franck and one or two others that Gloria and Roxy liked. The woman also sang. She was terrible. And this woman was the only human being Gloria identified with the house. On warm days she had seen that much of the woman that was between the shoulders and the knees. The woman did not close the window all the way down on hot days. She never had seen the woman's face, but only her torso. She had seen it in and out of clothes, and it was nothing to go out of your way to see. And that woman was the only human neighbor that Gloria knew anything about.

But a couple of yards away there was a garden; two yards with no fence between. Grass grew, there was a tree, there were some rose bushes, there were four iron chairs and a table to match with an umbrella standard in the center of the table. In that garden there was a police bitch and, just now, four puppies.

The last time Gloria had looked out the sewing-room windows the puppies were hardly more than little pieces of meat, not easy to count and completely helpless.

Now they must have been six weeks old, and as Gloria stood and watched them she forgot all about the woman who was playing the piano, for in a very few minutes she discovered something about the family of police dogs: the bitch had a favorite.

The bitch's teats had lost their fullness and had gone back into her body, but that did not make the puppies forget that they had got milk there not so long ago. The mother would run away from their persistent attempts to gnaw at her, but one tan little fellow was more persistent than the others, and when the mother and the tan had got far enough away, the mother would stand and let him nibble at her. Then she would swat him good and hard, but, Gloria noticed, not hard enough for him to misunderstand and take offense and get angry with his mother. The mother would open her surprisingly big mouth and lift him up and swing him away from her, then she would take a mighty leap and fly about the garden, chasing sparrows. Meanwhile the other puppies would be waiting for her and when she met them they would try again to take milk from her. Or maybe they were like men, Gloria thought; maybe they knew there was no milk there. And Gloria had a strong suspicion that the mother really liked their making passes at her. She guessed Nature provided the mother with the instinct to swat the puppies away from her. They were old enough to eat solid food now and as a good mother it was her duty to make them look out for themselves.

The mother was a marvelous person. Gloria found herself thinking this and since she was alone and not thinking out loud she went on thinking it. The mother was a marvelous person. Such good qualities as there must be in her, the way she held up her head and her ears stood straight up, and the way she would play with her puppies but at the same time not let them get too fresh or have their own way. Then the way she would lie down with her face on her paws, her eyes looking deceptively sleepy as she watched the puppies trying to eat grass or find something edible in the grass. It was really marvelous. There was one black fellow who wanted to play with himself, and every time he did the mother would get up and let him have it with her paw or else pick him up in her mouth and pretend to chastise him. She would put him down after a few moments and by that time his mind would be off sex. But all this time the tan was her favorite, and then Gloria saw something she did not believe. She saw it with her own eyes. She did not know anything about dogs, and maybe this was common practice among dogs, but she made up her mind to ask the next vet if dogs did this all the time. What she saw that she did not believe was a matter between the mother and the tan.

The mother was lying on the grass watching her children (about the way Ann would on the beach when she had hers). The tan was getting ready to squat for Number One. Instantly the mother got up and grabbed him in her mouth and took him to a bush. She put him down and grabbed his hind leg and lifted it. It was all new to him and he struggled, trying to get into a squatting position again, and he leaked a little, but the mother held on and shook him until he stopped leaking. That was all. It must have been one of the first times the mother had done this, but it was wonderful to see. It made Gloria wonder where the father was.

The father. That son of a bitch probably was out on Long Island or Connecticut or Westchester, where it was fashionable and cool, and here was the mother teaching her pup to stand up like a man and not sit down like a pansy. But the mother didn't seem to miss the father. She was self-sufficient, and that was a good thing about women. All that stuff about women must weep or wait or whichever it was. Give a woman her child or her children, and the hell with the men. It was incredible that before her very eyes Gloria had seen all the stuff about motherhood, which she thought was pretty much the bunk, being demonstrated by a police bitch and her litter. But it made her feel good again. It put Bill Henderson in his place as the mere father of Ann's children, and let him put his nurse up on the operating table or do whatever he liked. He wasn't important once he did his part toward making Ann's babies. If you loved a man, so much the better, but you didn't have to love him, you didn't even have to know him. They brought the stuff all the way from France and England and made mares have colts in this country, and they had done it successfully with people in New York, where the father was sterile and both parents wanted a child. Liggett. He had children. Gloria wondered about herself. Three abortions and all the things she had done not to have children probably had a very bad effect. For the first time she wanted a child, and she—

"Gloria! Eddie Brunner wants to speak to you," called her mother.

"I'll be there in a minute," she said.

Eddie might do it. But she didn't want Eddie. She wanted Liggett. Still, Eddie *would* do it. Only too glad.

"Hello."

"Hello, pal. This is Eddie."

"I know."

"I have good news for you, baby. I got a job."

"A job! Eddie, that's wonderful. Where? What doing?"

"Well, it isn't much, only twenty-five bucks a week, but it's something. Drawing for movie ads."

"Oh, swell. When do you start?"

"Right away. I work at home. They'll furnish the Bristol board and all that, but I can work at home. They called up this morning. Yesterday I was pretty sure I had it but I wasn't sure. I did some sketches for them and they seemed pretty sure I could do the kind of stuff they wanted, but this morning they called up and said it was definite. In fact it's going to be more than twenty-five bucks a week. That's what it was going to be originally, on a basis of part-time work, but now they said they could use some of my drawings on every picture. What they'll do is make mats and sell them. Do you know what mats are? Doesn't make any difference. I'll tell you at lunch. Will you have lunch with me?"

"Sure. But I don't want you to spend your money on me. We'll go Dutch Treat."

"Nuts. I buy this lunch. I'll be over for you how soon?"

"You can start right away. I've been up for over an hour. Come right over."

"I'll be over before you can say Jefferson Machamer."

"Jefferson Machamer," she said.

"That's not the way to say it," said Eddie, and hung up.

Eddie was full of plans, few of them making sense when his income was considered. All Gloria had to do was listen. "A small car, an Austin or one of those little Jordans. You know those little Jordans? They don't make them any more, but they were some cars. Or I keep seeing an ad in the paper for a baby Peugeot. I just want a small car."

"Naturally."

"Why naturally?"

"So you won't have to take anyone else for a ride. You want a car to think in, don't you, Baby?"

"That's right," he said. "A car I can think in."

"And Norma and I, we'll just sit around and sew on Sunday afternoons when it's hot. You go out to the country—the North Shore is nice and cool. You go out and you think and Norma and I will sit and wait for you, and then you come home and tell us what you've been thinking. Understand, if you don't *want* to tell us, or you're too tired, it'll keep. What else are you going to do with your money?"

"Well—" they were at the corner of Fifth Avenue and Eighth Street, halted by traffic. "You see those figures on top of the traffic lights?" At that time the traffic light standards were adorned on top with gilt statuettes of semi-nude men in trench helmets.

"Uh-huh."

"Well, I'm going to do something about them. I'm not sure what, but something."

"Somebody ought to."

"I may only buy them, all the way from here to a Hundred and Tenth Street, if they go that far, and send them to a silly old uncle of mine who loves to play with soldiers."

"No."

"No. You're right. I have a better idea, but I don't know you well enough to tell you."

"Certainly not."

"The idea is, how to control female jaywalkers. I would have instead of a light, when it is time for the red light to go on, all the little soldiers would uh, come to attention as it were."

"As it were."

"And all the women would stop, see? They would watch this phenomenon and meanwhile traffic would be rolling by. There's only one difficulty. When the women get tired of watching it we'll have jaywalking again."

"Ho-ho. Women—"

"I know. Women won't ever get tired of watching that phenomenon. This is a *nice* conversation."

"What about men jaywalkers?" said Gloria.

"We have a jaywalker for a mayor," said Eddie.

"Oh, stop it. That isn't even original."

"Yes, it's at least original. It may be lousy, but it's original. Anyway I never heard anyone else say it. That's always my trouble when
I make puns."

"What else with your money?"

"Buy you lunch. Buy you a present. Buy Norma a present—"

"And get a haircut."

Eddie was gay all through luncheon, long after Gloria grew tired
of his fun. She could see that it was more than the prospect of the
job that made him feel good. The other thing was without a doubt
Norma Day. Always before this when he was gay it did not last so
long without encouragement from Gloria; this time he went on, and
in a way that in anyone else she would have called stupid. Not stupid
in Eddie. Eddie did not do stupid things. And God knows he was
entitled to some fun. But twice in one day was too much for this:
first it was Ann Paul with her Mr. Fletcher—Mr. Henderson, rather.
Ann was all packed and everything and moving right out of Gloria's
life. And now Eddie. She could easily have said the hell with Ann.
She didn't like women anyway. Women had no spine. Gloria thought
they were more intelligent than men, but they didn't get as much out
of it as men did. Unless trouble was getting something out of it. Now
that Ann was safe and happy Gloria admitted to herself that what
their schoolmates had suspected might easily have been true. It was
nothing special against Ann. Gloria had a theory that there was a
little of that in practically all women; just get them drunk enough in
the right surroundings. And a lot of them didn't have to get drunk.
She had had passes made at her by dressmakers' fitters, show girls,
women doctors, and—and then she pulled herself out of this. For
every woman who had made a pass at her there were ten, fifteen, a
hundred, a thousand, who had not, and who probably had not the
slightest inclination in that direction. But admitting that she was

factually wrong did not get her out of the general mood. She came back to wishing Ann well, and found herself wanting to be away from Eddie. She was tired of being with him. The only person she wanted to be with was Liggett. She wanted to be home or with Liggett. One or the other. Away from the whole thing, all that was her usual life; Eddie, her friends, the smart places or the gay places, the language she and they spoke, and all about that life. But if she had to have any of it, she wanted all of it. Here, with the bright sun on Fifth Avenue, she was thinking that the only thing she wanted was to be with Liggett, lying in bed or on the floor or anywhere with him, drunk as hell, taking dope, doing anything he wanted, not caring about the time of day or the day of the week and not thinking whether it was going to end. And if not Liggett, then no one. Then she wanted to be home where she could be within sound of her mother's voice, surrounded by the furniture that she would not bump even in the dark. She wanted to be moral. She would stop smoking. She would wear plain clothes and no makeup. She would wear a proper brassière, no nail polish. She would get a job and keep regular hours. And she knew she could do these things, because she knew Liggett would be back. Maybe.

Eddie asked her to have more coffee but she said she had to go home and wait for a call. Like that Eddie understood. His gayety disappeared, he was considerate, he remembered that she had not been participating in his fun. "You go on home," he said. "I'm going uptown, and I'll take a bus from here."

"I'm sorry, Eddie."

"You're sorry? I'm the one to be sorry."

"It just happens today—"

"I know. Go ahead. Kiss me good-by."

"No," she said.

"All right, don't," he said. But she did, and at least made the waiter glad.

She went home, feeling like crying part of the way, and then halfway changing to pleased with herself because she was on her way home, which was a path to righteousness or something.

Three o'clock was striking when she let herself in. Elsie, the maid, was dusting the staircase and could easily have opened the door, but not Elsie. Sometimes Gloria suspected that Elsie, who was colored, knew something of Gloria's Harlem benders. It may have been that, and it may only have been the contrast between the respectful, almost slave-like obedience Elsie accorded Mrs. Wandrous, and the casual, silent manner Elsie showed Gloria.

"Packages come from the stores," said Elsie.

"For me?" said Gloria.

"Yes," said Elsie. She spoke it on a high note, as much as to say, "Why, sure. Who else would be getting packages in this house?"

"Then why don't you say so? . . . Oh, don't answer me." This was a swell way to start the new life, but this nigger irritated her. "What's your husband doing now? Is he working?"

"Why?" said Elsie.

"Don't ask why. Answer my question."

"He's gettin' along. Now and then he gets sumpn. Now may I ask why?"

"You may not." Gloria was on the verge of mentioning Lubby Joe, a Negro big shot the mention of whose name was enough to command respect among most Negroes. But it would be hard to explain how she knew Lubby Joe, and it was a thing that could not be left unexplained. This made her angry too, to start something she could not finish, especially something that would have given her so much pleasure as throwing a scare into Elsie. "Where'd you put the packages?"

"Uh cared them all the way up to your room," said Elsie.

"Yeah man!" said Gloria, in spite of herself.

She was upstairs, trying on the new clothes, when Elsie came in, dust-cloth in hand. "Some man called you on the phone. He lef' this here number."

"God damn you, you black bitch! Why didn't you give me this message when I came in?"

"Uh didn't think."

"Get out of here!"

She called the number, which was a private branch exchange, and the extension number which had been given Elsie. The extension did not answer. The number was the Biltmore. It could have been a *lot* of people, but it *couldn't* have been anyone but Liggett. She sat there half dressed, too furious to curse Elsie, hating the Negro race, hating herself and her luck. In five minutes she called the number again. It was always possible he was in the bathroom the first time. This time she left word that she had called. "Just say that Gloria phoned. The party will know." She only hoped it was Liggett. She was sitting there and she heard the front door close in the careful but not noiseless way her mother closed it. Gloria called to her to come upstairs.

"Certainly is getting warmer. When did you get back? Is Eddie really working?"

"Mother, this is the last straw. I want you to fire Elsie. Today."

"Why, what's she done?"

"I just had a very important message and she forgot to give it to me till just this minute, and of course when I called the party had left."

"Well, you know Elsie has a lot to do. She's got this whole house—"

"You can get any number of niggers that will do twice the work and won't forget a simple little thing like that. I'm sick of her. She's lazy—"

"Oh, no. No, she isn't lazy. Elsie's a good worker. I admit she has her shortcomings, but she isn't lazy, Gloria."

"She is! She's terrible, and I want you to fire her. I insist!"

"Oh, now don't fly off the handle this way over a simple little telephone message. If it's that important the person will call again, whoever it was. Who was it, and why is it so important?"

"It'd take too long to tell you now. I want you to fire Elsie, that's what I want you to do. If you don't I'll tell Uncle Bill. I won't stay here."

"Now look here, just because Elsie does something bad isn't any reason why you should be rude to me. You have your own way quite a lot it seems to me. Too much for your own good. You go around doing as you please, staying away at night and doing dear knows what, and we permit it because—well, I sometimes wonder why we do permit it. But you can't come home and disrupt the whole household because one little thing goes wrong. If you can't appreciate all the things we do, all for you—"

"I'm not going to listen to you." She went to the bathroom and locked the door. In the bathroom was a dressing table with triplicate mirrors and many lights. Even the front of the drawer had a mirror, and whenever she noticed this she thought about the unknown person who designed the table, what he or she must have had in mind: what earthly use could there be for a mirror on a drawer, just that height? What *other* earthly use, that is? It reflected your body right where your legs begin. Did other women really look at themselves as much as she did or what? Yes, she guessed they did, and it was not an altogether unwelcome thought. She wanted to be like other women, now, for the time being. She didn't want to be the only one of her type in the world. She didn't want to be a marked girl, who couldn't get along with the rest of the world. It had started out a good day, and then came Ann, and her joy for Ann didn't hold over an hour; she was bored with Eddie, really her best friend; she fought an undignified fight with Elsie, and she had a quarrel with her mother. Why did days have to start right if they were going to turn out like this? Was it to give you a false sense of security, an angry God, a cruel God, making you feel this was going to be a lovely day, about as swell a little day as you could hope to find, and then— smacko! Four times she had gone smacko! So what about this stuff of starting the day feeling it was going to be a good one? Or maybe it was a merciful God who did it. He gave you a good night's sleep, thereby making you feel good at the beginning of the day, because He knew you were going to have a tough one and you'd need all the optimism you could command. What about God, for that matter? She hadn't thought about God for a long time. Monday she would begin again, because she noticed one thing about people who believed in God: they were warmer people than those who didn't. They had a worse time, but they had a better time too. Catholics. Catholics had more fun on parties than anyone else. The Broadway people were mostly all Catholics or Jews, and they seemed to have a good time. At least the Catholics did. As to the Jews, they never seemed to have a really good time. They were too busy showing off when they were supposed to be having a good time. Like Italians. Gloria at this point changed her classification from Catholic to Irish. The people that seemed to have the best time, at least so far as she had observed, were the Irish Catholics who didn't go to Church. Some of them would confess once a year and then they could start all over again. That didn't seem right to Gloria, if you were going to have a real religion, but it certainly made those Catholics feel good. She decided she wanted to go to a Catholic Church and confess. What a story that would be if she ever told the father all she could tell. The party she went to thinking it was being given by a movie actress and it turned out to be a gangster party, where they had all the girls from a show and the gangsters tied sheets to one girl's wrists and hung her stark naked out the twenty-first-floor window, and when they pulled her in they thought she was dead. All the girls getting stinking as fast as they could because they were afraid to stay sober and afraid to suggest leaving. The two virgins. The dwarf. The very young and toughest of the mob, who never even smiled unless he was hurting somebody. She remembered how frightened she was, because that young man kept staring at her, but the lawyer with whom she had gone to the party told the big shot that she was Park Avenue, and the big shot got enough kick out of thinking his party was shocking her. And it was. She had seen wild parties, but this was beyond wild: the cruelty was what made it stick in her memory. She looked around the bathroom and it made her think of Rome. Rome never saw parties like that. Rome didn't have electric light and champagne and the telephone, thirty-story apartment houses and the view of New York at night, saxophones and pianos. Here she was, just a girl on the town, but about the only thing she had missed was lions and Christians, and she supposed if she hung around long enough she'd have to see that. With an effort she made herself quit this line of thought. It was so real to her that she was sure her mother could hear her thinking. She opened the bathroom door. Her mother had left the bedroom.

She decided to go away. Alone. Think things out. She opened her desk drawer where she kept her money, and she counted more than thirty dollars. Where to on thirty dollars, without asking anyone for more? This place, that place, no, no, no. Then yes: at five-thirty she could take a boat to Massachusetts. The *City of Essex* was leaving at five-thirty. She had enough to go there and back, pay all her meals, tips, magazines. She would take a small overnight bag.

"Miss Glaw-ria, telephone." Elsie from downstairs.

9

THE *CITY OF ESSEX* was built in the late 1870's, and though to this day she is a fairly sturdy craft, her designers were working to catch the custom of a public that was different from today's. Different in quite a few ways, the citizens of the Republic in the Rutherford Birchard Hayes administration were especially different from the Hoover citizens in regard to the sun. When the *City of Essex* was built, the American people, traveling on ocean-going and coastal steamers, liked to be in the shade, or at least did not feel like climbing from one deck to another just to get sunburned. Thus the *City of Essex* had a top deck that was little more than a roof for the dining-room. It had a sort of cat-walk around this roof, abaft the wheel-house.

If they were putting that much money into a boat today they would have a place on the top deck where people could lie and sit in the sun when the weather was fine. They would of necessity have proper handrailing along the edge of the deck. The handrailing would be high enough and strong enough to withstand the usual wear and tear on handrailing.

The *City of Essex,* however, was built in the late 1870's, and no matter how amusing passengers might find the elaborate decorations and furnishings of the dining-room, they could not say much for the handrailing along the top deck of this old side-wheeler. That handrailing was too low; it was dangerous.

But one of the last things Weston Liggett was worrying about, two decks below the top deck, was the handrailing two decks above him. The big worry was whether Gloria was on board the *City of Essex,* and there were other lesser worries. He was a man who a week ago

had a home and now had only a hotel room. He was insanely infatu-
ated with a girl young enough to be his daughter (he would not call it
love: he was too angry with her for that). He had reason to believe
that the girl was aboard this old tub, but he was not absolutely sure.
He was not positive. What was more, he did not want to take any step
toward finding out. He did not want to do any of the things by which
he could find out. He did not want to ask the purser (he did not want
to have anything to do with the purser, who was a round-shouldered
man with a neatly trimmed mustache; thin, and with a way of holding
his cigarette between the knuckles of his first two fingers that made
you think right away of a man fast drying up who at one time had
been a great guy with the women—a man who would be nastily
suspicious of any inquiry about a young woman, rather tall, well
dressed, about twenty-two). He did not want to ask a steward or
anyone else if such a young woman had come on board. Probably in
the back of Liggett's mind all this and the preceding day had been a
strong doubt that his marriage had busted up. The habit of married
thinking does not break so soon, not if the marriage has had time to
mean anything good or bad, and hence the precautions he had been
taking: when he telephoned Gloria he did not leave his name, because
he was not registered at the hotel under his real name but under the
name of Walter Little. He had made the reservation on the *City of
Essex* under the name of Walter Little (the initials were the same as
his own). When he tried to reach Gloria he had not left the phony
name because he was afraid she would not call back any Walter
Little. He had not left his own name because he was almost certain
she would not call any Weston Liggett. And so, all the precautions
before getting on the boat, and after boarding it. Aboard the *City of
Essex* he did not, as he thought of it, wish to show his hand.

So far as anyone could be sure, he was sure that Gloria had no
suspicion that he was aboard. She did not know where he was. He
had been in his room when she phoned, but he had deliberately not
answered. He had not called anyone else from the hotel, and it was
therefore reasonable to suppose that any call would be from Gloria.
He did not at first know why he had not answered, but the moment
the phone stopped ringing he congratulated himself on a master

stroke. Gloria's phoning meant that she was home. It just possibly meant only that she had phoned her home to find out if there had been any messages for her, but that was unlikely. It was more likely that she was home when she phoned his room at the hotel. Acting on his hunches and as part of the master stroke he took a cab to within a block of her house. He dismissed the cab. He was going to be patient. He had his mind made up that if Gloria was in that house he would wait ten hours if necessary until she came out. He bought a couple of afternoon papers at the newsstand at the end of Gloria's block, and looking at his watch very big, so that anyone who saw him would think he had an appointment, he stood with his papers, one open, one folded and tucked under his arm. He did not have long to wait. Less than ten minutes after he—as he thought of it—took up his vigil, Gloria appeared, carrying a bag. He got out of her sight until she got into a taxi. Liggett got into a taxi across the street. He pretended to be undecided about where to go (as he certainly was until Gloria's cab got under way). Then noticing that her cab was turning into a one-way street he told his driver to go through that street until he made up his mind. His mind was made up for him. From one one-way street Gloria's cab went to another one-way street, westbound as was the first. He followed her cab and watched her get out at the Massachusetts and Rhode Island Steamship Company pier. He kept his cab a few blocks longer, got out and took another cab to the M. & R. I. pier, having given Gloria time to get aboard. He knew enough about the M. & R. I. ships, because he had taken them many times when Emily would be spending summers with her family at Hyannisport. He knew that they never left on the dot of 5:30, and he could take the *City of Essex* at the last minute if he so chose. He did so choose, because at next to the last minute a thought came that almost made him give up today's chase: What if Gloria was going on a trip with some other man? Some cheap fellow, to be going on a trip of this kind. It was common and cheap. Worse than Atlantic City. He almost didn't go, but then he thought what the hell? If she wanted to do that, now would be the time to find it out, and if she didn't, it would be a swell opportunity to talk to her and get her to listen to reason about the coat and all the other things he wanted to discuss

with her. He felt weak and impotent when he thought how much of
his life depended on her consent. Just her consent. A whim, perhaps.
She might say no now to something that next week she would say yes
to. So much depended on her consent, and her consent depended so
much on his approach. If he went at her threateningly she might tell
him to go ⸺ himself, but if he went at it in the right way he might
easily get her to agree to everything. And one of the things he was
beginning to want very much to have her agree to was that she should
sleep with him tonight. So when he came aboard the *City of Essex* his
plan was to lie low and after dinner he would talk to her and then see
what happened. He hoped she wasn't the kind that gets seasick on
Long Island Sound.

On the *City of Essex* there is a narrow space of deck belting all the
outside cabins except four on each side of the ship. On the starboard
and on the port side are two sets of four cabins each which the
reader must remember never to take when traveling in the *City of
Essex*. These uncomfortable cabins are just forward of the housing
that covers the side-wheels which propel the ship. Liggett had one of
these cabins.

There was nothing to do but sit and look out the cabin window.
The cabin was very narrow, and Liggett parked his ass on a little
stool and put his forearms on the window sill and smoked cigarettes.
He took off his coat and was more comfortable, and really it wasn't
bad when you looked out the window. The *City of Essex* goes at a
pretty good clip down the North River and up the East, under the
bridges, past the (Liggett was on the port side) wasted municipal
piers of the East River, the unheard-of tramp steamers docked north
of the Brooklyn Bridge, and on up into the section from Mitchel
Place north, occupied by Beekman and Sutton Place buildings which
Liggett knew, inhabited by people he knew. He knew by the sound
when he was near and under the Queensborough Bridge. There was
so much hysterical noise of thousands of straphangers and motorists
hurrying home to their hutches in Queens and Nassau counties. All
the way up the river, and especially in the vicinity of Hell Gate
Liggett kept thinking what a big job it is to be mayor of New York.
All the dock employees, the cop on Exterior Street, the hospital

people, the cops of the Marine Division, the people who worked on Welfare Island (which Liggett of course could not see), the hospital people on one island and the rat-fighters on another, the woman who had to live on a city-owned island because she spread typhoid fever, the men running the ferry-boats, the fellows making repairs under one of the bridges—there were enough of them to make up a good-sized (and probably very horrible-looking) city. And the only name they all knew was James J. Walker. Liggett wondered if Walker ever thought of that—and if he did was it a good thing for him to think of? Maybe he thought of it too often. It was too much of a job for one man. Liggett decided that the next time he saw Walker he would tell him he ought to have a rest (although Walker had just got back from one). Still daylight, and too early by his watch for Liggett to hunt out Gloria.

Blueprints. Did the average person know how many blueprints had to be kept on file for, say, a coal hoist like the one he was passing? There were prints of all the elevations of the building itself, and floor plans and so on; but the prints that a plan engineer had to use, for instance. The average man would look at a switchboard and not know that there was a blueprint for the board itself, then prints for the wiring and insulation, prints for a dynamo, a separate print for various parts like a bearing. Good Lord! what if you could invent a blueprint material that would be a lot better than any now in existence, and marketable at a profit but selling a little lower than any other today? You'd make a fortune that would be like gold. For all the blueprints Liggett had looked at he knew nothing about how the paper was made. Oh, well. That wasn't his line, but all the same it was a fascinating thing to think about. All those thousands of blueprints. Why, in one plant alone, like the Edison plant . . .

A commuting boat, owned by a fellow Liggett knew, and supported by five acquaintances of Liggett's, caught up with and passed the *City of Essex* like a bat out of hell. The commuting boat, a two-step hydroplane with Wright Typhoons, was up out of the water and going like a bat out of hell. Why did people take such chances in the East River, when a floating cigar box hitting the hull when the commuting boat was going that fast, would smash through the hull and

raise hell, probably kill all the passengers and the small crew.
"Jesus, but some guys are God damn fools," said Liggett. If that
was their idea of a thrill, all right; but as a way to get home it was
lousy. Granted that the Long Island was not the ideal railroad, it
would still be better than getting killed in a boat like that. It would
be safer and quicker to take a plane, because you could land a plane
near the yacht club which was this boat's home port. It wouldn't be
more expensive to use a plane, either. *What* God damn fools some
fellows were! Every single one of them a married man with at least
one kid, and at least one of the fellows really was not in a position to
pay his share of the tremendous cost of this boat. Why did they do
things that way, or anyway why go so fast?

But Liggett was only thinking from momentum after reminding
himself that those fellows were married. He wasn't thinking much at
all; because the sight of a boat speeding husbands homeward did not
make him feel good. The next time he went home there would be
strain even between the girls and himself. Emily, naturally you
would expect it of her. But it would have communicated itself to the
girls—if indeed Emily had not actually told them that their father
would not be living at home any more. Ruth. The thing that made
him kiss her hand in the station wagon. The way she had taken
charge at the family luncheon. Oh, the things he wanted to do for
her, the things he wanted to do with her. He realized that for a
couple of years now he had been having the beginning of anticipa-
tion of the day when he would be able to take her out to dinner and
the theater and a night club, to boat races and football games. Probably there wouldn't be many times like that; she was a beautiful kid.
"Jesus, sometimes she takes your breath away," he thought. Not
beautiful in a conventional way. It was more in the eyes, the set of
her chin when she was sitting quietly on a porch or in a corner, not
knowing she was being watched. He guessed there were no new
things that a father could feel about his daughter. But he guessed no
father felt so deeply, little though he might show it. You couldn't
show it much with Ruth. Kissing her hand like that on Sunday—it
had just come over him and he had done it, and he knew she liked it.

That was good. Her liking it. She liked him better than she did Emily. No, but in a different way. And he liked her so much better than when she was a little kid. She got bigger, and your love got bigger. She was more completely a girl, a person, and your love was more complete. He wanted to be with her all the time she was pregnant, when she was having her first baby by the swell young guy she would marry. Not some older guy who had gone around and laid a lot of girls and was out of college five or ten years, but someone her own age. Like those two people in one of the Galsworthy novels, only they were cousins, weren't they? And they had to be careful not to have children. Ruth. Lovely, dear Ruth, that a father could love.

The tears were in his eyes and one or two out over the lower lid, and he became aware that he had not noticed it at first because dusk had come and darkness was coming. The light was gone. You were conscious of the curtains in the windows of the small yachts that the *City of Essex* passed. He was hungry. The clean feeling he had from loving Ruth did not last long. He remembered what he was to do on this boat.

GLORIA was hungry too. One more discomfort. The other was that ever since she had come aboard the *City of Essex* she had wanted to go to the bathroom, and she was afraid to go. She had used toilets in speakeasies where to breathe the air seemed pretty risky. But there was something intimate about a speakeasy in the family. No one who went to the same speakeasy as you did would be so mean as to give you something. That was almost the way she felt about speakeasy toilets; but she always took elaborate precautions anyway. But on this old boat everything was so *old.* The women's toilet (as distinguished from the ladies' room in a speakeasy, the johnny at school, the little girls' room at a party in an apartment, and the wash-my-hands on a train) was clean enough, and an elderly Negress was there to sell you safety pins. Gloria took one look, went into one of the toilets, and then came right out. The old Negress probably thought she was crazy, but this was not Gloria's day for caring what old or young Negresses thought. Finally, after failing altogether to win out by "not thinking about it," she gave in, went to the bathroom, came back and was ready for a fight or a frolic and a small steak.

She was working on the steak when a woman spoke to her. Gloria was alone at a table for two, the woman was alone at a table for four. "Always a nice breeze on Long Island Sound, isn't there?" said the woman.

"Yes, isn't there?" said Gloria.

"It's my first ride on one of these boats, although ha ha I've been to Europe several times. But I wanted to take this ride to see what it was like."

"Yes. Mm-hmm," said Gloria.

"Just about what I expected. I wonder where we're off of right now do you suppose? Think we passed New Haven? Because I have friends live there. I'm from— I'll bet you didn't come as far as I did for this trip. You're a New Yorker, I can tell that, aren't you?"

"You can tell it to anyone you please," was what Gloria wanted to say. "Yes, New York," was what she said.

"Want to come over and sit at my table? There isn't anyone else sitting here, and we're the only ladies traveling by ourselves I notice."

"Well—do you mind if I finish my steak? It'd be so much trouble to move now. But thank you. I'll have dessert with you if I may." She wished she had what some girls had: the ability to get rid of bores, instead of talking nervously and not thinking what she was saying. She didn't want to have dessert with this school-teacher or whatever she was.

"Then I'll come over to your table. I'm all finished eating, but I'd like to have a cigarette, only I hate to light one here when I'm sitting by myself. It looks funny. Yih know? When yih see a woman eating by herself smoking in a public restrunt. Where are you from? Oh, you did tell me, New York. Tsih. I want to go to New York for a real stay some time. I'm always going some place when I go to New York, on my way to Europe or else home after being to Europe. Oh, did I burn you?" Hot sulphur from the woman's match was scratched loose and stung Gloria's wrist. "Here, let me have a look. . . . No, it's all right. It may burn a little. I'd put something on it if I were you. Awful the way they make these matches. I suppose that Ivan what's his name made these. The match king, from Denmark. No, Sweden. Do you see that man over there with the cigar? That's the reason why I wanted to sit with somebody. He's drunk."

"He *looks* sober," said Gloria.

"Not, though. Drunk as a coot. Tight as a tick."

"Tight as a tick. Did you make that up? Just now?" said Gloria.

"Oh, no. Why, we say that all the time at home. Tight as a tick? Didn't you ever say that?"

"Never heard it before in my life. What does it mean? What is a tick?"

"Well, I've always wondered that too, but I guess it must be something tight. It couldn't mean the tick of a watch, because I don't see anything tight about the tick of a watch. What do they say in your crowd when someone is three sheets to the wind?"

"I have no crowd."

"Well—I mean, your friends. What do they say when someone is under the weather?"

"Oh," said Gloria. "Well, I don't think you'd like what they say."

"Really? Why? Is it risqué?"

"Yes, a little."

"Tell me. What is it? I won't be shocked."

"Well," said Gloria. "Most of my friends, my *men* friends, they say, 'I was stewed to the balls last night.' My girl friends—"

"Really. I took you for a lady but I see I was wrong. Excuse *me,* " said the woman, and stood up and left the room.

"I didn't have to do that, but I guess I had to," Gloria told herself. "Now I'd like a drink, and isn't it nice? I won't be able to get one." She smoked a cigarette, hoping the strange woman would come back and think she looked funny. She went out on deck, and on the radio on deck the Connecticut Yankees were plugging Mr. Vallée's recording of "The Wind in the Willows." The air was pretty good. There was no moon.

This was one of Gloria's nights for not looking at men. At a party or at a ball, in a railroad station or a public speakeasy, on the street,

at a football game, Gloria always did one of two things about the
matter of looking at men. She either did one or the other: she either
got the eye of a stranger and stared him down, giving him a complete and unmistakable going over the way few American men have
the nerve to do with American women; or else she all but did what
they call in the movies "fig bar." Fig bar is a term which covers the
whole attitude of the very bashful child; the toes turned in, eyes
lowered, and especially the finger in the mouth. Gloria could be
bashful when she wanted to, and she frequently wanted to. She never
got over her real terror of a strange crowd. She could not recall a
time when this was not true. It was true of her as a child, and on one
occasion it had made her do something she never got over regretting.
It was at a party, and it was that she had stayed with a man with four
other people looking on; two men, two women. The other women
wanted to do it, and did, but Gloria was the first. It was one of the
few times in her life that she did something that made her repeatedly
ask why she had done it. When she discovered that the reason probably was that she was showing off more intensely than ever before,
and that the reason for wanting to show off was this unconquerable
shyness—it didn't make the whole thing any better. She was glad
when one of the women who had seen it, a second-string movie
actress, died. That made one less person who had seen it. She
wished the others would die, too. But she did not wish it very
strongly, because she knew that the other woman, not the actress,
probably wished Gloria dead too. And it did nothing to cure her
shyness. It only made it worse. Sometimes just as she was about to
enter a bar she would remember the time—and she could hardly
force herself to enter the bar. Other times she would be passing a
row of tables and she would hate her evening gown for the very
things that had influenced her selection of it: its décolletage, the way
it fit over the hips. Full well she knew the movement of her own hips
as she walked, as though each hip were a fist, clenching and un-
clenching, and the rhythm locked forever, reminding her of a metro-
nome. She knew, because she had watched other girls. A girl walks
across a room, her hips going *tick-tock tick-tock.* The girl becomes
self-conscious and stops at a table, interrupting the rhythm with the

hip resting on *tick;* but when she resumes her walk, *tock* goes the other hip, and *tick-tock.*

It was dark on deck and on Long Island Sound. The thin bars of light on Long Island and Connecticut shore were better light than the cheap lamps on deck. Gloria told the steward to put a chair in the middle of the deck for her. She did not notice anyone.

Thus she did not see Liggett, who was leaning against the rail on the starboard side, looking at Long Island and being honest with himself in that he was guessing, and guessing only, the position of the *City of Essex.* When he heard Gloria's heels on deck he tightened up. He knew the sound for the sound of a girl's shoes. He turned and saw that she did not look in his direction. He watched a steward put a chair down for her. He left and went to the dining-room.

The Negro waiter was none too pleasant about giving him something to eat, as it was past the dinner hour, but Liggett was not in a mood for humoring waiters. When the Negro brought the soup Liggett said: "Take that back. It's cold." He knew the Negro was making a face at him and when he began to mumble Liggett looked up and said: "What?" so quickly that you could hardly hear the *t.* All aspirate. Then the white headwaiter came over and asked if there was anything wrong, and Liggett said no, thank you. The Negro picked up the plate and the headwaiter followed, obviously asking him what the hell was going on. The Negro answering the man said the soup was cold, the headwaiter telling him well, then for Christ's sake bring *hot* soup and be quick about it, and the Negro whining that cole soop want his faul, chef to blame for cole soop and anyway looka what time tis. Liggett was pretty well pleased with the way he had handled the situation, not snitching to the headwaiter.

Abruptly, he stood up. The headwaiter rushed over to him. "Anything wrong, sir?"

"I don't feel well. I think I'd better have some air." He didn't feel sick but he certainly didn't want to eat his dinner. "Never mind the dinner."

"I'm sorry, sir," said the headwaiter.

" 'T's all right," said Liggett.

He went up on deck again and Gloria was not in her chair. She was standing at the rail on the port side. It was noticeably colder and the only other people on deck were an Italian-American and his wife and two children, the Italian trying to get his money's worth of sea air, and the sleepy wife and children looking up to him for the signal to go to bed.

"Hello," said Liggett.

Gloria turned to give him cold stare Number 25, but said: "Good God!"

"I'm quite a stranger," said Liggett. "I'll say it for you."

"I wasn't going to say that. What—how did you happen to be on this boat?"

"You don't think I just happened to be on board, do you?"

"No, but how did you know I was going to be on this boat?"

"I followed you."

"Ooh. What a cheap trick. Followed me."

"Well, I had to see you."

"You didn't have to follow me. You could have called me again."

"Then I'd have missed you. You left your house a short time after you got my message."

"It was your message. I thought it was."

"Yes, it was my message. Do you want to sit down?"

"Not particularly."

"I do."

"I'd rather stand. Aren't you afraid people will know you?"

"Who, for instance? Those Italians? They look like friends of mine?"

"You never can tell."

"Anyway, there they go," said Liggett. "Now listen to me for five minutes, will you please?"

"I'll sit down now. I'm weak."

"Why?"

"Well, the way you suddenly appear."

"Been on the boat since five-thirty."

"You kill me."

"Here. Do you want to sit here?" he said. "Now look here—"

"Oh, no, thanks. I don't want any of those now look here discussions."

"I'm sorry. How shall I begin?"

"Are you all right? I mean after the fight? I thought you'd be hurt pretty badly."

"I may have a rib kicked loose."

"Well, don't fool around with that, then. I knew a boy had a rib kicked loose in football and finally it punctured his lung."

"You wouldn't want that to happen to me, would you?"

"No. Whether you believe it or not, I wouldn't."

"Why not? Simple humanitarian instincts or what?"

"No. Better than that. Or worse."

"What?"

"I love you."

"Aw-haw. That's a laugh."

"I know."

"What makes you think you love me?"

"I don't know. Nothing makes me think I love you. It's closer than that. It isn't as far away from me as something making me think I love you. It's knowing that I do love you. I don't expect you to believe it, but it's true."

"I beg your pardon. Have a cigarette."

"Oh, how nice. American cigarettes. There's a big fine if you're caught smuggling them into Massachusetts."

"Don't kid."

"All right."

He reached for her hand, but she would not let him hold it. "No. You wanted to talk. Talk, then."

"All right," he said. "Well, in the first place, I've left my wife. Or rather—I don't know how to put it. Technically I *have* left my wife—"

"Permanently?"

"Permanently? Why, yes. Of course permanently."

"Of course permanently," she repeated. "As a matter of fact you don't know whether it's permanently or not. I can tell by your tone, you haven't even thought about that phase of it."

"No, I guess I haven't figured it out by months and days and years. Are you cold?"

"Yes. But we'll stay here."

"You don't have to be nasty about it. I merely asked."

"I'm sorry."

"Well, to get back to the subject. My wife and I have split up. Permanently. I told her about you—"

"Why did you do that?"

"I didn't mention your name."

"That isn't what I meant. Why did you tell her before you told me?"

"I didn't have much chance to tell you, remember."

"Even so you should have told me. You should have waited. What did you do that for? I'm not a home-wrecker. You have children. It's the worst kind of luck to break up a home. You should have told me first."

"I don't see what difference that would have made. It had nothing to do with the facts."

"What facts? You mean my sleeping with you? Did you tell her I slept with you in your apartment? Did you?"

"Yes."

"Oh, you fool. You awful fool. Oh. Oh. Oh, Liggett. Why did you do that? You poor man. Ah, kiss me."

He kissed her. She put her hand on the back of his neck. "What else did you do? What else did you tell her?" she said.

"I told her everything except your name."

"What did she say?"

"Well, I didn't give her much chance to say anything. I told her I loved you."

"Yes. And didn't she ask you my name? No, she wouldn't want to know that. She'll find out soon enough, I suppose."

"I didn't want to tell her your name. I wouldn't have if she'd asked me."

"She wouldn't be in any hurry to know that now. What are her plans?"

"I'm not sure. I told her I'd give her a divorce in New York if she wanted it. I'd give her grounds."

Gloria laughed. "You already have."

"That's exactly what she said."

"Is she going to accept your kind offer?"

"I think she plans to go to Reno."

"Why go to all that expense? Get her to get one in New York. I'll be the unidentified woman in the lacy negligee."

"No. Reno's better."

"It's expensive. It costs a lot of money to go to Reno, so I'm told."

"But I think she wants to go to Reno, so whatever she wants to do is all right with me, except we'll have to have some arrangement about my seeing the children."

"How old are they?"

"Ruth, the older one, she's going on sixteen, or maybe she is sixteen, and the younger one, Barbara, she's two years younger."

"Yes, I remember now. You did tell me. But that's not so good. Isn't the older one going to have a coming-out party?"

"I doubt it like hell. Those things cost. Two years ago, yes. But not this year, or next year."

"Next year we're going to have a revolution."

"Where do you get that kind of talk? Revolution. In this country? We might have a Democrat president, but—or is that what you mean by revolution."

"I mean bloody revolution. Heads on staffs or staves or whatever you call them. Pikes. Your head, for instance. All the rich. Your head and a straw hat with a Racquet Club band on it. That's the way they're going to tell which heads to cut off. Dekes, Psi U's, Racquet Club, Squadron A."

"Will you marry me?" he said.

"I was trying to get your mind off that. You don't have to feel you're bound to ask me that."

"It's pretty obvious that I'm not doing this because I have to. It's because I want to. Do you *want* to get married?"

"To you, yes, but—"

"There are no buts. If you want to, we will. There isn't any other consideration."

"On the contrary, there are thousands of other considerations, but they don't matter."

"That's what I meant."

"No, it isn't. But we won't argue the point. Yes, I'll marry you. You get the divorce fixed up and all that and I'll marry you and I'll be a good wife, too."

"I know you will."

"Oh, not for the reason you think. You think because I've been around like a man and I'm ready to settle down. That's not the real reason why I'll be a good wife."

"Isn't it?"

"Absolutely not. Do you want to know the real reason? Because it's born in me. My mother. I was thinking today what a wonderful wife she was to my father, and still is after all these years. In a way of course you're right. Living the kind of life I've led then finding out that there's only one life for a woman. I know you'd rather not have me mention the kind of life I've led, but I can't just pretend it never existed."

"Where's your stateroom?"

"It's on my key. Where's yours? I'd rather go to yours."

He told her how to get to his. "I'll go down now," he said.

"I'll be down in five minutes," she said.

In his stateroom he thought what an awful place it was to bring her to. Then when she knocked on his door he was embarrassed some more. He sat on the lower berth and she faced him and he put his arms around her at the hips. Here she was, just under her clothes, standing with her hands holding the upper berth and ready for anything he wanted.

"No!" she said.

"What?"

"I don't want you to," she said.

"You will," he said. "Sit down."

"No, darling." She sat down on the berth beside him.

"What's the matter?" he said.

"I don't know."

"Yes, you do. What is it?"

She looked half way around the tiny stateroom and then brought her head back to looking straight ahead.

"Oh," he said. "But it won't always be like this."

"But I don't want it ever to be like this, ever again. Not even now."

"Then we can go to your room," he said.

"No. It isn't much better. It's bigger, but not better. It's still a dirty little stateroom on the *City of Essex.*"

"Only for tonight," he said. "I want you so much. I love you, Gloria."

"Yes, and I love you even more. Ah, no. Look. Look at that bed. Those sheets. They weigh a ton. Damp. Cold. And we can't both stand up at the same time in this room. Oh, the whole thing. Like a traveling salesman and his chippy."

"You're no chippy, and I'm not a traveling salesman. We're as good as married now. Signing a lot of papers won't make us more so."

"Yes, it will. Not signing the papers, but what the papers imply will. I'm going up to get some air and then to my room. Do you want to come along?"

"To your room?"

"No. On deck. I won't stay with you tonight, on this boat. If you don't want to come with me, all right, darling. I'll see you in the morning. When we get off the boat we can go to a hotel and I'll go right to bed with you. But not here."

"Mm."

"It isn't scruples. You know that. It's just so God-damned—"

"Cheap and vulgar, I suppose. You're a fine one to talk."

"I know. That's just it. Good night. If you don't want to see me in the morning, all right. Good night."

He did not answer, and she left. He sat there, hating her for a moment, for the truth was he wanted her in this room almost as much as he wanted her at all. The very smallness of the room would make it good, like being in a box. It would be new.

And then he began to see what she meant. He was sorry for what he had said (but knew he could make it up). What he wanted to do was to see her before she went to bed, tell her he was sorry, and tell her she was right about the room. She was no common tart, and she had a right to object to lying on this bed. He put on his vest and coat and left the room.

The sounds that the boat made muffled the heavy thump of his feet on the deck. That was the only way he knew how noisy the boat was. Ordinarily he made a lot of noise walking, but the big pistons that turned the side wheels, and the wheels themselves, and the nose of the *City of Essex* pushing into the water, and the rather stiff offshore breeze—it wasn't sail. "Jeep," he said, when he meant to say Gee. The breeze filled his mouth and made him gulp.

One deck, two decks, and no Gloria. He saw a sign hanging from a cord, Passengers Not Allowed on Top Deck After 8 P.M. That's where she would be.

He climbed over the cord and the sign and walked slowly up the stairs. There was no need to proceed quietly. Apparently every passenger had gone to bed and it was Liggett's guess that no deckhand would be at work on the *City of Essex* at this hour.

At the top of the steps he could see only the outline of the wheelhouse, and the *City of Essex*'s single stack and some ventilators. There was one short string of light on the shore, and it was all dark otherwise. Then he saw Gloria, he guessed it was Gloria, sitting on the dining-saloon roof. She turned at that moment and saw him, her eyes having become better accustomed to the darkness. She got up and ran forward. Then she stopped and looked around.

"Oh, all right," he called, and turned and started down the stairway. Half way down he heard a scream, or thought he heard a scream. He ran down the few remaining steps, and this time he knew he heard a scream. He looked down at the water just in time to see Gloria getting sucked in by the side wheel. Then the boat stopped.

"There was nothing I could do," said Liggett to nobody.

10

THERE IS NOT much room between the blades of the side wheels and the housing that covers each wheel. It was half an hour before they got what was left of Gloria out from between the blade and the housing, and nobody wanted to do it then. If she had fallen overboard abaft the housing she would have been shot away from the *City of Essex* by the force of the wheel, but where she fell was just forward of the housing, and there is a tremendous suck there. The *City of Essex* is always pulling in floating timber and dead dogs and orange peel, and sometimes when the wheel makes its turn the stuff is kicked out again. Sometimes not. The men in the wheelhouse heard the second scream and signaled to stop. By that time Gloria was caught by the blades and was pulled up into the housing, counterclockwise, in one long crush. She probably was killed the first time a blade batted her on the skull, by the same blade that pulled her up into the housing. There was no place in her body where there was a length of bone unbroken more than five inches. One A. B. fainted when he saw what he was going to have to do. The captain of the *City of Essex,* Anthony W. Parker, had only seen one thing like it before in his life, and that was a man in the black gang of the old *Erma* when the *Erma*'s boiler burst off Nantucket in 1911. Captain Parker directed the removal of the woman's body from the wheel. He and two A. B.'s entered the housing from inside the boat. The A. B.'s carried an ordinary army blanket. One of the A. B.'s accepted a slug of brandy from the captain's flask; the other man was going to take one, but he decided he could work better without it. They put the blanket over the body first, then gently rolled the body over and into the blanket. Captain Parker helped them carry the body inside the hull. "Go on back and see if you can find the other hand," said Captain Parker. "She may have been wearing a ring. Have to find out who she is." The search for the other hand was unsuccessful.

"Keep that covered up," said Captain Parker, when the blanket fell open. "Go on back with you," he said, to the engine room crew who had collected.

The chief steward was called and he sent for one of the stewardesses, a middle-aged Negress. She screamed and was hard to manage, and it took five minutes for them to persuade her to examine just the girl's clothing, which they showed her by lifting a corner of the blanket. It took ten more minutes to get some answer out of her, and then she said yes, she recognized the dress, and gave the number of Gloria's stateroom. The captain sent someone there, and the someone returned, saying it must be her, her bed hadn't been slept in and the room didn't look occupied.

"She only come aboard to do the Dutch act," said Captain Parker. It was a hell of a thing. A young girl. Probably in the family way. The thought never crossed his mind that it was anything but suicide. A young girl, maybe eighteen, maybe twenty-one, according to the stewardess, who came on board alone, ate alone, according to the chief steward (who remembered her come to think of it, after hearing the stewardess describe her; and was corroborated by the purser), and was not seen talking to anyone. Captain Parker had to make a complete report for the owners and for the port authorities in New York and Massachusetts. Some assistant district attorney that wanted to get his name in the paper probably would be down snooping around and trying to make something of it. But here was one case of premeditated suicide and no two ways about it. It was too bad she didn't jump off the stern, but if you wanted to die that much it probably didn't make much difference which way you did it. Captain Parker hoped for her sake she got one on the skull when she was drawn in, otherwise it was a terrible death, judging from the looks of her. A terrible death. Well, girls got themselves in the family way these days irregardless of all the ways they had now that they didn't use to have to keep from getting that way. Captain Parker wondered whether he ought to say the Lord's Prayer over the body, but he looked around at his officers and men, and no, no Lord's Prayer in front of them. Fanchette, one of the A. B.'s, from Pawtucket, had crossed himself when he saw the body. That was enough. If the girl's family wanted to, they could have a service and all the prayers they wanted.

The *City of Essex* resumed her trip, and the next morning in port the passengers were asked to give their names and addresses before leaving the ship. Otherwise to most of the passengers the trip was as usual, and many left the boat unaware of what had occurred. Liggett had one awful moment when he almost forgot to write Walter Little instead of his real name. He took a taxi from the pier to the railroad station and from there took the first train to New York.

11

THE TRIP TO New York was old, old scenery for Liggett—the years in prep school and college and at Harvard and on leave during the war and visiting Emily at Hyannisport. But he never took his eyes off the scenery, old or not. There comes one time in a man's life, if he is unlucky and leads a full life, when he has a secret so dirty that he knows he never will get rid of it. (Shakespeare knew this and tried to say it, but he said it just as badly as anyone ever said it. "All the perfumes of Arabia" makes you think of all the perfumes of Arabia and nothing more. It is the trouble with all metaphors where human behavior is concerned. People are not ships, chess men, flowers, race horses, oil paintings, bottles of champagne, excrement, musical instruments, or anything else but people. Metaphors are all right to give you an idea.)

Liggett thought he knew what had happened, and he called himself a murderer. Then he stopped calling himself a murderer, because he began to like it, and this was no time to like what you were calling yourself. A murderer is a man in an opera box with a black cape and a dirk; a man with a .38 automatic and an unfaithful wife; a man in leather chaparejos with many conchos, and a Marlin rifle. It is a hard thing to get away from the thinking you do as a boy, when you learn that a murderer is a noble criminal. You have to unlearn it. Liggett had seen one murder in his life. In France. He had seen many men killed, and some in hand-to-hand fighting, but only one murder. One of his men was fighting a German and getting the best of the German, with the German beginning to bend over backward against the trench. The American could easily have taken care of the German, but one of Liggett's sergeants, taking his time about it, came up and fired his pistol twice into the German's ear. That was murder. And in his way the sergeant was a murderer. He belonged to the long line of murderers and not of warriors. Gang killings were murder.

It was a reprehensible thing, but murderers bore some relation to history. What he had done bore no relation to history, and never would. He hoped it never would. He didn't want it to. He hated having this secret but he wanted no one else to have it—and knew that he was leaning forward in his seat so that the train would hurry and he could spill it all to Emily.

Now there was Emily. Always before there had been Emily and always would be. He thought away from that, the way on a train you think away from things. A good thought comes and is the big thing in your mind, but it sticks there and the click of the car wheels over the joints, especially on lines that use 90-pound and other light rail, lulls you to sleep with your eyes open, the thought sticking in your mind, then forgotten, supplanted by another thought.

Thus the thought of Emily, giving way to the thought of what had happened last night. He could see it all, including what he had missed. When Gloria ran and he called to her, he believed she could hear his voice, the angry tone, but not the words; and so she ran again when he called, "Oh, all right." She was headed for the stairway on the port side, behind the wheelhouse but pretty far forward, hoping to get away from him by running down the stairs. But in the darkness and on account of the motion of the ship she ran smack into the rail, which is extremely low on the top deck of the *City of Essex*. She most likely hit the rail just below or just about at her ʼnees. The forward throw of the upper part of her body—and she into the water. The scream, and then the second scream, and he ʼhe could not save her, knew it the fraction of a second after he ʼended what was happening. Well, he could have died with

He would tell it all to Emily. Yes, he knew he was afraid not to tell her. If she told him to go to the police and tell what happened, he would do it. But he would not tell them without being told to do it. Yes, he knew he hoped she would tell him not to go to the police.

At Grand Central he went through the passage and up the steps to the Biltmore, got his key, went to his room, came down and paid his bill. Back to the Grand Central, he gave the bag to a Red Cap (he did not want anyone to see him carrying it). He told the Red Cap to check the bag and bring him the check. He bought the afternoon papers. The story was on the front pages of the *Journal* and the *Telegram*—the *World-Telegram,* they were calling it now, and it looked like something they got out during a printer's strike. There was nothing in the *Evening Post,* the paper Emily read. The *Journal* had a headline: MYSTERY DEATH N. Y. GIRL IN L. I. SOUND. The story was to the effect that mystery surrounded the death of Gloria Wandrous, 18, brunette, pretty, and her leap to death from the *City of Essex.* She was identified by *her clothing!*

Liggett read no more. What about Emily's coat? Where in God's name was that coat? If Gloria had kept it at home it would be easy to identify it. The police never had any trouble identifying a thing like that, an expensive mink coat. They would go right to Emily. It was all right for her, but where was her husband that night? What was her coat doing in Miss Wandrous's apartment or house? Did she know Miss Wandrous? Did she know of her husband's relations with Miss Wandrous? Was she shielding her husband? Where was her husband that night? Then that cop in the speakeasy. He would make a report. The bartender would see it in the papers and he would comment on it to the cop, and the cop would report that the girl had had trouble with a man's attentions the Tuesday before she killed herself—*if* she killed herself. Then the people in the speakeasy the night he introduced himself to Gloria. They were the kind of people who reveled in anything like inside information when there was a scandal. "Did you read about poor Gloria? Gloria Wandrous? Yes. Why, yes. Why, we were with her and what's his name, Weston Liggett, at Duilio's the other night. Isn't it awful? The poor kid. I thought Liggett had taken quite a shine to her." Then there was that kid, Brunner. Just a friend, Gloria had said, but a friend would be worse now than a lover. All her lovers were checking their alibis for last night, and they would be only too glad to keep out of the whole thing, but not a friend. Liggett went home.

He still had his key and he let himself in. The maid answered his questions: No, there had been no callers or telephone messages; yes, Mrs. Liggett was out and would be back around three o'clock. She was shopping, the maid said.

Liggett chain-smoked cigarettes and poured himself a drink but could not drink anything but water. Then he sat down and wrote Emily a note. "Emily," he wrote. "Please meet me at '21' at four o'clock. This is terribly important and I beg of you to come. W." Then he called Lockheed, next in charge at the office, and told Lockheed he had been ill—"confidentially I've been on my semi-annual bender"—and Lockheed said everything was under control, no messages of any importance, he would send up bids on the Brooklyn job for Liggett's approval, but it didn't look like they would get the contract as old John McCooey was sore about something. . . .

Liggett had had an idea. He would go to Brunner and ask him quite frankly whether he knew anything about the fur coat. He was sure Brunner did know about the coat. It was the kind of thing Gloria would regret doing, and she would discuss it with a friend. And Liggett believed it possible for Gloria to have a friend. He believed Brunner was her friend. He had had a girl the other night. Not bad, either; and a man who was having an affair with Gloria wouldn't be likely to bring along an attractive girl. Anyway, Liggett's plan was to tell Brunner he had read about Gloria, how sorry he was, how much he loved Gloria. He might even go so far as to say he and Gloria planned to get married, but he would have to be careful how he did that. He would have to be ready to say that now that she was dead, there was no use having a lot of trouble—two young girls—the coat. If he knew how to get the coat or where it was, he was sure that was what Gloria would want done.

Liggett found the address in the telephone book, and went there by subway and on foot. Brunner, thank God, was in. He recognized

Liggett, which encouraged Liggett but also put some worry in reserve.

"Mr. Brunner, I don't know whether you remember me," said Liggett.

"Yes. Mr. Liggett. What can I do for you?"

"Well—no, thanks. I've been smoking too much all day. I guess you know why I came."

"I imagine something about Gloria. You knew she—"

"I just saw it in the afternoon papers," said Liggett. "I don't know how to start. You were her best friend, she told me."

"Guess so."

"Did she tell you about us, about our plans?"

"Well, I knew you were having an affair," said Eddie. Eddie stood up. "Listen, did you come here about that God damn coat? Because if you did, there it is. Take it and stick it. I don't want you coming here with a long face and all you're worried about is are you going to get mixed up in a public scandal. You want the coat, so take it. I'm sure I don't want it. She didn't want it either. The only reason she took the God damn thing was because you tore the clothes off her. Guys like you put her where she is today. I wouldn't be surprised if you were the real—" The doorbell rang.

"Who's that?"

"Probably a friend of mine." Eddie pushed the release button and then poked his head out and looked down the hall. "Who is it?"

"Mr. Brunner? My name is Malloy and I would like to talk to you spare a minute of your time I'd like to ask you a few spare if you—"

"Talk sense, what do you want? Oh, it's *you.*"

"I think I'll run along," said Liggett.

"All right," said Eddie. "I'll send you those drawings. Where do you want them? Home or your office?"

"Uh—home, if it isn't too much trouble," said Liggett.

"Just as much trouble to send it home as to your office," said Eddie. "Good day, sir."

"May I come in?" said Malloy.

"Not if you're going to get tough you can't."

"Oh-h, I remember you."

"Yeah, you oughta," said Eddie. "Well, what do you want? Are you looking for a piano player?"

"No, this is business. I'm a reporter. From the *Herald Tribune.*"

"Oh."

"Well, it's a living. Or was till today. I think this may be my last assignment, so help me out, will you? I got drunk yesterday on the Crowley story. Jesus, did they shoot up that place! You know the story?"

"I haven't been out to get a paper."

"Two-Gun Crowley? They got him yesterday. They had the whole Police Department up there, Ninetieth Street, West Side. Crowley and another guy and Crowley's girl."

"Oh, did they kill him?"

"No, not him. But he'll burn. Whenever you kill a cop you burn. When two lines intersect the vertical angles are equal, and when somebody kills a cop they burn, and when I get excited on a story I usually get stewed. I told them I got some tear gas, but I didn't get away with it."

"Tell me some more about yourself, Mister."

"No, not now. Some other time. Maybe tomorrow. I came here to ask you about this Gloria Wandrous. You were a pretty good friend of hers, weren't you? You were, weren't you?"

"Not the way you mean."

"Well, that's what I want to know. Who was? I want to get a line on her friends. I'm not writing the story. I'm just what they call digging up facts. Me digging up facts, for Christ's sake. I *write.* I'm not a digger."

"You're an artist."

"In my way. So are you. You probably think you're a good painter. Another George Luks or uh, Picasso, to name two. The only two I can think of."

"Listen, Bud, if it's all the same to you."

"Well, when did you last see Miss Wandrous?"

"About a week ago. No, I saw her Sunday night."

"Mm. That's very funny. Then it couldn't have been you having lunch with her only yesterday at the Brevoort. She left first and you took a bus uptown. But of course if you say so."

"Are you going to put this in the paper?"

"That's what I'm supposed to be, a reporter."

"Well, then you'd better get it straight."

"I won't get it straight if you hold out on me or lie. Listen, is this the first time you were ever interviewed by the working press? If it is, let me tell you something. The rest of the boys will be here in a little while. The *Trib* isn't a scandal sheet so you'll get a better break telling me the truth than telling me a lie. If you tell me the truth I'll know what to print. But if you start telling those boys from the tabs lies they'll have you tied in knots. They're real reporters. I'm not. I'm the kind of reporter that wants to be a dramatic critic, but those babies will tear this place upside down—"

"And where will the police be while all this is going on?"

"Probably outside to see that you don't get away. There's one guy on this story that was born in this neighborhood, and he knows all the angles. Now you come across with some straight talk and then I'll give you a lift uptown. Was she depressed when you saw her yesterday?"

"Yes."

"Why?"

"She didn't tell me. I thought she had spring fever."

"She didn't give you any hint of why she was depressed?"

"Nope."

"Was she pregnant?"

"Liss-senn."

"Who was she that way about? Quite a few, I gather, but which one in particular?"

"Nobody that I know of."

"Was she married?"

"No. I'm pretty sure of that."

"Now here's one you won't like. Is it true she took dope?"

"No, not since I knew her."

"How long is that?"

"Two years."

"Well, she didn't tell you everything. She took dope all right. What about her relations with her mother and uncle? What about that uncle, by the way?"

"They seemed to get along all right. The uncle gave her a lot of money, or as much as they could afford. She had a good allowance and she always wore good clothes. That's all."

"One more question. Did she ever speak of suicide to you?"

"Sure. The way everybody does. I speak of it. Even you I imagine."

"But specifically, jumping off the *City of Essex*. Did she say anything about that yesterday at lunch? Or any other time? What I'm trying to get at is, was suicide on her mind?"

"No, I wouldn't say it was."

"That's what I think. There's something screwy about this whole thing. I've read enough detective stories to know that a young girl, pretty and all that, she doesn't pack her bag the way Gloria did just to knock herself off. That was a love trip, if you don't mind my saying so. One more question, Mr. Brunner."

"You said that a minute ago."

"This is important. I just want to show you I'm not a complete dope. Have you been in communication with the family since yesterday?"

"No. I tried to get them by phone but they wouldn't answer. I guess the phone—"

"Has been disconnected. I thought you'd say that. And so has yours been disconnected. And you weren't out to get a paper today. So how do you know about this?"

"Say, you're not trying to—"

"Just giving you a sample of what you'll get from the boys and girls on the tabloids. Multiplied by fifty and you have an idea."

"Well, my phone isn't disconnected, so you're wrong."

"Yes, and you're lying. Oh, don't worry. I don't think you did it. Come on, I'll take you away from the wolves."

"Will they really break open the apartment?"

"Oh, probably not. I'm just taking you uptown as a friendly act.

They aren't interested in you as much as in some elderly guy. That's all I know about him, and that's all they know. He was part of her past. A very big part, I should say. Coming?"

"All right."

"I'll buy you a drink. Jesus, guy, you don't think I like this, do you? Have you heard any of the new Louis Armstrong records?"

"No new ones. What ever happened to the little dame you had that played the piano?"

"Married. That's what we all ought to do. You too."

"I'm going to."

"I have a novel almost finished. As soon as I finish it and get the dough and stay on the wagon three months. You better lock your windows just in case."

12

"I'M PREPARING A paper on New York newspapers," said Joab Ellery Reddington. "Will you reserve a copy of all the papers for me every day?"

"Yes, sir. We don't get them all, but I can order them for you if you tell me how long you'll want them."

"A month. Shall I pay you every day?"

"That'll be all right," said the newsdealer.

And so every afternoon Dr. Reddington would go from his office in the high school building, down to the railroad station, and back to his office. He would open each paper so that the financial page was on the outside, and he would sit and read every word about the Wandrous case. With fear and trembling he watched the beginning, the growth, and the decline in references to an older man, a middle-aged man, an elderly man. Dr. Reddington still had in cash the money he was going to pay Gloria for her promise never to mention his name, and he carried this money with him all the time. He never knew when he was going to have to use it. He did not know where he would go, but he would go somewhere. Then one, then two, then all the papers described the man. A Major in the Ordnance Department during the War, whose name police refused to divulge. The police were good and sick of the case and only kept it open because one of the tabloids would not let it die down. The police said they only wanted the Major for questioning.

Then one day the police announced that the Major had died in 1925 of a heart attack on a train between St. Louis and Chicago. The body had been cremated and the urn reposed in a Chicago funeral home. After that Dr. Reddington continued to read the New York papers, but there were no more references to an elderly man, and in late August the doctor stopped the papers and joined his family, who were vacationing in New Hampshire. The Reddingtons always went to a hotel where the women guests were not permitted to smoke.